BAD FORTUNE

A MALCOM WINTERS MYSTERY

THOMAS J. THORSON

Thorshammer Books
ISBN: 978-1-7358366-5-2
For ordering information, visit: www.thorsonbooks.com

Cover and interior design by Stephanie Rocha
Photo by Laura Chouette/Unsplash,
iStock.com, Vectoreezy.com

Printed in the United States of America.

PRAISE FOR *HEIRS APPARENT*

"Thorson is an accomplished writer with a gift for crafting a compelling narrative, amusing characters, and crisp dialogue...A diverting read that never lags."

—*Windy City Reviews*

"Thorson's meticulous prose and clever insights keep things moving en route to a massively entertaining second act that will keep readers up well into the night."

—*Best Thrillers*

PRAISE FOR
THE CONNUBIAL CORPSE

"The story was filled with some of the most extraordinary characters I have ever come across...a must-read for anyone who appreciates a great mystery thriller."

—*Readers' Favorite*

"Fascinating...[with] the flair of a novel unafraid to take risks."—*Independent Book Review*

"Intelligently delivered and intriguing...A pure pleasure... This intricately plotted foray into the violent world of murder, intrigue, and superstitions is sure to wow the fans of finely constructed mysteries."

—*The Prairie Book Review*

"A fast-paced and action-oriented mystery novel... [with] some of the weirdest characters in the history of mystery fiction...Excellent. 4.7 stars."

—*The Indie Reader*

PRAISE FOR
THE COSMIC KILLINGS

"A thought-provoking thriller... This wild ride is cleverly penned to perfection, for an eerie, original, and endlessly entertaining thriller."

—*Self-Publishing Review*

"[A] captivating tale with an irresistible appeal to fans of sleuth... *The Cosmic Killings* is convincing, powerful, and an ingeniously written yarn. The expert development of themes of religion, murder, and politics remains one of the strongest strengths of this spellbinding story."

—**Jane Riley,** *The Book Commentary*

DEDICATION

As always to my daughters Tierney, Lourdra, and Gilleece, with love and a never-ending desire to make them proud.

ACKNOWLEDGEMENTS

Just as all of my novels feature the same four characters, the look and feel of each book as one of a series is due to the consistently high quality of work from the same geniuses toiling behind the scenes. My editor Kristen Weber, who disguises commands as suggestions so that spending weeks reworking the entire first six chapters of the book somehow seemed like my own idea, and who is almost never wrong in knowing how to make it better. The incomparable Stephanie Rocha, whose vast talents are not only evident in the stunning cover art but reach onto every word of every page. And of course Steve Kirshenbaum of Looking Glass Books, my children, my friends, and my readers, who offer encouragement even when they don't realize they're doing so. I blame myself for continually starting to write another installment after thinking the prior book would be my last, and credit each and every one of you for helping me get it done.

ONE

Boredom is a totally foreign concept to me. The fact that I've spent the last hour and sixteen minutes searching my memory for even a single moment in my adult life where I've considered myself in such a state of languor only emphasizes how deeply I'm immersed in this mood. Not less than twenty-one of those minutes were spent ruminating on the difference between boredom and inactivity, which has led to some less than profound insights. It was commonplace in my prior career working for a government agency with no name or public profile to spend long hours sitting perfectly still while waiting for someone to exit a door or to finish a sandwich, but the fact that at those times my life was simultaneously in peril clearly classified such endeavors as something other than boredom. Maybe it's time to throw the definitions of tedium and ennui into the mix and to ruminate on those distinctions for another twenty-one minutes. I am, after all, supposedly an English professor.

Even the life I stumbled into after leaving the shadows behind has been an adventure that requires constant vigilance in keeping my newly minted identity as an author and teacher at the University of Illinois Chicago intact against the constant scrutiny of my boss Stuart Vanguard, whose justifiable suspicion that I'm a fraud has him seeking any opportunity to fire me. Throw three separate recent murder investigations into the mix, my living quarters above a would-be diva named Ted during working hours and Rebecca at all other times, as well as a faux Cuban chef who claims he's in witness protection for trying to assassinate Fidel Castro, and each moment of each day has been worth the price of admission and free of both boredom and tedium.

Until now. School is out for the summer and I resisted the administration's suggestion that I teach a six-week "The Relevance of Shakespeare in the Modern Era" class to incoming freshman, only in part because I'm pretty sure I'd run out of things to say after the first ten minutes. The main reason, though, comes in the form of a short-in-stature, tall-in-reputation superstar in the world of molecular biology, my best friend—and sometimes more—co-worker Vinn Achison. Between our teaching duties and corralling a cult-obsessed killer, we spent our spring planning a trip to that mecca of vacationers everywhere, the Atacama Desert in Chile. A glorious technicolor of sand dunes during the day, at night it offers the best stargazing in the world. Or so says the internet. Perhaps sensing that my level of enthusiasm didn't match her own, she also offered to throw in a side trip to see the penguins on the islands of Magdalena and Marta at a natural monument called, creatively enough, Monumento Natural Los Pinguinos.

"They're cute," she argued at the time, a hint of annoyance entering her voice. "They're also endangered, so we may never get the opportunity again. Besides, who can resist the chance to observe 100,000 penguins waddling around on a single chunk of rocky substrate?"

Well, me for one. Would a beach in Oahu be so bad? I bit back the first several replies that came to mind and focused on coming up with the words I hoped she wanted to hear in order to preserve intraspecies harmony.

"Just spending time with you is enough to make me happy, no matter where we are," I tell her. Moments like these make me ponder if I'm truly a nice guy or just completely bewitched by her beauty and brains. Or maybe a complete fraud.

"Hmmph" is all I got in return, as if she could see through my brilliant attempt at deflection.

As it turns out, we're not going anywhere. While I sit staring at my feet trying to decide whether testing my tolerance for the spiciest peppers known to mankind would get me out of my funk or simply take my mind off it during a trip to the hospital, Vinn is languishing in her condo a few neighborhoods over in self-imposed quarantine, the victim of a malady that even she hasn't been able to identify. As of this morning the possibilities range from something only seven people in history have ever had to a plague that was supposedly confined to islanders somewhere off the coast of Guam in the sixteenth century. Such is the way the mind of a scientist works, which would be amusing if it didn't mean that she's exiled all humankind, including myself, away from her presence. That would include the other 489 passengers on the airplane that left yesterday morning for South America.

With Vinn off limits and my travel plans dashed, I'm uncharacteristically at a loss as to what to do with myself and my time. This morning I took out my stash of exotic teas from around the world and organized them first alphabetically, then by country of origin, then by age, then by the amount of flower in the fragrance, and finally by how the teas ranked in terms of something called hui gan, a concept I was introduced to by a tea master in the mountains outside of Guangzhou, gan being the equivalent of how one's mouth feels when taking in a breath of fresh winter air and hui the way that same mouth remembers the gan. Or something like that. I confess that I don't understand it myself. That exercise was enough for my weary consciousness to signal my inner self that I need a hobby, but a coin collector I'm not.

As I remain lost in thought, an unidentifiable and distinctly unpleasant aroma drifts through an open window from the apartment below, a signal that Rebecca is home from work and deep into an attempt to recreate a meal she consumed at one of the local restaurants. Her success rate is perfect, not having come close even once. Whether out of pride for her creation or a burning desire to rid her refrigerator of the resultant mess, she invariably chooses to share half of the meal with the nearest individual who won't shoot or stab her for trying. That rules out Leo in the garden apartment and leaves only me. Now sufficiently motivated to break out of my malaise enough to avoid this catastrophe, and recognizing that I haven't eaten all day, I slip on a pair of sandals and move down the stairs past Rebecca's door as quickly and quietly as I can. Probably not necessary, as she wouldn't hear a tornado siren over her belting of a song from "South Pacific."

Once on the ground, I detour and move down several steps to Leo's door to see if he'd be willing to share some of the obscure and always potent liquor that he serves from unlabeled bottles along with his equally mystifying bits of unsolicited life advice. He has an eerie habit of knowing when I intend to drop by and opening the door a crack before I'm even in sight, so it's no surprise that there's no answer to my knock when I make it all the way there without his appearance. Time to put on my thinking cap and actually make a decision as to what to do now that doesn't include traipsing back upstairs past Rebecca's door or burning the lining of my stomach with a ghost pepper.

That same stomach reminds me that I'm overdue for dinner, so I head down the block to fulfill my role as a hunter-gatherer. My brain, however, has other ideas as it shifts my focus and moves into overdrive with a combination of self-pity and wildly divergent thoughts as to what I should be doing with my life, not only in the next few weeks but in the years to come. Distracted and disoriented, I wander without paying any attention to where I'm going until the smells of braised pork and ginger make me break out of my haze. Before me in a cinder-block building painted dark gray with dashes of yellow and orange is a Filipino bakery I've never noticed before. Peering inside, I see movement that indicates it's still open despite the hour as well as a neat line of small, empty tables up against the wall. The longer I stand the more prevalent the aromas, until my stomach directs my hand to reach for the door before my mind can make a conscious decision to move.

Ignoring the tempting towers of pastries next to the register, I grab a chair and order siomai, a duck dumpling with hot spices in a mushroom broth. My disappointment at missing out on one of Leo's mystery brews still lingering, I succumb to impulse and add to my tab a mug of calamansi punch, a citrus drink often found in the form of lemonade, but here fortified with pisco, a cousin of brandy, and a healthy portion of fresh ginger, the aroma of which lured me inside. I'm well into my second drink before the food comes, but now that it's here I'm having trouble stabbing any of the dumplings which keep moving around on the multiple plates that I see in front of me. I finally aim for one in the middle and find success. The dumpling melts in my mouth and is absolutely heavenly. I'm a big fan of symmetry, so having had two drinks, I order another plate of the duck to even it out. Somewhere in another part of town, Vinn is scowling.

Whether it's the comforting effect of the meal or the stimulation of the alcohol, a fraction of a kernel of a partial plan begins to form in my mind. As much as I hate to admit it, I've never felt more alive than when investigating the killings Vinn and I have been drawn into, rubbing shoulders with a violent criminal element, losing sleep over the inability to put the discordant pieces together, the threat of imminent bodily harm around every corner, and the ultimate euphoria—usually accompanied by significant pain—when we bring a small piece of justice to our corner of the city. Each of those adventures were brought to us unsolicited, sucking us in despite our best efforts to resist, but things have been quiet lately. Maybe if trouble isn't going to come our way, it's up to me to go looking for it.

With a sudden, invigorating feeling of triumph and a renewed sense of purpose, I rise to my feet, take a bold, purposeful step toward the door, and promptly fall flat on my face. Perhaps this new attitude in spirit requires a sober body to keep pace. I sheepishly rise, exit the restaurant without making eye contact, and begin walking toward the great and thrilling unknown, with only chance to guide me.

TWO

So far today isn't starting out any better. Maybe the local Next Door app isn't the best source of information on crime. About half an hour in, I've found postings on seven missing dogs (two of which were later found), three missing cats, and an apparent rash of thefts of garden gnomes. I can see it now: after three long nights on stakeout, I witness the culprit snatch a particularly portly fellow then follow him to a farm in Indiana with acres of gnomes, elves, and other statuary. It's the type of fame that I can live without.

As it turns out, none of the myriad other websites devoted to the vast array of transgressions in the city are any better, mostly because they focus on statistics or are too sparse on specifics to give even a hint of whether it would be something worth pursuing. The Chicago Police Department's Twitter page, at which I'm now staring, is little more than a celebration of the crimes it solved. Cheerleading I don't need.

Frustrated and thirsty, I make my way to the kitchen and pull out a long-neglected stash of ginkgo biloba tea leaves and begin to heat water. I'm not fond of its earthy, almost bitter taste, but it has a reputation for bringing on mental clarity, so what do I have to lose, other than my taste buds for an hour or two. I steep the leaves long enough to make it sufficiently strong to clear even my muddled mind.

And it works, sort of, as two new ideas almost instantly pop into my brain. First, that I really, really don't like ginkgo biloba tea. Second, maybe I should stop by to see Officer Jenkins, the baby-faced campus cop who's been on the periphery of a few of our earlier investigations. It's possible he can be throw me a bone or at least point me in the right direction. I reach for the phone, think better of it, and instead exit my apartment and head to campus.

"Sorry, Mal, but things are slow right now." Jenkins sits dwarfed behind his massive desk in the corner of the squad room. "Students are mostly gone and the summer term isn't due to start for a couple of weeks yet. Had a mugging a few days ago, and the usual laptops stolen from the library, but that's about it. Not exactly scintillating enough for you I would guess. Oh, and someone reported that they thought they saw a chimpanzee."

I exhale in exasperation. "What about your connections to the city cops? Don't you guys get together in cop bars, drink too much beer, and gossip about weird cases or the unsolved crimes that never leave your head? How about cold cases from the 1940s? Serial killers? Criminal masterminds that everyone knows about but are too good to get caught?"

I'm not sure if Jenkins' stare denotes sympathy or pity. What it definitely does not do is give me any hope that he's about to throw me a nibble.

"Mal, go home. Do what everyone else does. Buy a jigsaw puzzle. Binge watch a show on cable that will have you asking why you wasted ten hours of your life. Take up karate. Or better yet, just wait. People in trouble seem to have a habit of finding you whether you want them to or not."

"Fine. But see if I ever nominate you for U of I employee of the month." Jenkins throws a pencil at me and goes back to whatever I interrupted, which I think was filling in a crossword puzzle. Maybe things really are slow. Maybe Chicago has become a crime-free city. Maybe I need to stop talking to myself and do what I should have done in the first place. She may be sick, but if I know Vinn, she's as stir crazy as I am.

"No, I'm not going to let you in. I'm in quarantine. Go away." Vinn's voice sounds nothing like someone who's contracted a deadly disease, or even someone with a bad cold. Time to turn on the charm.

"Not a chance. I'm going to sit here outside your door and hold my breath until you open up." Okay, so maybe that's less charm and more the behavior of a two-year-old, but I follow through with a very loud inhale as I slide my back against her door.

"Mal, seriously, I'm ill. Do me a favor and just go back to your place. You have a phone. Call me. Text me. Just leave me." Maybe she is sick after all. She's classic rock all the way, but it sounds like she's reciting the lyrics of a country song.

"Can't hear you," I mutter indecipherably as I turn blue. "Na na na na..." I put my fingers in my ears for effect. When I was young my parents could see through walls when I misbehaved, so why not Vinn?

Suddenly I'm falling backward and I feel a strong grip on my collar as I'm being pulled forcibly into her apartment. A sockless foot enters my line of sight as it kicks the door shut behind me. I turn around slowly, not sure what to expect. Looking up from my prone position, a menacing figure towers over me, cheeks flushed and angry. Her hair is mussed and she's wearing nothing but a pair of panties and one of her many t-shirts with a chemical equation across the chest. I smile but get a glare in return. Maybe this is one of those times where it's best to let her talk first.

"What part of 'quarantine' don't you understand? The only reason you're in here is that Mrs. Potts across the hall will raise hell with the condo board if she can't hear her game shows because of the racket you're raising. Now that you're in, you can't leave. You're in isolation too."

I eye her suspiciously, wondering whether she's serious or if I've just been kidnapped for her sexual pleasure. I make the mature choice, deciding that I'll keep my fantasy to myself while still totally ignoring the point she's trying to make.

"I missed you," I begin, "and even though I have no idea as to what you think you were exposed to in your lab, it can't be as powerful as my love." Even as the words leave my mouth I realize how ridiculous I sound, but they have the intended effect. Far from her heart melting at my sentiment, a slight quiver begins to show at the corners of Vinn's mouth and, try as she might, she can't hold back. She loses the battle of self-control and is soon laughing loud enough to raise the hackles of Mrs. Potts. Music to my ears, but I can't let her know that.

"I'm crushed," I tell her, pouting.

"Oh shut up and come sit here next to me on the couch. I missed you too." Vinn collapses onto her vintage rosewood sofa and I quickly join her. We interlock fingers and sit quietly for a few minutes before she speaks again. "And for the record, I'm about 89 percent certain that I'm not contagious. I'm pretty sure it was food poisoning from a sandwich I bought at the school cafeteria. If it really was what I feared based on the work I was doing at the time, I wouldn't be talking to you now."

We're settling into a comfortable haze together when

my cell phone notifies me that I have a text. From the tone I can tell that it's Rebecca, so the decision to ignore the text is easy. I don't need to know what fashion faux pas her friend Tracy committed at the baby shower, or hear her whine that her hair stylist is moving away, or that she needs to borrow some sugar, stat. Two minutes later my phone sounds again. As before, I ignore it. No sooner does my pocket stop vibrating than the phone sounds with the familiar ringtone of the song "Lola."

"You'd better get that," Vinn tells me with a sigh of resignation. "Maybe your building is on fire or she's out of mascara."

"What is it Rebecca?" I snarl into the phone without any pretense of being polite, putting the call on speakerphone so that Vinn can share in the drama.

"I need to talk to you Malcom, and it can't wait. Can I come up in five?" Vinn clears her throat loudly enough for Rebecca to hear. I hope she takes the hint. "Oh, is that you Vinn? I'm glad you're together. You should hear this too. Are you upstairs? Are you decent?"

Vinn shakes her head silently then pantomimes hanging herself by the neck, complete with tongue lolling out of her mouth and eyes staring vacantly. Rebecca may not take Vinn's hints, but I do.

"Rebecca, I'm actually at Vinn's place now. She's a bit under the weather and I need to take care of her. Can we do this tomorrow morning? Say around 9:00?"

My suggestion is met with thirty seconds of silence. Rebecca wants us to know that she's pouting. "Fine," she finally intones. "But no later. And Vinn, drink lots of tea with lemon. I need you here as well."

I disconnect the phone, lean back, and put my arm around Vinn. "She does sound distressed," I tell her.

"I know," Vinn says.

"And she's our friend and my tenant," I continue.

"I know," she replies.

"And..." I begin.

"Okay, just shut up Mal," Vinn says without enthusiasm. "We might as well sleep at your place tonight to save us having to get up early tomorrow. While I'm getting ready, do you want to order some dinner? I don't think I can look at another can of soup or a soda cracker again for the rest of my life. Sushi okay? We can pick it up on the way."

THREE

I'm awake and up early, quietly shutting the bedroom door behind me so that Vinn can sleep in. I decide to kill a little time by dropping in on Leo again. Including my trip to his door yesterday, I haven't seen him around for several days, which is unusual. I'm not in a panic, but as tough as Leo is, he's also of an age where he's more susceptible to a stroke. It doesn't hurt to check.

His entrance is hidden below ground level behind dozens of potted herbs and other plants lining the top of a stone wall. As I get closer, I pause momentarily. My ingrained and well-earned paranoia at walking into any area blind as to what might lurk there has the hairs on the back of my neck stand up and tingle as I round the corner at the top of the steps despite having made that journey hundreds of times before. The fact that it's usually Leo anticipating my arrival isn't any less unsettling, as he's usually adorned with a bloody apron while holding a large equally bloody cleaver. I've always assumed that he just arrived home from his restaurant, the Kuban Kabana, but can't be entirely sure.

I let out the breath I didn't know I was holding as the landing below is devoid of clandestine assassins, then proceed down and knock loudly. No response. It's not likely he's asleep, as I've never known him to sleep, and the sun is now up and shining brightly. He could be at work, but again despite the facts that it's his restaurant and that he's the sole employee, he never seems to spend much time there. This lends credence to his claim that he's in witness protection after having done something he doesn't want to reveal, as does the fact that one sampling of his food is clear proof that he doesn't know how to cook. Still, he has to go there periodically if for no other reason than to support the charade of his identity, and he's shown himself to be tough for his age. Tough for any age, in fact. It's also possible he's shopping for shoes or garlic. So nothing to worry about, right?

Maybe. The extended time since he's responded to my knocks is unusual for someone who's rarely away and who can always be counted on to be around to host an alcohol-infused late-night session at his kitchen table, so his absence is raising alarm bells inside my head that are too loud to ignore. I check my phone for the time and realize I should go back upstairs and start breakfast. I'll come back down again later.

Despite her occasional expressions of affection, I'm convinced that the real reason Vinn keeps me around are the breakfasts I make whenever she stays over. I'm a cold cereal and fruit kind of guy in the mornings when I haven't shared my bed the night before, so a part of me could argue that that the same breakfasts are why I stay with Vinn. Of course, it could be the deepening love we have for each other, but food is a much more tangible and plausible hook.

Whatever the reason, small mounds of batter that will turn into delectable corn fritters are just hitting the hot oil when Vinn stumbles out of the bedroom rubbing sleep from her eyes. Her coffee, made from a blend of rare beans she concocted herself, is already made and ready and she acknowledges my effort with a silent nod. My tea of choice is a Monkey-Picked Oolong, which supposedly breeds wisdom in the drinker. I don't think that's true in my case, just as I don't believe monkeys actually pick the leaves. All I know is that it happens to taste good with fried breakfast food.

"Mmphmp," Vinn mutters as she douses the first few fritters I slide onto her plate with bourbon-infused maple syrup. I frown at the lake that forms on her plate, wondering if the syrup is meant to complement my fritters or the other way around. Experience tells me to wait for the clouds to lift before beginning any conversation. Today it's a long wait before Vinn opens her mouth to form her first words of the day.

A loud, persistent knocking interrupts whatever thought she was about to express, and the irregular rhythm vaguely resembling a show tune easily identifies who's on the other side of my door. "Rebecca." I tell Vinn as I head to answer her summons. She's twenty minutes early.

"Well it certainly took you long enough, Malcom, you weren't still in bed, were you? Oh, hi Vinn, nice to see you. Do you sleep in sweatpants? I can't even imagine. I mean I swear by my Olivia von Halle silk nightshirt. You know the one I mean? It was on the runway in Milan. Not this year, last year, but it's still fashionable. The floral one, not that horrid print with the cubes. Oh, are those corn fritters? Wonderful. Malcom, be a dear."

I can tell Vinn is trying to suppress a giggle at the same time she's contemplating slapping Rebecca just to see if that would work as a reset button. I'm trying to envision Vinn sleeping in anything other than sweatpants and a ratty t-shirt but am having no luck. No one's imagination is that good. Instead, I turn the heat back on under the cast iron pan but choose not to honor our guest with fresh oil.

Rebecca moves to sit in the one chair in my living room that she finds tolerable, which for her means that its neutral tones don't clash with whatever ensemble she's wearing at the time. Today it's a diamond-patterned red and orange skirt with a lime green blouse and blue designer sneakers. I've been tempted on several occasions to ask if she's color blind, but even from across the room I feel Vinn's elbow striking my rib cage.

"Rebecca, do you mind getting to the point? I thought you had an appointment at the nail salon."

"That's not until—oh I see, you're making fun. Shame, Malcom. And yes, of course I have a reason to be here. You remember my friend April, the one we call 'Calendar Girl' behind her back? She had that incident with the tummy tuck last winter. Well, she was having lunch with Trish, my stylist, and said that her friend—April's, not Trish's—had the most wonderful palmist that gave her just the best advice based on what she read in her lines and that her life had just turned around completely. So maybe there's something in all of that mumbo jumbo but I never believed it before. I still don't, not really, except..."

We wait while Rebecca stabs a fritter and chews. Then she stabs another, but pauses, staring at her plate. A slight reddening begins to appear beneath her foundation and a small tear trickles out of her left eye. It doesn't take a genius to tell that the fritters are a means of stalling. She's having trouble with whatever part of the story comes next. Vinn finally intervenes.

"Rebecca, why don't you give me your plate? I have a feeling that whatever you're about to tell us would be better said with a cup of coffee. How does that sound?"

Rebecca just nods and remains silent while she waits for Vinn to return. When she does, Vinn and I assume our own accustomed spots for when we have company, but scoot closer to allow Rebecca to speak without having to project. Rebecca scans Vinn's face for residual signs of illness before sliding her chair a foot further away. We wait patiently for her to gather her thoughts.

When she does speak, it's Ted's voice that we hear, a sure sign of how out of sorts she is.

"I've never been so upset in my life. Let me start at the beginning."

FOUR

"Please be patient with me as I go back in time five or six years, because I think it's important to give you the background." Rebecca closes her eyes to concentrate, stress clearly etched in her face. Vinn and I look at each other with concern. "No, it might be longer than that. But I guess it doesn't really matter.

"I met a woman through a mutual friend. I was not, um..." She pauses to find the right words, "presenting in this way at that time, though the desire was there. In other words, I was the same person inside then that I am now, other than whatever changes we go through naturally as we age a little. I apologize, I don't mean to get off track. Anyway, we dated casually at first, but over time became exclusive. After about six months we moved in together."

"Does this woman have a name?" Vinn asks as she signals to me to start taking notes. Her mind is exactly where mine is. Just two minutes into Rebecca's narrative, it's looking like she's going to ask our help for something more involved than a simple tailing job or tracking down a lost love. And no matter what it is, we're going to do it for her.

"Oh, yes, I'm sorry. Sara, no 'h.' Last name Engers. A real looker, then and now. Pretty smart, too, although somewhere in her brain there's a loose wire. I'll come back to that. And everything I know about fashion I learned from being with her. Anyway," she continues, "things were going well for the first several months, on all fronts. We both loved the same music, liked to try new restaurants, hated sports, and...Do you need to know about our sex lives? I mean, in detail?"

"Not unless it's relevant," I reply quickly. I really, really hope it's not relevant. "If you like, why don't we skip over that for now and if Vinn or I think we need to come back to it we will."

Rebecca nods, relieved, although probably not as much as I am. "But you can see where this is going. As time went on, cracks began to appear in our relationship. I know I'm biased, but at a time when I still saw her as the perfect woman and worshipped the ground she walked on, she began to find fault with me. Mostly little things at first. 'Are you going to wear that shirt with those pants?' 'Why do you have to steal the covers?' 'You keep the apartment too cold.' Then 'You keep the apartment too hot' an hour later. I loved her, or thought I did, so I was more than willing to assume the blame for any rifts, or at least stay quiet and let her anger blow over. But it only got worse.

"I started keeping track of how many times she said something affirming to me and how many times she was critical. Got that from one of those self-help relationship books. After a week the tally was astoundingly and devastatingly one-sided. I began to have doubts about the state of our relationship, in particular her feelings about me, but wanted above all to make everything work. To get back to where we were. That's when the jealousy started."

I call for a pause to refill everyone's drinks, as much for my benefit as for Rebecca's. Her story so far isn't an uncommon one, but Rebecca has an internal strength that would allow her to eventually stand up for herself and walk away from a toxic relationship before it became irreparably damaging. Knowing that, there's more here than she's told us so far and her story is likely going to take a very dark turn. I'm in no hurry to get there.

Coffee in hand, Rebecca takes in a long breath and

continues. "She began to imagine that I was being unfaithful, if not physically at least through my inner desires. She became the thought police, always assuming that I was lusting for a woman we passed on the street or fantasizing that I was making love to someone else when we were, well, doing it. She started monitoring my phone, scrolling through all of my texts and call history and even after finding nothing there accusing me of erasing damaging evidence. Our storybook romance disintegrated in record time."

"Rebecca, don't take this the wrong way," I say gingerly, "but were you having an affair?"

She thinks about it, scowls at me, but ultimately decides not to take it the wrong way. "No, not even in my mind. I was fantasizing all right, but not about other women, only about getting away from the one I had. I wasn't eating or sleeping and my health was suffering. People at work started to take notice. In retrospect it took me way too long to make the decision, but I eventually came to the conclusion that I had to cut ties, the sooner the better. So one day when I knew she wouldn't be home I left work in the middle of the day, packed a bag, and left. She could keep the furniture, the champagne glasses, the fluffy towels, the works. I just needed to escape. And that was that. End of relationship."

Rebecca leans back in her chair, exhausted from the telling of her tale. Vinn and I exchange puzzled glances. "That" was obviously not "that" or Rebecca wouldn't be here. Vinn takes the lead.

"Um, Rebecca, it sounds like that was a horrible experience and we appreciate you sharing it with us, but can we assume your story doesn't end there? There must be some reason that you're so distressed this many years later."

Rebecca sits back up straight, her lips compressed.

"About a month ago Sara showed up at my job, insisting that she see me. The receptionist called and I told her not to send that woman back to my office under any circumstances. Apparently things got loud and profane after that and would have turned violent if building security hadn't arrived. They escorted Sara out and she's on the building blacklist, so she can't get past the front desk. But that didn't deter her.

"You know that I'm very active on social media—well, as Rebecca anyway. I love to post photos when I'm out on the town, or just of food I've created, or of a dress I got as an absolute steal on eBay. You know, Malcom, you follow me. But always as Rebecca, never as Ted. Somehow she found me anyway. I guess it wouldn't be that difficult if you were determined enough, and she must have been determined. My mistake, although I didn't know it at the time, was posting my plans to meet up with friends at Three Dots and a Dash, that adorable tiki bar north of the Loop. Have you ever tried their Down Periscope? Tequila, mango brandy, pineapple, and I don't know what else. It's to die for."

I grin as she reverts to Rebecca for just a flash. But almost immediately her frown returns and she gets back on point. "There were five of us, just hanging out and having fun. I was wearing an Elie Tahari floral that just flows and makes me happy every time I put it on. Times were good. Then before I knew it she was there among us. Sara, as gorgeous and as crazy as ever. Inches away from me. At first she didn't say a word, just looking me up and down as if she wasn't sure it was me, getting in my face. Then she started laughing, treating that part of my identity as a joke, and insisting that she accompany me back to my place so that I could put on a pair of pants. When I refused and tried to ignore her, she started getting hostile, saying ugly things. My friends tried to intervene and that's when she brought out the claws, getting louder by the second and even trying to rip off my dress. They restrained her until a bouncer came to help out. He carried her out the door, banning her from the place, but not before she screamed a parting shot at me. I can even tell you her exact words. There was a lot of profanity, but the relevant part was 'I know someone who will put a curse on you. Your life is now cursed.' She used that word twice. Of course we laughed it off. I'm not laughing anymore."

We wait silently while Rebecca sips on her drink. I realize my note taking stopped as she described the incident at the bar, except for writing down the name of her drink. I make a few notations to catch up. Vinn prods her. "Go on, Rebecca."

"I want to make clear," she begins with some passion, "that I don't believe in ghosts or Bigfoot and especially not in curses or crystal balls, April's palmist notwithstanding. But ever since that night, my life has been hell. Nothing major at first, just a lot of little incidents that added up to make me miserable. My car was keyed. A stranger spilled coffee on my best suit, then the dry cleaner lost the suit. Someone used my Visa number to charge over $1,000.00 at a smut shop. After that things accelerated. My clients started getting anonymous emails telling them that I had a long arrest record. Rebecca was outed to my boss. She didn't care, in fact she already knew. But still. And my bank just stopped a hacker from emptying my savings.

"I know she's behind this, Malcom. Vinn. But I have no proof and don't know how she's doing it. I'm worried it's going to pick up even more. I need it to stop. I need you to stop it. Tell me how much you need to get started."

Vinn and I both instantly turn down her offer of pay,

talking at the same time but using different words, leaving Rebecca confused as to what we were trying to say. I hush Vinn, something I'll probably regret. "Rebecca, don't even think about paying us a dime. When all this is over, you can bake us a cake." Out of the corner of my eye I see Vinn wincing. "I'm sure we'll have a lot of questions for you once we digest what you've told us, but for now I think we have enough to get started. Let us know, though, if anything else happens."

I lead her to the door but suddenly have a thought and pull her back, earning a perturbed look in return. "I'm sure it's nothing to be worried about, Rebecca, but have you seen Leo lately? He hasn't been around and I'm a bit concerned."

Rebecca's expression of annoyance fades and is quickly replaced by one of worry, giving me her answer before she even opens her mouth to respond. "Come to think of it, no. Let me think about the last time I saw him." She concentrates, biting her ruby red lip as she does so. "It was last weekend when I dropped by his apartment to borrow some fresh cumin and an onion, and you were there with him wearing that go-dawful yellow shirt you seem to like, and the two of you tried to get me to join you but you were already so drunk and besides I had a pie in the oven and the color of whatever was in the bottle on the table was almost neon green so I would have passed anyway."

"Thanks, Rebecca. I think that's the last time I saw him as well. Probably just haven't been on the same schedule. Or maybe he took a trip somewhere."

"I'm sure that's it," she says, not sounding convinced. "Yes, no big deal. He can take care of himself. But Malcom," Rebecca puts her hand on my arm, her voice turning tender, "please let me know when you find him."

FIVE

"Be careful what you wish for," I tell myself as I return to my seat. I must have said that out loud, because Vinn looks at me curiously. "I'd been getting a little edgy, bored even, and was thinking that dabbling in a little crime solving might be the solution to my ennui," I explain hesitantly, expecting ridicule in return.

Vinn grins slyly. "Not just you, cowboy. Great minds think alike. Or, maybe more accurately, one great mind and one trying to get there."

I throw a pillow at her, which she easily dodges, before she turns serious. "I could see the sour look on your face as Rebecca told her story, and I'm sure your first thought was that her problem not only is a bit pedestrian for our skill sets, but the lack of useful information means that we're stuck before we even get started, which would put us in familiar territory. But maybe not. I might have a starting point, but instead of trying to explain it, it would be better to show you. For that, we need to go back to my place."

I give her my best puppy-eye look trying to learn more but it has no effect, so I do the next best thing and put on my shoes and grab my keys.

Vinn's unit is usually as meticulously neat as a science lab, but as we enter I'm struck again with a feeling of disconnect by the clutter that greets us. Yesterday I assumed it was part of her research into her illness and decide to ask.

"Is all of that test results?" I point in the direction of several stacks of papers spread across her coffee table. More papers which appear to be computer printouts are piled on chairs, the floor, and her kitchen counter.

"Um, no," she sheepishly replies. "For the first several days of my confinement I was focused on nothing but figuring out what I had. As I began to realize that I wasn't going to die, and that egg salad may be the culprit, I knew I should continue to isolate just to play it safe, but at that point I began to get restless. More than that, I was going insane. I needed to find something to do. Like you, I began to read local crime reports. At first it was just out of curiosity, something to keep me busy and to glimpse into the underbelly of the city—you know, the darker side of human nature is so much more fascinating than the goings on of the yachting set. But then I began to see that the news I was reading about crime dovetailed neatly with gossip among philanthropists. And delving further, what they were talking about mirrored the talk of everyday people. It was fascinating, and ultimately may giving us an entry point with Rebecca. Want to see what I found?"

Without waiting for an answer, she continues. I've learned that anyone who works hard and methodically toward a conclusion to a puzzle has an innate need to share every detail about how they got there, and as a scientist Vinn is no exception. The train may take a while to get to the station, but I have no choice but to sit back and enjoy the ride.

As she speaks, Vinn begins to get more animated and the listless figure who grew exhausted on the walk over takes on a vibrant energy. She's never more excited than when on a scientific quest with a puzzle waiting to be solved if only she can discover the correct data to insert into the variables. Only two minutes in, she can tell that she's already losing me and change tactics.

"Perhaps a visual aid will make this clearer," she says as if talking to a first grader. "I made a chart." Of course she did. She bounds off the couch, riffles through a stack of documents, and returns with a handful of notes.

"There are four different groupings to reference, each with their own perspective," she says with enthusiasm. "The official logs of the cops, of course, although you need to dig a little deeper than Facebook to get to any meaningful reports and even then detail can be lacking. Then you have neighborhood groups such as the one you looked at, but you have to sift through a lot of dregs to get to the good stuff. Gossip and nosy neighbors can be a great source of information but you have to look at it with a wary eye.

"Then there's newspapers, mostly digital now, both regional and local. They generally only report on the stuff that will sell papers and tend to focus on sensationalist aspects but few facts. Finally, there are the unofficial crime reports like CrimeWatchChicago and WatchYourBack, which fall somewhere in the middle of this spectrum but are by far the most useful. The people who put these out are passionate about getting facts that you won't find anywhere else and who aren't afraid to include minor incidents such as stolen puppies or an attempted purse-snatching along with the murders and assaults. Even some white-collar stuff."

Vinn scoots closer to me on the couch, opens her laptop, and motions me to concentrate on the screen. By the time I sit, she's pulled up a chart with seemingly every color of the rainbow on it. I can tell that she's beaming with pride. I'm about to observe once again the organizational skills that in part exhibit why she's the esteemed scientist that she is.

"I've outlined the boxes resulting in a death, whether

intentional or not, in extreme spectral red. Other serious
crimes such as rape or armed assault also get red, but as you
can see as the crimes diminish in seriousness, the wavelength
of the coloring shortens as well until you reach the low 600s
in nanometers, so that by the time you get to attempted
kidnapping or armed robbery, they're not even spectral. That's
when we get to threats of harm, arson, that kind of thing that
start out more orange and run down into yellow. Stolen cars,
bad checks, and such are green, cyan, or even turquoise. See?
Really short wavelength colors. Your stolen puppy? Indigo.
Pickpocket? Purple. You can instantly identify how bad
the crime was by the color shading. Then if the crime was
actually solved, which wouldn't interest us, the entire box is
shaded as if you were looking through sunglasses."

If you don't know Vinn, you'd think she was showing off
how she has brains far superior to every other mere mortal on
the planet. The truth is that it would never occur to her that
not everyone categorizes colors by their wavelengths or knows
the difference between spectral and non-spectral colors. Or
for that matter, what "spectral" even means. Me? I see a chart
full of pretty colors. Apparently Vinn is just warming up.

"Now if we skip down a few pages, you can see that I've
listed crimes by frequency and cross-referenced them by date
and neighborhood with my own subjective ranking from 1-18
as to the ingenuity required to pull them off. I figured if we
were going to dive back into the detective business, we might
as well pick an adversary that's our intellectual equal, right?"

If Albert Einstein were alive and went to the dark
side, she might have a point. Just as I'm about to raise this, I
notice Vinn's shoulders beginning to sag and the brightness
in her eyes is fading rapidly. A small voice in my head had

begun expressing doubts about whether Vinn's illness had been contrived as an excuse to stay home and play around with figures and colors, but I now see the fatigue resulting from the effort it took to walk her from my apartment and present her chart. She doesn't argue when suggest a short nap, take her by the hand, and lead her to her bed. She's asleep before I leave the room. Unfortunately, she wore out before connecting all of her research to Rebecca's string of bad luck.

Alone in front of her laptop, I have no choice but to attempt to analyze the data she collected in my own primitive and slow-witted manner. Over the next few hours I begin to see patterns emerge that may be worth a deeper look. Strings of what appear to be related incidents involving thefts of high-value items, confidence games, odd types of muggings that occur too frequently to be random, and victims reluctant to cooperate with authorities begin to emerge. At this point, my brain is too muddled to postulate connections or to even begin to theorize as to what these patterns, if they really do exist, really mean and how they relate to Rebecca. In the past I've always found it best to bounce my thoughts off another mind better trained to recognize patterns, but she's sound asleep in the next room. I do what I always find works best in such situations. I close the laptop, go into Vinn's bedroom, and join her in slumber.

SIX

Vinn looks better in the morning but insists that she needs one more day to recuperate and to run tests to make sure new symptoms haven't appeared between yesterday and today. She emails me copies of her charts, research, and other data, hands me a mug of keemun tea and a piece of toast with pear preserves we bought together at the farmer's market and pushes me out the door. I could choose to be offended but opt instead to appreciate the light but slightly smokey aroma of the tea and the fact that she keeps it on hand for me. The sun is barely up but it's already warm and the skies are cloudless, so I decide to walk the three miles back to my place.

The quiet of the early hour and the fresh air allow me to try to make sense of the vague patterns that may or may not have existed from the statistics and crime summaries Vinn so meticulously put together, and to try to find a connection, if it exists, to Rebecca's mini crime wave. Unfortunately, as much as I try to find a way in, the information we have is just too sparse to proceed, or even to decide if we want to or should continue in this direction, without gathering more specifics. And that means talking to victims and witnesses, which requires finding contact information for multiple parties, which means having to deal with cops, reporters, and neighbors. Not being a people person, or so I've been told, this isn't the answer I was hoping to find. Maybe I can subcontract the work. It's something to think about and to raise with Vinn, but for now I'm at least satisfied that we have our summer planned. Kind of. And better yet, one that doesn't involve a lot of sand and aquatic sea birds, although it does require working with a high-maintenance crossdressing diva.

As I close my squeaky front gate closed, I take another short detour down the stairs to Leo's front door. Again, no answer to my knock, and there's no way to see through the darkened windows. I debate using my copy of his key to enter to make sure he's not inside and in need of medical help, but his extreme desire for privacy and the odds of my getting a knife in the gut if I enter while he's home make the decision more difficult than it should be.

I trudge up the stairs to my own front door, the weight of Leo's absence and the decision I have to make about whether to break into his apartment canceling out the bright feeling I had from my stroll in the beautiful summer weather. As I step into my unit, internal alarm bells sound and I quickly drop to the floor. Something isn't right. There's a disturbance in the air, a faint but odd smell that shouldn't be here along with the unmistakable feeling that I'm not alone. I cautiously look in all directions as I slowly make my way to the kitchen, the location of my nearest stash of weaponry.

Just as I clear the island, I suddenly come to a halt, my heart stopping along with the rest of me. Lying prone and unconscious, clothes filthy and blood-stained, is the very man I was looking for moments before.

"Are you sure he's alive?" Rebecca, now dressed for work as Ted in a Brooks Brothers suit that must have put a serious dent in her budget for cocktail dresses, repeats for at least the third time. Leo isn't tall, but he's got a lot of muscle packed into what's there and it took the two of us almost twenty minutes to move him to my couch, which I covered in an old sheet. It didn't help that Rebecca refused to hold him in any place where she might get blood on the suit. "I mean, you checked again, right? Because he doesn't look so good."

To her credit, Rebecca doesn't raise the possibility of calling for an ambulance or seeking professional help. Leo avoids public interaction anywhere he isn't in complete control of the situation, perhaps because he simply values his privacy to a pathological extreme, but more likely because he has a mysterious past that requires that he keep off the radar. Reaching out for help even in circumstances such as this would have severe repercussions I'd rather not imagine.

"He's fine, Rebecca," I answer hastily before realizing how idiotic that sounds given what we see before us. "Well maybe not fine, but his pulse is good and he's breathing. I do think we need to do some further examination. Would you mind helping me take off his clothes?"

Rebecca turns pale but whatever response she intended to make is delayed by an insistent pounding on the door. Not expecting anyone, I cautiously approach it and utter a word not used in polite company as I swing the door open.

"Forgot my key in my rush to get here. Where is he?" Vinn asks breathlessly before glancing in the direction of the living room and hurrying that way.

"Vinn, when I sent you the text I was just looking for advice. You're not well and didn't have to come here. Probably shouldn't have come here."

"You're still sick?" Rebecca croaks, shrinking away from the couch as she glances first at Vinn then back at Leo before muttering something about an important meeting and quickly making her way to the door.

"It's Leo, Mal," Vinn explains in an exasperated tone. "He's family. So, what do we know?"

"He's breathing and seems stable, but for this tough

old man to fall unconscious he must have been subject to something pretty severe. We were about to strip him to look for injuries—well, I was—when you knocked."

Vinn nods. "Right. Can you bring a scissors? Might be easier to just cut them off. Given the multiple rips and blood stains, they're not worth saving anyway."

I let the scientist with the steady hand do the honors, which she performs with an enviable precision as if this were an everyday occurrence. As the fabric falls away from Leo's chest, Vinn and I both gasp. Thick, dark scars from unknown prior encounters which he's never mentioned cross both torso and stomach, but they're clearly not the cause of his present condition. Blood oozes from at least a dozen stab and slash wounds of various depths. None fatal, but clearly the source of a lot of pain and loss of blood.

"Mal, hand me my bag, would you?" For the first time I notice a canvas grocery bag with the familiar four stars of Chicago's flag on the side sitting just inside the door. As I glance inside while picking it up, Vinn's usual compulsive orderliness is nowhere in evidence. She obviously threw whatever's inside together in a hurry.

"See if you can find a bottle with a blue ointment inside and a plastic bag with some strips of cloth. While I'm cleaning him up, pull out the bandages and compresses." It takes me longer than it should to find the ointment, giving me new understanding of the woman who can't find her car keys in her purse. Vinn mutters a quiet "thank you" while I rummage for the bandages, finally choosing to empty and organize all of the bag's contents.

Watching Vinn work over Leo's wounds is strangely disconcerting, as it's Leo who in the past has treated each of us with colorful mystery ointments and his skills with needle and thread. Were he conscious, I'm sure he'd insist on doing this himself.

"All right," Vinn interrupts my reverie, "I'm going to need your help. Press the sides of this cut together while I sew, working your way from up here on down. The larger ones we'll use needle and thread, then Steri-Strips for the others. He really needs stitches, but knowing Leo I doubt he's ever seen the inside of a doctor's office or hospital."

Vinn is slow but efficient and eventually Leo's bleeding is contained. After a moment to take a breath, she glances at his pants. "He's not going to like this," she says as she picks up the scissors. Minutes later the pants join his shirt in tatters. Thankfully there are no further cuts, but some yellowed areas of severe bruising that'll darken later cover both legs. Vinn gently runs her hands down each leg looking for breaks before shaking her head.

"I think I'd better be the one to look down there," I tell her. Vinn nods, a slight smirk finding its way to the corner of her mouth. I lift the waistband of Leo's boxers and bend my head for a closer look, bumping the top of Vinn's head in the process. Whether she was looking for professional purposes or simple curiosity I didn't ask. We find everything that should be there in place and nothing that shouldn't be there.

"We need to turn him," Vinn tells me, a task I anticipated but don't look forward to. There's no way to gently roll a man of his girth and neither of us makes any attempt to be gentle. Thankfully there are no additional wounds that we can see, a sign that Leo at least kept his attacker where he could see him. It may have saved his life.

As we lower Leo back to a prone position, Vinn emits a sudden high-pitched girly shriek, which thankfully covers my own. Leo's eyes are open and an angry stare greets us as we finish our task. Neither of us speaks as he rises to his elbows and scans down the front of his body before accepting Vinn's work with the slightest of nods and lying back down, pain clearly etched in the deep lines of his ancient face.

"You lost a lot of blood, Leo," I tell him, although I assume he's aware of that fact. "Otherwise there's nothing that caused you any permanent damage. You'll add a few more scars to your collection, have to be careful not to open up Vinn's patch jobs, and your legs may be sensitive to touch for a while. In other words, you need to take it easy for a couple of weeks, maybe more."

"No," he croaks before passing out, his head landing with a thud on my cushions. Vinn and I look at one another, each of us with a slight smile. It's exactly the answer we would expect from a mentally-sound Leo and an indication that he'll be motivated to get better. A good sign. On the flip side, it also likely means that he's going to seek out whoever did this to him and put himself in danger as he seeks his vengeance, possibly before he's ready. Nothing Vinn nor I can say or do will stop him.

Vinn begins packing up her bag, this time in a meticulous fashion. "I guess that's about as much as I can do for now, and I assume Leo will be more comfortable applying his own magic ointments from here on. He'll want to be in his own place and Rebecca can help you get him down there, so if he wakes again before she gets back from work try to keep him resting until she does. I need to get back to my own sick bed."

I give her a quick hug and a whispered thanks and within moments am left alone with an unconscious Cuban in my living room. I can feel the tension course through my body like a living thing, not the best state for me to think clearly. I move to my kitchen, one eye on Leo in case he wakens, and pull out a bag of Egyptian Chamomile tea leaves to brew. Not something I'd buy myself, it was a gift from the seniors in my "Monsters and Myths" fiction class that just ended. Chamomile supposedly calms the drinker's nerves, making me wonder what my students were trying to tell me. This seems as good a time as any to test it out.

Whether it's the tea or the passage of time, I do begin to relax to the point where I can start considering the first thing I should do when Leo regains consciousness and how to keep him from trying to leave too soon. Of course. There's one thing I can do that solves both issues and that he won't resist.

I grab what I need and move quickly and quietly outside and down to Leo's door. My keys do nothing to open the locks I had installed, indicating at some point that he changed them, and there are two new ones I hadn't noticed before. I know exactly which picks to pull out and proceed to work on getting inside. Vinn could have done it in under three minutes, but I'm still proud of the five that it takes me. I've been with Leo at enough of his late-night drinking sessions to know where he keeps his hooch, but still waste time wondering which bottle to snatch. I finally choose a nearly-empty bottle of purple-orange liquid, figuring if it's almost gone it must be a favorite. Tucking it under my arm, I hustle back upstairs.

It's nearly two hours before I sense movement in the direction of the couch. Leo is trying to sit up, a task that appears beyond his current ability. I cup his shoulder and push as gently as I can and within a few seconds in which he's obviously suffering intense pain, he's upright. I pull a chair close and produce the bottle and shot glass. Leo's eyes light up as he reaches over to grab each in a different hand. His hand is steady as he pours an inch into the glass before downing it in one swift movement. He pours again, not quite as steadily, takes a sip, then sets the glass down on the coffee table.

I sit in silence. Even when he's at his best, Leo only talks when he's ready. He closes his eyes for a long moment, opens them, then repeats the process, as if mentally preparing himself for whatever he has to say. "Don' ask," he mumbles, staring at me with suddenly sharp, focused eyes.

"Okay fine," I respond. "But when you're ready the first thing I'll want to know is how you got into my apartment." I've made some dangerous enemies over the years and thought I had installed an extremely good security system when I first moved in. All it's missing is the dragon and the moat. Leo emits a soft chuckle, reminding me that his own secret past probably equaled mine in giving him the skills to bypass the best barriers money can buy.

"The second thing I want to tell you is that if there's someone out there who wants to hurt you, which seems fairly obvious, Vinn and I have your back. I know you prefer to work alone or at least on terms that the two of us may not be comfortable with. But when it comes to you, all rules go out the window."

Leo nods again, clearly about all I'm going to get out of him today. I realize that he may not have eaten all day and will need food to fuel his recovery, so I walk to my fridge to pull out some cheese and a leftover end of a crusty baguette, then bend down to rummage around for anything else that might appeal to him. When I turn back to put my findings on the island, the couch is empty and my door is open. I should have known better. He did leave the bottle behind, which isn't like him, but when I pick it up and look inside there isn't a single drop left. When I pulled it out of his apartment there was enough for at least four shots the size of what he poured himself, yet I never saw him drink past a sip of his second glass.

I peer down the stairs to make sure he's not lying at the base then close and set all of the locks on the door, checking them twice. I text Vinn to make sure she also made it home and to give her an update, then go to the kitchen to eat some cheese.

SEVEN

"He hasn't come out of his apartment at all?" Vinn asks as she stuffs half a potato varenyky into her mouth, her appetite the best indication yet that she's fully recovered. Having lived in the Ukrainian Village neighborhood of Chicago for a couple of years now, I've learned where to find the best native foods. While a couple of restaurants are known for their own version of these dumplings, locals know that every so often if you're lucky or keep your ear to the ground, you can catch Daryna over on the next block with her own version of a pop up restaurant in her back yard selling these freshly-made wonders with homemade sour cream in a plastic cup on the side. Today she also had a few filled with fresh blueberries, choosing to fry instead of boil them, a dozen of which are warming in my oven.

"Not only that, he won't even answer his door. I know he's in there because the empty booze bottle collection in the recycling bin has been getting larger by the day. Rebecca says she can hear his rumblings late at night. I'm concerned but not sure what I can do about it."

"He's a big boy, Mal. It's only been two days since you found him. Give him time. If he needs our help, he knows where to find you. In the meantime, we need to spend less energy worrying about the old man and more time working on Rebecca's issue. Time to brainstorm."

We clear our dishes from the island and she makes way to the living room to power up her laptop while I pull dessert out of the oven, transferring several dumplings to two plates before throwing a dollop of sour cream over them. It's melted perfectly by the time I sit down beside the resident genius. For the hundredth time we study the detailed table and flow chart she brought up on her screen while we engorge ourselves and utter compliments Daryna will never hear under our breaths.

"I don't know about you," she opens up after wiping her mouth with her sleeve, "but I think we should work on the assumption that all of the attacks on Rebecca are the work of a single person, or at least are coordinated by one. There's no shortage of crime in this city, and nothing that Rebecca reported to us is in itself unusual, but what is unlikely is that one individual would be the victim of so many diverse offenses within such a short period of time.

"Yep." My pride forces my brain to race to think of something else to contribute to the conversation besides a three-letter word. "And the obvious choice is Sara, Rebecca's ex. But my initial impression from what Rebecca told us about her is that she isn't the type to get her hands dirty. Possible, but let's put her on the back burner for now. Joining her back there is the idea that there's a curse involved. A literal curse of course is nonsense, but someone could always create the impression of one, but let's skip that for now. First up, we need to look for patterns. See if other people in the city have also been subject to the same string of so-called 'bad luck.' Broaden our database. Maybe there's a bad guy out there who specializes in this kind of thing."

Vinn looks at me like I just grew a flower out of my nose. "Exactly my thought. Maybe you're getting smarter in your old age, Winters. So any ideas about where to start looking for this one-of-a-kind mastermind?"

"Nope." Four letters this time, although granted one of them is silent. "That was my brilliant contribution to this discussion. You're the scientist and this is your data. I could probably come up with something in five or six minutes, but I want to see if you're on the same page."

Vinn opens her mouth to say something but thinks better of it and refrains. Best not to alienate the man who feeds you warm blueberry varenyky. I watch her as she counts to ten in her head, sighs, then decides to move on, resigning my role to hanging on tight to her coattails.

Vinn looks at me curiously. "Not really. If I remember correctly, there were at least a couple of reports of a series of incidents against the same person that the cops eventually wrote off as people posing as victims over and over just to gather some attention. I can see where they draw that conclusion, especially if the so-called crimes were all petty things not worthy of official intervention. But we were looking at a starting point and I think we have it. We need to go talk to those people and compare their stories to Rebecca's."

"I don't suppose those reports had the names and phone numbers for these people?" I ask. Vinn shakes her head and smiles sadly. Wonderful.

"Don't look so doleful, Mal. We're still brainstorming, remember? Let's take a little bit of a leap. The average mugger, thief, or vandal either wants a quick buck or to perpetrate a single act of revenge. Let's go back to your thought that a single person or organization is behind Rebecca's string of incidents. Joe Criminal isn't going to be imaginative enough for the variety of actions she's suffered, nor have the capability to break past a credit card's security system, or have the gumption to call her boss. If one person is behind all of this, I have to think money is involved, and not piddly sums.

"Back when I worked for the government, we had a

case similar to this. Wasn't our area of expertise but some VIP was the victim and the local cops couldn't get a handle on it. Same MO—a series of small but increasingly expensive crimes against him. Turns out it wasn't anything exotic, just a high-stakes grifter looking to extort a large sum from a rich man in order to get the incidents to stop. All of which is my way of saying it may be that simple. Let's expand our net to include grifters, con men, and the like."

I make a face but it doesn't deter her. "I know," she continues, "I may be off base, but my gut says we should at least look into it. And if I'm right, it'll actually narrow the number of victims and hopefully make the pool of witnesses easier to deal with."

"Okay, fine," I tell her. When you have nothing much else to go one, a gut feeling at least gives us something to do. "So what do we do?"

"We start by focusing only on the neighborhoods with a high density of people with money. Lots of it. We're not looking for three-card monte players on the el. And we're going to have to read between the lines because all we're going to see from the data we collect is the end result of the con. The victims themselves may not even know how they were taken. Unexplained financial losses, the larger the better, would be perfect. For now let's error on the side of highlighting anything that doesn't have a detailed explanation and where the loss is in the upper five figures or more. We don't want to miss anything and can do more filtering later. You take Streeterville, I'll take the Gold Coast. We'll do city first, then North Shore. Okay, go."

It may have sounded terribly thrilling the way she described it, but our best effort to find a way to alleviate our boredom starts out, appropriately enough, with extreme tedium. Hours go by and our list grows, but at first glance all we have is an assortment of vague summaries of who knows what and no indication that any two of our collected crimes are related. I start to suggest that we call it a night but after my first seven words realize that I'm talking to the air. Vinn is sound asleep with her fingers poised over the keyboard of her laptop. I wake her gently.

"Vinn, I think we've both had enough excitement for one night. Before we head off to bed, though, I do have one thought. If what we're really after are high stakes grifters, many of the victims will be too embarrassed to report the crime to the cops, but they're rich for a reason and won't want to lose a penny. I think we need to find someone to hack into insurance company databases for us, and maybe we can even palm off some of the so-called research we've been doing ourselves onto someone else. I'm not sure my standby hacker J.J. has resurfaced and this kind of job might be too pedestrian for him anyway, so I'm wondering about using a student to help us out. I have a name or two I can reach out to, unless you think that would be crossing a line."

Vinn looks at me as if I just turned purple. "Mal, we not only blurred that line a long time ago we erased it completely. As long as you can trust them, go for it. Now about…"

I'm pretty sure she was about to add something snarky, but her words are interrupted by a gigantic yawn, her head flops down and she slowly sinks into the couch, dead to the world. I shut her laptop, lift her into my arms, and head down the hall. Tomorrow's another day.

EIGHT

"Sure, that's possible. But why would I do that for you?"

I'm sitting in a rickety chair across from Officer Mendez in the detectives' room of a police station a stone's throw from Vinn's condo. In contrast to Jenkins' orderly and nearly empty desktop, papers litter Mendez's desk with no apparent organizational system, affirming that unlike the campus bad guys, the rest of the city's criminal element doesn't take off for summer vacation. Having already gleaned that Jenkins either won't help obtain details on the various crimes listed in Vinn's database or can't because the campus cops aren't a part of the city department, I reached out to Mendez. We first met when our paths crossed in a prior investigation where he grudgingly admitted that we were instrumental in taking some very bad people off the streets. Whatever capital Vinn and I may have banked as a result of that adventure apparently had an expiration date.

My approach to Mendez would normally have been reaching out to him as an old friend, which we're not, or as a casual buddy, which we are also not, but I had to quickly veto that when I realized that for all our interactions previously, I don't even know his first name. So instead I came with hat in hand simply asking him for his help. It's not going well.

"Because I'm a law-abiding citizen requesting the help of the local constabulary?" His face tells me no. "Look, Mendez, we're trying to help a friend in need. Remember Rebecca? She's been the victim of a series of incidents that started out small but seem to be escalating, and we have reason to believe that they're all originating from a single source. From our limited research, she isn't alone. There appear to have been a number of locals who also have been having unusually long streaks of bad luck, and some of them are in the upper regions when it comes to assets. Might be a feather in your cap to put a stop to this targeted crime wave."

Mendez makes a face that he'd better hope won't freeze that way. "Wouldn't be me, I don't work bunko. But yeah, I'm aware of what you're talking about and it isn't anything new. Scam artists, con men, and more have been around for thousands of years. The new twist is the situation you're describing, where the same people all of a sudden have a string of things happening to them. They always think they know who's behind it, but the person they finger invariably couldn't be doing the crimes themselves, so they must have help. Help that stays under the radar. What exactly the person the victim IDs gets out of this we don't know because we can't find them to ask them. Again, though, not my department."

I stay silent as Mendez disappears into a cloud of thought. When he emerges, it's clear that a decision has been made. "Okay, here's the deal. Same as last time. I'll get you a couple of names but they didn't come from me. And if you get something hot, you tell me before you run headlong into a situation you might not come out of. Got it?"

I hide my smile. "Got it, officer. Scout's honor. I promise, we'll be good."

Mendez scowls. We both know that's not true. "Before you go—and you are going soon—give me the details of Rebecca's misfortunes and I'll run it through our database to try to find other recent patterns that come close to matching."

I fill him in on the little we know. One part of him seems disappointed at the paucity of information but another part appears thrilled that I won't be hanging around here much longer.

"If that's all you've got that's all you've got." He tells me with a sigh. "Now get out of here and I don't want to see you here again. Ever. Look for a text later. A text not from me."

The temptation to make a pithy remark is overwhelming, but I'll be getting what I came here for and don't want to screw it up. I rise quickly without comment and hustle to the stairs.

"Just names?" Vinn expresses her disappointment as we sit on her couch sipping on her homemade brew of pineapple, apricot, and lime punch. It could use a splash of vodka but we need to keep our wits about us, at least for now. "I guess we should be thankful for his help but he could have at least attached a phone number or address. And only two names at that. We'd better hope that at least one of them pans out because it doesn't sound like he'll be in the mood to give us more. Which one do you want, Chastity Horowitz or Ruby Phillips?"

"I'll take Chastity. Sounds like there can't be too many of with that name around and just the name alone smells like money." I wasn't wrong. No sooner do I push the return button on my laptop than my screen is filled with images of an elderly woman with platinum blonde hair, and in every picture she's wearing a designer dress or a fur. It would be too much to expect that her address or phone number would be publicly available, so it'll take further digging.

I move to Facebook, Twitter, and Instagram, the triumvirate of platforms to inadvertently reveal too much about yourself. Sure enough, a large number of photos were taken in the courtyard of the same building and one had a link to an article from a local news scrap that interviewed her in her home. A giant picture window in the background presents a perfect view of the Chicago skyline and from the perspective indicates that she has to live at least fifty stories up. Her windows face south and east.

I drag together a montage of pictures of Chastity inside and in front of the building and of the view from her luxury suite. "Vinn, do you recognize this building? You know the city better than I do."

Vinn studies the photos in silence, a crease appearing on her forehead as she scrunches in concentration. "I can't name it," she finally tells me, "but I've seen it and so have you. From ground level of course. And from the view, it's got to be near the Water Tower. Very close I would guess. Try Googling "Luxury apartments Magnificent Mile Chicago."

It takes two seconds of typing and the push of a button to get links to lists of the top apartment buildings in the Streeterville area, and less than a minute more to identify the one I'm looking for. Vinn was slightly off on its location, as it's a couple blocks both south and west of the Chicago Water Tower, one of the few structures to have survived the fire of 1871, but close enough to be able to brag about its proximity to Michigan Avenue.

"It's called the 'Pinnacle,' 21 E. Huron," I tell her. "Who names these places anyway? Why couldn't it be called 'The Cellar'?

Vinn doesn't react. "Put the name and address in your notes, Sherlock. When we find our hacker, it shouldn't be difficult for them to get into the building's directory, or if she filed a claim the insurance company's records will have her unit number and phone. In the meantime get over here and help me out. Mine's not as easy."

It's hard to believe that anyone can't be located on social media these days, but if Vinn's research is to be believed there's no adult, and only one child under the age of five, named Ruby Phillips living within the city limits. We try different spellings, expand our search out to the adjoining suburbs, then enter in all sorts of variations of her first and last names with details from the crimes against her, which were mostly vandalism, phone harassment, and the like. After over half an hour we run out of even bad ideas and are forced to admit defeat.

Vinn closes out the search engine and pulls up her notes. "The police report I found isn't specific, but it looks like she lives somewhere on the near west side. Along with hundreds of thousands of other people. Before we go knocking on doors, add that to the hacker list. Then go get me some cheese."

I've learned from past experience that once the cheese comes out, our investigation comes to a halt for the time being. Moving to the kitchen, I'm surprised to see that the skies are dark outside. We've been at this a long time. I slice up some Havarti and Muenster from a dairy we visited near Madison, scrounge through her cabinets to find some stale crackers, then put them on a plate and return to her side on the couch. By that time she's browsing Netflix and we settle in for the night.

My former employer had some of the top IT specialists in the country on staff and would often use them for less-than-legal purposes, but I found that hackers who learned their craft at top computer science schools like MIT or the University of Illinois tend not to get their hands as dirty as they sometimes need to be. They seem to have a built-in level of restraint that they may not even know they have. That's why field operatives such as myself ended up tracking down our own sources who honed their skills in dark basements or their parents' garages. J.J. was one of those, and in my view one of the best. Unfortunately he went dark after hacking into the Russian intelligence community some months ago and I'm not sure he's resurfaced or, for that matter, is still alive. Vinn and I used a student on campus last time we needed a hacker and she was wonderful. We both ignored moral and ethical lines in using her services last time, and I'm hesitant to suggest that we do so again. Vinn does have her principles.

"What's your issue Winters?" Vinn asks me condescendingly. "Of course we can approach Malika again. What we need her to do is nothing compared to last time. The only reason I didn't suggest her in the first place is because I'm not sure if she stuck around campus for the summer and I deleted her cell number from my phone in case there was any fallout from that whole mess. Didn't want anyone in authority to be able to trace her through me. You did the same thing, right?"

When I don't answer right away Vinn stares at me with narrowed eyes. It's disconcerting. As a distraction, and also as a stall tactic, I pull out my phone and begin scrolling through my contacts. There she is under the Ks. Think fast, Winters.

"Um, this is probably a different Malika." Okay, so I'm not always fast on my feet. Vinn snorts, grabs my phone, and looks at the screen.

"Uh uh, it's entirely possible that there are two Malika Kumaris in this world and that you've met both of them. I swear, Mal, you can be a real moron sometimes. Fortunately in this case your idiocy can serve our purpose." Before I can grab my phone back, Vinn's already punched a button.

"No, Malika, this is actually Vinn Achison, but Professor

Winters is right here. I'm just using his phone. How have you been? Great, good to hear. Look, we don't mean to bother you, but…. Well, yes, it is something similar. Yes, it's also something just a tiny bit illegal. Of course, yes, it's for a good cause, at least we think so. Malika, don't you even want to hear what we're asking you to do before you agree? Okay, fine, let me get our notes, but promise me if you have any doubts no matter how small that you'll say so."

Vinn puts her on hold. "We've created a monster, Mal. She's so excited to get involved that any moral constraints don't even cross her mind. I guess when she gets locked up after hacking Fort Knox we'll only have ourselves to blame. Hand me your notes on what we need from her, will you?"

I do so and Vinn gets back on the phone. "Malika, all we're doing is trying to track down two people who were victims of a series of crimes. We have names and for one we have an address but need her unit number. And phone numbers for both if possible." Vinn supplies her with what little information we have. "For Ruby, we don't have any suggestions. We already tried all of the usual sources. I guess just run her name through whatever databases you think might turn her up. For Chastity, we thought that you could tap into the condo association's directory and if that doesn't work, maybe she filed a claim with her impotence company. Wait, that can't be right." Vinn throws me a caustic look. "Sorry, insurance company. Winters' handwriting is almost indecipherable. Great, thanks. Sooner the better, and this time instead of course credit we'll pay you. Sound good?"

"I think that girl would pay us to do the job," Vinn sighs as she hangs up the phone. "So I guess now all we can do is wait."

NINE

Despite her enthusiasm, we don't expect to hear back from Malika today or anytime soon. Crime takes time, or so a former mentor once said, and as stupid as it sounded at the time it happens to be true in this case. Not knowing quite how to fill our time while waiting, Vinn and I are like two schoolkids a week into summer vacation. We're restless, unfocused, and are starting to get on each other's nerves. I awkwardly scan Vinn's living room looking for answers but the walls aren't giving up their secrets. Finally, with no better option and no excuses to delay it, we decide to see what we can find out about Sara Engers, Rebecca's nemesis. Vinn grabs her laptop, which has a bigger screen than mine, and we snuggle close together as she enters the name into Google.

In a nanosecond, ten thousand links fill the screen and at first glance all of the hits on the first few pages appear to be about the same person. Rebecca's statement that the woman is attractive was an understatement. Sara is stunningly beautiful in every picture we pull up even as she went through stages experimenting with a rainbow of hair colors. Especially notable are her sharp facial features and piercing blue eyes, the kind that seem to be able to penetrate deep into your soul. Even the butterfly tattoo on her left wrist is tasteful and seems to enhance her looks rather than detract from them. It's easy to understand why Ted, who from what I can tell would have been and may still be as chauvinistic as they come and the type to judge a woman only by how she looks, was instantly attracted to her and reluctant to give up on the relationship. Sara's eyes also suggest a deep-seeded evil lying right below the surface, although that might be me projecting.

"Before we go any further, let's make sure that this is the right woman," Vinn suggests as she navigates to Sara's webpage. Buried deep among the hundreds of selfies and links to various new age websites selling crystals and meditative services is a detailed biography of her life, which reads as if she deserves some sort of medal just for being who she is. My stomach turns and Vinn scrunches her nose in disgust as she continues to scroll. "Wait, here we go," she eventually says. "She actually uses her own point system to evaluate everyone she's ever dated. Ugh. At least she has the decency not to use last names. Or maybe she's afraid of being sued."

"Quite a long list," I observe. "There—about a quarter of the way down. Let's read what it says about 'Ted.' 'Mildly attractive in a Cro-Magnon sort of way with a basic personality to match. Tried to be the manliest of men but only succeeded in presenting as beastly. Living with him was like being trapped in an elevator with a hillbilly from hell. Score: 2 ½.' I've got to give it to her, that's our Ted. Definitely the right woman." For no reason other than morbid curiosity, we take turns picking reviews to read. None are positive and a few even make Ted sound like a catch.

"Let's at least glance at her links," I suggest after reading a particularly viscous skewering. "Maybe one of them will be to a 'Hire a Thug' website." Vinn throws me a glance that I know all too well means she's wondering why she sticks with such a moron, but decides to humor me anyway. "Let's see, lots of information about the healing powers of crystals, which chakras to press for which ailments, links to herbalists, and even a shout-out on the virtues of fortune telling. All right, never mind. Let's move on."

"Facebook next," Vinn tells me with an air of authority to leave no doubt that she's taking back control of the mouse. Facebook already helped us track down where Chastity lives and we hope to stay hot with Sara giving up way too much private information while trying to look like one of the cool kids. Travel preferences, personality preferences of friends, political views, favorite foods, fashion photos, and the like are often invaluable in suggesting a path to take in an investigation. With Sara, however, not so much.

"It just seems to reinforce what we already gleaned from her own page," Vinn bemoans, clearly disappointed. "Although I guess if it becomes important to know that she prefers her future read by palmistry instead of a crystal ball we're already a step ahead."

"It does look like she's unfriended a number of her long-time pals lately, since she profiles each one and announces what transgression they committed to get on her naughty list," I tell Vinn. "Might suggest that she's as unstable as Rebecca seems to think she is. Maybe even enough to commit a series of petty crimes to show how she feels."

We continue peering into Sara's life for another half hour, including trips to LinkedIn, Twitter, Instagram, and at least half a dozen similar sites that Vinn seems to have an awareness of but I don't. Except for confirming that she visited the Cayman Islands in 2019 and looks great in a bikini, it was a waste of thirty minutes with the notable exception of the fifteen seconds Vinn allowed me to look at the bikini photo. We then move on to the profiles of some of what appear to be her closest remaining friends to see if they slipped up and mentioned the time they were with Sara when she keyed a car, but no luck there either.

"I'm not sure that got us anywhere," Vinn sighs. "And unless you're seeing something that I'm not, we're nowhere nearer to first figuring out if this woman is behind Rebecca's series of misfortunes and second, if she is, how to approach the problem."

"Afraid not," I admit. "And there's really nothing that we could pass on to Malika to pursue that'll move us forward either. We know her name, Rebecca gave us her address and phone number, and her life seems to be an open book on social media. No rocks to turn over. Short of catching her in the act, we're stuck."

"Well, let's not tell Rebecca that as of yet," Vinn says. "If she asks, we're in the process of assembling a personality profile that will enable us to...to... I don't know, you're the English teacher. Add some words."

We sit glumly for a few moments before I nudge even closer and put my arm around Vinn's shoulders as she leans her head into me. Finding comfort in being close, I'm half asleep and almost don't recognize the tone coming from my phone as a text. Vinn grumbles as I shift to reach my phone and identify the annoying texter.

I'm not sure what sound I emit, but Vinn correctly identifies it as a mix of surprise and concern, and sits up, immediately on alert. "It's Leo," I tell her. "He wants to talk."

Vinn instantly recognizes the significance of what just happened. Leo is the very definition of an old-school, crusty old man, and it wouldn't surprise me if this is the first text he's ever sent. More remarkable, though, is the fact that he's reaching out at all, which again he's never done that I know of. Self-sufficient to the core with a background of shady activities that would probably make Vinn and I look like schoolchildren, to acknowledge his need for assistance with whatever's been going on in his life signals that the danger he's facing is major with a capital 'M.'

I text back that we're on the way while Vinn arranges for an Uber. The nine minutes we spend pacing while waiting for Amil to arrive in a burnt orange 1982 Chevy Citation seems much longer. As we step into the rear seats of the car we hope will get us back to my place in one piece, Vinn expresses the same thought that's been stuck in my brain since Leo's text.

"What's the story with your tenants, Mal? That's two for two, although I have the feeling that whatever's eating Leo is a little more serious than a car getting keyed."

I offer no response and we ride the rest of the way in silence. If Vinn's imagination is going the same places that mine is, we're both expecting that whatever we're about to hear will be life-changing, not only for Leo but for the two of us.

The Citation's engine starts smoking about a block from our destination and the driver skillfully turns off the engine and coasts to the curb, a maneuver that was so smooth I have the feeling that this isn't the first time. Vinn and I quickly scramble out and begin half walking, half running to my building, but not before the driver shouts at us that he hopes this won't affect his tip.

As we enter the gate I pause, a part of me wondering if Leo's waiting for us up in my apartment. Rather than trek upstairs, we decide to try his place first since we're practically there already anyway. Our loud knock elicits no response, so

I try one more time. We're about to give up and head upstairs when I hear a series of no less than five locks and two bolts being thrown. That's new. We're no sooner past the threshold than Leo slams the door behind us and goes through the lock process in reverse.

The apartment is dark, the only source of light a small portable lamp on his kitchen table, and even that has a towel over its lampshade. Notably absent are the usual bottle and dirty glasses on the table, which might be another first. I can't remember ever visiting Leo where a mysterious and always potent drink isn't waiting for me. Consuming it was mandatory, the price of admission to his home.

"Fuckin' thing worked?" Leo mutters softly in his faux-Cuban accent as he looks at his phone like it's a foreign object. "Didn't wanna call in case someone listening."

I don't have the heart to add to his worries by informing him that if someone's able to tap his phone they can also read an exchange of texts. "So what's going on Leo? I've never seen you like this before." Vinn nods her head to show we're all on the same page.

Leo is a man of few words, but that's usually by choice. If he has nothing to contribute to a conversation, which is almost always, he keeps his mouth shut. That being said, I've never seen him struggle to talk when he actually wants to. After a few moments of uncomfortable silence, he sighs, rubs his face with both hands, and begins to speak quietly. Vinn and I both lean forward in order to hear him.

"My past. It is back." It's not unthinkable that that's all he's going to say, but both Vinn and I remain silent on the assumption, and hope, that more is coming. Thankfully we're right. "I know you don' believe me about Castro. You are right. Not true. But is true about someone else. Also dictator. Also dangerous. Our job to kill him.

"We failed. Only I make it back alive. Move here, to this country, start new life as cook. Many years ago. Thought everyone on government side dead by now. I was wrong." Leo stops, sweat drops appearing on his forehead. He grabs a nearby towel and mops them off. "Can't tell you which man or which country. Bound to silence, part of my deal. Tell you, and problems get worse than they already are. Will be target of both sides."

"Leo," Vinn interjects, "we appreciate that you need to honor whatever arrangement that you agreed to in return for your new identity. Mal and I both understand consequences of breaking silence in such matters due to our own circumstances. But you must understand that you haven't given us enough if you want us to help you. At a minimum, we need to know who's found you, how to find them, and what you want us to do."

Now that my eyes have adjusted to the dim light, I suddenly realize how tired Leo looks, as if he hasn't slept in days or even weeks. Seeing this strong man so vulnerable makes me ready to do whatever I can to get him back to the old Leo. But Vinn's right. We need more. Leo's eyes reflect the debate going on behind them, when they suddenly assume a newfound calm. He's made a decision. He twists around and reaches behind him.

"Here," is all he says as he slides a manila folder across the table, its outside covered in a myriad of colorful stains. I choose not to speculate as to what they're from but make a decision to put on gloves before I touch that folder. Perhaps emboldened by having conquered a mystery plague, Vinn is less queasy than I am as she reaches forward and moves to open it.

"No!" Leo quickly shouts before remembering he's trying to remain quiet. "Not here. Not in fron' ah me. Later."

We simultaneously nod in acknowledgment and just begin to push our chairs out when the old man pulls a dark green bottle out from some hidden alcove with one hand and quickly follows by producing three shot glasses in the other. Vinn and I exchange a look that recognizes we're going to regret the next few hours as well as tomorrow morning but don't have a choice in the matter. We sit back down as Leo pours.

TEN

The aroma of coffee wakes me in the morning, not because it makes me salivate for a cup, in fact just the opposite. There are few smells that can make me queasier after a night of alcohol imbibing, or at almost any other time, than that of coffee, and at this particular time I didn't need any help feeling sick to my stomach. Somewhere in the back of a cabinet I have a kudzu flower in a glass jar that I've been saving for just such an occasion. Steep it in some white tea with a thumb of ginger then add a little orange zest, and it should help my head clear. At least that's what I tell myself to motivate me to get moving. Vinn can drink myself and virtually any man alive under the table, so I brace myself for her typical energetic "good morning" and the smug expression of someone who sees anyone who can't survive a long night of drinking as a wimp. I've played that role with her too many times.

I'm totally unprepared, then, for the sight that awaits me in the kitchen. Vinn is half on and half off one of the stools at the island, her head face down and cradled in her arms, eyes puffy and closed, a line of drool hanging from the corner of her mouth. The coffee she must have so desperately wanted that it pulled her out of bed sits unattended in the coffee maker I bought only after she resisted all of my attempts to convert her to tea. An unladylike snort tells me that she's left the conscious world. If ever I needed an incentive to quickly overcome my own hangover to appear unaffected by last night, this is it. I quickly heat water until the bubbles reach the crab eyes stage, with light wisps of steam barely forming, then pour it over the kudzu flower and ginger in the largest mug I have. One four-minute shower, a quick shave, and a dash of zest later, and I'm sitting across from her waiting for the dead to rise.

Surprisingly, the tea actually does seem to be helping, and over the next half hour I'm able to force down a piece of toast spread with a generous portion of Amish peach jam. I've just finished my second cup of tea when movement catches my eye. The mighty genius is awakening.

"Hwar I gemm hoar?" she asks with a husky voice that on any other day would have driven me crazy and led to activity in the other room.

"Excuse me? Would you mind repeating that?" I surprise myself with the false amount of chipper in my voice. I move to grab Vinn's favorite mug and fill it with coffee, partly out of sympathy and partly to move out of range.

Vinn struggles to sit up, strands of unwashed hair falling across her eyes as she does. Even in this condition, or maybe in part because of it, she's as sexy as any woman I've ever met. She clears her voice as she accepts the coffee. "How'd I get up here?"

Now that I've had my fun with her and allowed myself the unusual satisfaction of feeling just the slightest bit superior for once without her even knowing it, I have two paths in front of me. Just looking at her now, I quickly decide that in the interests of harmony and to score a few brownie points, I would ignore the temptation to gloat and instead switch to the loving and sympathetic partner. That doesn't mean I can't rub it in a little by sounding alert and cheerful.

"I honestly don't know," I tell her brightly, which is true. Vinn scowls at me and I'm suddenly glad she isn't armed. "The last thing I remember is you singing the University of

Minnesota fight song."

"Oh gawd, I haven't done that since college," she moans. She takes two large gulps of coffee and the smallest hint of color returns to her cheeks. "I don't know what was in that bottle of his, but I never want to see it again. Damn you, Leo." Vinn slides off her chair and lurches toward the refrigerator, where she pulls out a fried chicken leg she finds in the butter drawer.

"Speaking of Leo..." I nod in the direction of the greasy manila folder, which somehow made it up here intact and is sitting neatly on my couch.

"Uh uh, no way. I mean not yet." Vinn pauses to scrape half the meat off into her mouth. "I don't want to even think of that man for the time being. Besides, my brain isn't where it needs to be deal with whatever we're going to find in there. I need lots of fresh air and some waffles." She wrinkles her face, takes a not-so-discreet sniff of her armpit, and makes a decision. "But first I need a shower and some fresh clothes."

Forty-five minutes later we're seated at a picnic table outside of Cracked, a breakfast place just far enough of a walk away from my place to allow both of us to breathe a lot of fresh air and apparently to work up an appetite. No waffles on the menu, but Vinn's breakfast burrito with hash browns and my chilaquiles verdes are disappearing rapidly.

Pausing between bites, I pull out my phone. "I want to see if Malika has come through for us yet," I explain to Vinn, to whom the concept of using hands for anything other than consuming food at the moment seems to puzzle her. "Yep, email from late last night. Let's see what she says."

Vinn moves around the table to sit side-by-side, using the movement as an opportunity to stab a forkful of my breakfast. "Looks like she's still working on Ruby, but she scored with Chastity," she observes. "There's no buzzer code since the building uses a doorman, but here are her unit number, cell number, even tax returns and the combination to her locker at the tennis club." Vinn frowns. "I'm proud of that girl, but maybe we need to have a little talk to her about boundaries."

"Later. For now, what do you say? It's a beautiful day, we have no other plans unless you're ready to dive into Leo's past, how about we go pay a visit to our good friend Chastity?"

"I'm in," Vinn replies with a level of enthusiasm indicating that she's nearly recovered. "But first, do you see our server? I wonder if they have dessert in this place."

On any sunny summer day such as this one, tourists are elbow to elbow for several blocks in either direction of Michigan Avenue, jamming intersections, crossing against lights, or just standing in the street to gawk at the tall buildings. If we take an Uber, we may have to start talking about dinner plans before we arrive at the Pinnacle. Walking might be faster, but better yet is the el, which runs underground in that area, and the Chicago Avenue stop is a short walk from our destination.

If I had a background in architectural design I might be impressed by this tall glass building which was designed by an local architect of note, but to me it's just one more building that looks better on the drawing board than it does on the street. As we near the entrance to the condominiums, which appears well hidden to discourage the curious from venturing in, I guide Vinn to the edge of the sidewalk away from the throngs of shoppers.

"Do we have any semblance of a plan?" I ask her, pretty much knowing the answer. Our best-laid plans have rarely if ever succeeded, providing plenty of incentive to just wing it. Problem is, looking back at our history of investigations together, barreling ahead without a plan hasn't exactly worked for us either.

"Just follow my lead Mal," she tells me, using the very words I feared. "An older woman might relate better to a woman than to a man, especially given the likelihood that it was a man that robbed her." As we merge back into the crowd, it occurs to me that Vinn didn't really answer my question, which I assume was intentional. Winging it it is.

Vinn pulls up Malika's email on her phone as we move into the doorway. She finds whatever she's looking for and stashes it in her purse. There's no panel of buzzers or anything else to indicate that any of the unit owners wants to be contacted by the outside world on this side of the door, so we move into the inner sanctum. Our progress is immediately halted by a tall black man in an impeccably tailored uniform. A doorman in name only apparently since we handled that chore ourselves. More like a security guard in traditional doorman attire to momentarily confuse trespassers such as ourselves.

"May I help you?" he asks in a deep baritone, his tone making it sound like the only thing he's likely to help us with is to immediately escort us back outside. Vinn, already prepared to take the lead today, puts on a somber face and lowers her own voice half an octave. I have to suppress a smile.

"My name's Achison and this is Winters," she tells the gatekeeper. "We're investigating some, uh, incidents involving Chastity Horowitz. I believe she's expecting us."

"Very well, Officer. If you don't mind stepping away from the door and waiting over here, I'll call up."

So Vinn's plan is to impersonate police officers without actually identifying ourselves as one. At one time we would have debated the ethics of such a move and discussed the fine points of not crossing the line into an arrestable offense. Seems like one of us no longer sees a line at all and the other doesn't see fit to object.

The doorman returns wearing an expression of someone who's about to tell us about a death in our family. "It seems like Mrs. Horowitz doesn't remember making this appointment," he tells us, probably scanning our backsides to look for the best areas to plant his foot, "but she is very glad you came nonetheless. She of course has been very distressed by events of late. If you would follow me."

Vinn raises an eyebrow at me as we walk, surprised at her own success. We're turned over to the elevator man, who has the physique of an ex-Marine and a scowl to match. He lets us in one at a time, evaluating us with every step. Hairs raise on the back of my neck. I have the uncomfortable feeling that if we say even an unkind word to Chastity, he'll sense it and we'll have to take the stairs back down. It would be a long walk, as he pushes the button for the 46th floor. From what I read online, condos on the upper levels in this building start at around three million.

The ride is smooth and fast and before we know it the elevator eases to a stop and the doors open. Immediately outside the door is yet another bulky man in an identical uniform as the elevator guy. Not a marine this time. More like a retired linebacker for the Bears.

Without a word, he motions us to follow him down the hall. We stop before the door to unit 46C and wait as he knocks gently with a gloved hand. Moments later the door opens, first a crack and then as wide as it will go. Before us stands a woman in her 80s, hair as blue as Lake Michigan, thick glasses safely secured by a diamond cord, wearing a silk housecoat that must have run her an amount equal to a year's worth of my salary. She looks like what every grandmother should look like. Slightly rotund, a kind face, and an air of having seen it all. I half expect her to produce a plate of cookies from behind her back.

Moving to the edge of the doorway, Chastity Horowitz peers at us, then slowly scans us from our feet to the top of our heads. "Well?" she says loudly with a raspy voice. "What in the hell do you want?"

Despite the circumstances, Vinn and I both have trouble suppressing a chuckle. She recovers first, assumes a more serious expression, and takes the lead, as planned. "Mrs. Horowitz, my name's Vinn Achison and this is Malcom Winters. We understand that you've been unhappy with the lack of progress the police have made regarding your complaint, in fact I'll bet you wonder if they're making much of an effort at all. The two of us have substantial investigative experience along with a history of success where the police have failed, and with your permission we'd like to assist you. There would be no fee. In truth, we have a close friend who may have fallen victim to a similar scheme, maybe even by the same source, and by allowing us to help you, we hope to help her as well."

Whatever Vinn saw in this woman when she answered the door led her to switch tactics on the fly, so that we've given up all pretense of being official. Maybe I can cancel my reservations for that jail cell. Her assumption that Chastity is less than thrilled with the police response isn't much of a risk, since almost every victim of a crime in the history of the world is unhappy with the cops when their case isn't solved and lingers for weeks if not longer. The mention of a friend with a similar matter is a nice touch. Hopefully Mrs. H. won't jump to the logical conclusion that we have the slightest idea what the circumstances of her situation are.

After a long pause, Mrs. H. nods her head. "Might as well come in then. If I don't like what you're pushing, though, I'll call Ron here and he'll boot you out on your asses." She looks at the man who was stationed outside the elevator, who remains impassive and silent. He stays in the hall as we follow Mrs. H. into her unit. I close the door behind me. Take that, Ron.

I'm immediately impressed by what three million dollars can buy. The unit itself isn't all that much different than my own except for the size and the fact that everything in it from the carpeting to the blinds to the microwave probably cost more than my entire building. It's the view, though, that sets it apart. With windows facing both east and south, she has a nearly unobstructed view of Lake Michigan and the Loop. On a clear day, she can probably see Indiana. My living room overlooks my kitchen.

Mrs. H. settles into a designer chair while we plop ourselves onto a designer couch and rest our feet on the designer carpet. We are not offered cookies. Vinn doesn't waste any time.

"The details we have aren't as specific as we'd like them to be. If it's not too much trouble, can you run us through what happened to you?"

Smart move. Most people, especially crime victims, are more than happy to talk about themselves. Mrs. H. quickly shows that she's no exception.

"This whole thing started out small and then snowballed. I didn't even notice it at first. And don't you go thinking I'm senile just because I'm old, young man, I'm as sharp as ever. Although for a while I wasn't sure myself. I couldn't find my watch one day even though I always keep it in the same place. Then a few days later a credit card was missing out of my wallet. I swore it was there the day before but still called every shop where I might have left it. Nothing. One evening I went to prepare some chicken fillets for dinner but they weren't there even though I know I bought them. That's how it started.

"It accelerated from there. My bank misplaced a deposit. Someone stole my identity on Facebook. Don't look so surprised, I can use a computer, thank you. Whoever it was posted all sorts of lies under my name. Lost a few friends. Then I'd get calls in the middle of the night but when I'd pick up there'd be no one there. My number's unlisted and there's no way that anyone but a few friends and family know what it is."

And Malika and Vinn and I, of course, but I don't interrupt with that information. Mrs. H. isn't done. "There were some other things but you get the picture. At least you'd better or I'll call Ron because you'd be too stupid to help me. Anyway, I was playing bridge with a few ladies in the lounge on game night when I may have mentioned my troubles between hands. One of the other players suggested that I go see a medium. Of course I thought that was rubbish but she said it had helped her and I thought, what the hell, why not?"

"Mrs. Horowitz," I interrupt, "can you tell us who it was that suggested the medium?"

She looks at me like I'm a fool. "Wouldn't I have told you if I knew? It was some young whippersnapper in her 40s or maybe a little older, brown skin, maybe she's black but could be Spanish. I don't know her name or what unit she lives in. Had never seen her before. Game night is open to all residents, even those on the lower floors, so it's not always the same players." Vinn and I exchange a meaningful glance but say nothing, not wanting to interrupt the flow.

"So she gave me the name of some woman that she used and said that she works out of her home in the South Loop, but would meet in a client's home for a little extra. Pays to be rich, you see. Like I said, I don't believe in that mumbo jumbo but I figured if nothing else it's be a story to tell later. So I set it up."

"When was this, Mrs. Horowitz?" Vinn asks.

"Two months ago? A little longer? Somewhere around there. And you can call me Chase." She's looking directly at Vinn when she says this as if I weren't in the room. Great. Now I have no idea what to call her and will end up having to be careful not to address her by name at all.

"And you know what? She wasn't some old hag, she was maybe 40 or so, although everyone younger than me looks 40. Clean looking, dressed normally. No crystal ball or any of that crap. She just closed the blinds, made sure everything was quiet, then took my hands into hers. Told me to relax and let my thoughts run free. Then she proceeded to tell me all about myself, stuff that she never should have known. And about my family, saying that my mother who's been dead for thirty years asked about events that happened after she died. I know this all sounds crazy when I talk about it, but she knew things. You had to be there.

"Eventually she gained my trust and I figured maybe she really can find the reason for my string of bad luck. I won't go into details, but she discovered that someone—she couldn't tell me who—put a curse on me and that I'd keep having bad luck unless she did something to lift that curse, or block it, or something.

"She told me she would need $10,000.00 to make it all

go away. Seemed like a lot but I can afford it and it would be worth it to stop all of the annoyances. I paid her and she said she would need to gather some herbs and do some incantations, or some such thing for a week straight and then have a ceremony with me at the next full moon. The ceremony was right here, she was sitting where you are. There were glowing orbs, and chanting, and holding hands, the whole works. Even then it seemed ridiculous, but you know what? It worked. All the petty little annoyances stopped happening."

"So you paid $10,000.00 and it all went away?" Vinn asks, trying not to sound judgmental. "I thought I read something about a necklace."

"I'm coming to that," Chase says defensively, "because the problems started up again. Same kinds of stuff. I called Madam Isadora—that's the name she uses—and after putting me on hold she said that there was a hole in the chakra or some babble and that the first go-around wasn't powerful enough to ward it off. Don't give me that look. So she needed $5,000.00 more and scheduled another session. This time she brought an assistant. Anyway, they darkened the room and even put a blindfold on me and then burned incense. Something was glowing on the table and they put on music. After about fifteen minutes, Isadora told me we needed absolute silence for fifteen more. I waited and nothing happened, so finally I took off my blindfold. They were gone. So was most of my jewelry, including that necklace. Total value was close to $200,000.00."

By this time, tears had formed at the corners of Chase's eyes and the confident voice of only minutes before had deserted her. We talked for a few more minutes but by then her energy level had sunk to zero. We exchanged numbers, told her we'd be in touch, and slipped out the door.

ELEVEN

Back in my apartment, Vinn and I once more ignore Leo's folder. Though we haven't said it out loud, I think both of us are hesitant to poke into Leo's past for fear of what we might find. We choose instead to focus on evaluating what if anything we had just learned from our conversation with Mrs. H. "This may just be me and as you know I'm prone to latching on to wild theories, but did you sense a link between Chase's problems and those of Rebecca?" I ask Vinn, being careful not to provide any more details to see if she picked up on the same notion that I did without leading her directly to the same conclusion.

"Glad to hear you bring it up first, that way if it's actually as much of a stretch as it's likely to be, I can blame you for wasting our time," she replies, only half kidding. "Why don't you call Rebecca to see if she can add anything to her profile of Sara." She slides my phone over to me.

"Rebecca, this is Mal. Not yet, we've barely started. I do have a question to ask you about your ex, though. We know she had an interest in alternative remedies and the like. Was Sara's interest in the occult just for show for her followers or did she ever actually visit mediums, fortune tellers, or anyone like that? Okay, good, when was that and do you know the details? I see, thanks. No, it's probably nothing. You know us, we're looking at this from every angle and most of what we're doing at first won't amount to anything. We'll let you know."

As I hang up, Vinn is looking at me with raised eyebrows. I know better than to leave her hanging. "Bingo. Besides the interest in anything new age that shows up in her social media presence, Sara regularly visits palm readers, fortune tellers, and other mystical sources for guidance as to decisions she needs to make or just general life choices. It was one more thing that bothered Rebecca about her. She put more stock in what they said after looking at lines on her palm or reading tea leaves than anything Rebecca would contribute. Sounds like she's a true believer."

Vinn looks less than thrilled by this development. "Matches up with what was on her website, but I was hoping that wouldn't be the case," she sighs. "We could be going down a rabbit hole by looking into this aspect of things only to discover that there's no pot of gold at the end of the rainbow."

"Mixed metaphor aside, I agree with you. But as of right now, and I can't believe I'm saying this, that's our best lead. First, there's no question that the stranger that Mrs. H. played cards with set her up, don't you agree? And this Madam Isadora and her assistant clearly robbed her, that can also go in the undisputed-fact-until-disproven-otherwise column. With Mrs. H., then, the fortune teller is our first and so far only line of investigation. It really won't add much effort to throw Rebecca into the same pile, and it's no longer that far-fetched. Besides, the only reason we're helping Mrs. H. is because we suspect it'll help us with Rebecca. Remember how Sara told Rebecca that she knew someone that could put a curse on her? Might not be the same woman that stole from Chase, but they're definitely neighbors in Crazytown."

"All right, even if all of that is true, what next?" Vinn asks. "Unless there's a side of you that I don't know about, neither one of us has even the tiniest familiarity with mysticism. If these people are a fraction as skilled as drifters as they appear to be, we can't go into this cold."

"Way ahead of you. I just called for an Uber."

The Occult Book Store, located on the first floor of a four-story brick building on Grand Avenue about a five-minute drive from my place, markets itself as the oldest spirit shop in the country, having just celebrated its centennial anniversary a couple of years back. Expecting a dimly-lit room with beaded doorways and the scent of incense, I'm surprised at the bright, open space that greets us as we enter. The walls on either side are lined with bookshelves, glass cases in the center offer spiritual kits and supplies, and everything appears as neat as a pin.

Clearly out of our element, a bearded man in his thirties quickly makes his way over to assist us. "Help you folks?" he inquires quizzically.

"Not sure," I admit. "We're looking into a couple of possibly related crimes in which fortune tellers appear to have played a key role." I see the alarm in his eyes and quickly act to assuage his rising defensiveness. "Before I explain further, we're not here to accuse anyone. We're simply trying to gather background information on alternative spiritual beliefs, especially as they relate to people who abuse them for profit. Figured your bookstore would be a good place to start."

My attempt at calming our greeter doesn't appear to have been totally successful. "Well," he says guardedly as he gives Vinn and I the once-over. "No one associated with this shop, employees or customers, would be involved in anything like that. We sell rare spiritual books and conjuring supplies to those who practice or study the beliefs of ancient civilizations. We supplement this with readings, lectures, and social gatherings. But let me be clear that we would in no way be a party to anything immoral or illegal."

Vinn tries to ride to the rescue. "Again, we're not accusing you or any of your true believers of anything. Our evidence shows that someone, or maybe more than one person, is using spiritualism as a front for committing crimes. We would think that honest practitioners such as yourself would want us to prevent such people from sullying your own names by association."

That seems to have struck home and our host's features soften ever so slightly. "I'm not sure any one or two of the books we carry would be enough for your purposes, and it's easy to focus on the wrong information without guidance. I do have an idea that may help you. Feel free to look around and I'll be back in a few minutes."

As we wait, we browse the shelves. Books on ancient alchemy, pagan rituals, astral realms, tarot, and more wait for someone to bring them home. The glass case contains an array of cauldrons, wands, crystal balls, and spell kits. I make a mental note that the next time I'm bored to come by and spend an afternoon.

I'm considering which spiritual bath salts to purchase when the man returns, paper slip in hand. "Here's the phone number for Angela Boswell. She knows more about the history of the Roma than anyone else around. She's expecting your call."

Before Vinn or I can ask what or who the Roma are, we're escorted to the door and told to have a great day. Once outside, Vinn wastes no time in pulling out her cell and punching in the numbers. The conversation is short. "Tomorrow at 10:00 a.m.," she says. "I guess we won't know if we're on the right track until then."

For the second time in two days, I'm surprised and a little disappointed at the lack of a mystical ambiance for our foray into the world of the occult. Angela Boswell, who our research revealed is a well-known and highly respected reader among those who follow such things, lives and works out of her bungalow in the Portage Park neighborhood on the northwest side of the city. We're currently sitting at her kitchen table. While she processes our consultation fee, she catches me glancing around.

"Not quite what you expected, is it?" she says with a smile. "To the uninitiated, they think that we all work out of a dark room sitting at an embroidered table with a glowing crystal ball in its center and dress in colorful low-cut robes and a scarf. Some do, but that's all for show and not at all necessary. Frankly, the more bling the less likely the reader is legitimate. Now, what can I do for you?"

"We're college professors with backgrounds that endowed us with skills friends and colleagues have found useful in helping investigate certain matters that have been ignored or given a low priority by more official channels," Vinn responds, being deliberately vague. "We've recently been drawn into two separate matters that have a common denominator, namely a fortune teller at the center of a serious crime. We're not impugning your craft, but someone out there appears to be using it for less than honest purposes. Before we dive any further in, we're hoping to find out what we're up against."

Angela nods. "Very delicately put, thank you. And yes, there's a segment of our population, like any other, that preys upon the innocent and the stain of their crimes splatters the rest of us in the eyes of many. We could devote an entire day to the subject, but I'll try to give you the condensed version. That still requires a history lesson, so settle in and get comfortable.

"Frank at the bookstore mentioned the Roma when he called, which is the first direction many people go when talking about gypsies and scammers. That's a rash overgeneralization but he may not be wrong and it's as good a place as any for you to start. I'm Roma myself, as are many if not most of the spiritual readers in the area. Our history stretches back over a thousand years to an oppressed people called shiviranuchara, who survived a series of wars in India by hanging on as camp followers to the armies for both sides. After the wars, we were expelled from the region and emigrated to Eastern Europe, mostly the Balkan areas as well as lands that are now parts of Turkey and Greece. Most of us ended up as slaves to the native populations. Roma women—never the men—even then had a reputation for clairvoyance and the ability to tell the future and used these crafts in order to survive. Our skills appear in written works dating back to the 1400s and we've been doing it continually over the centuries.

"Anyway, to jump forward, in the late 1800s Roma from Serbia and Hungary came in droves to Chicago, where the men worked sharpening knives or as musicians while the women read palms and told fortunes. As late as the 1970s it wasn't unusual for Roma women to work out of the backs of wagons or for a so-called "gypsy caravan" to lead a funeral procession on the north side of the city. That still happens but in a much less public way."

"I was at a wedding a couple of years back where a gypsy band played," Vinn interjects. "They were incredible."

Angela appears to beam. "You don't remember their

name do you?" Vinn shakes her head. "Many of my family members play at weddings and other festivals. Our traditions live on through music. But you didn't come to hear about that."

She sighs. "Not all Roma women have the gift of foretelling, but many act as if they do. And there are entire families, gangs even, that take advantage of our reputation to line their pockets. Mostly it's simple fraud. Let me give you a common example. You make an appointment with me for a reading, wanting advice about your life. Before you come, I do my research on you. Social media nowadays makes it so easy to find out everything I need to know. By the time you're sitting across from me, I can 'divine' so much about you that you'll swear I really do have special powers. I'll be vague, letting you fill in the blanks, look for subtle reactions to my comments, quickly backtrack if I get off course. To draw out more facts I don't know, there's the principal of subjective validation, which is a fancy way of saying that you create a personal connection to a generalized statement I make in a desperate desire to make it true. And voila, I'm a psychic."

Angela pauses to take a sip of water before continuing. "You pay me for a series of meetings and by the time you realize you've been had, I've got thousands of your dollars in my pocket. And you won't go to the police. First, what I did isn't necessarily illegal and can be cast as entertainment. Chicago itself doesn't even have any laws against it. Secondly, you'll be so embarrassed to have been conned that you don't want to tell anyone about it anyway. It's not that different from what I do except that I legitimately focus on healing, don't fleece my clients, and I don't create elaborate fictions."

"Fascinating," I tell her, and I mean it. "But have you

heard of any bigger scams, where people lose larger sums, even fortunes? And how would we find the women who practice the big con, so to speak?"

Angela looks wary. "Yes, there are always rumors. You need to tread very carefully, Malcom. These aren't just skilled con artists, these women and the men behind them are dangerous. One errant step and your life may be over. As far as finding them, again all I can provide is what I pick up in gossip. There's a shop called the Lucky Hoodoo on the South Side. They provide occult supplies but also perform ritual services that include cursing your enemies. As far as I know, that's as far as they go. But drop the right phrase or two or let it be known that you're looking for an effective curse, and you may be approached after you leave the shop. That's when you're invited to enter a very dark world."

Andrea rises to refill her glass. "I've said enough, but I'd appreciate it if you could keep me informed on what you find." She looks at the clock on her wall. "You still have a few minutes left on your consultation. Would either of you like me to do a quick reading of your palm?"

Vinn shrinks away, but I shrug my shoulders and stretch my right arm in her direction. Angela takes my hand in both of her own, rubs my palm gently, then lowers her head until she's about three inches away. Without uttering a word, almost immediately she pushes my hand away while emitting a small shriek, her features darken, and she appears absolutely terrified. Waving her arm wildly in the direction of the door, we take the hint and quickly leave her home.

TWELVE

"After Angela's performance there at the end, I'm not sure I want to be anywhere near you for a while," Vinn remarks, "and I can't help but feel it had something to do with whatever lies within that envelope."

We're sitting at my kitchen island snacking on cheddar popcorn, which coats our fingers in an orange powder that transfers to anything we touch. My subconscious most likely influenced me to pull it out over something less messy as a way of stalling for just a few more minutes before we have to face the inevitable and read whatever it is that Leo gave us. Its selection may have been a product of my subconscious, but eating too much popcorn to the point that I'm nearly ill as a stall tactic was definitely intentional. I don't want to see what's inside the packet any more than Vinn does.

"I guess we can't put it off any longer," I sigh as I move to the sink to wash my hands. "You ready?"

"No, but I never will be." Vinn's voice quivers a little, which makes me more nervous than I was seconds before. We've both had run-ins with some very nasty people funded by foreign governments before, if that's what this is, so you would think this would just be one more incident and no big deal. In reality it's precisely because of our experiences with international thuggery that we're reluctant to go down that path again. If this wasn't Leo, we wouldn't even consider it.

I slit the top of the envelope open with a kitchen knife and slide a slender stack of documents out onto the counter. On the very top is a high-resolution photo of the face of a man roughly seventy years of age who in some ways resembles Leo. His features make him look like he's led a trying life, with deep wrinkles and troubled eyes, though his thinning hair remains dark. A scar that begins above his eye runs diagonally across his nose and out of the frame of the picture. A scowl that seems to warn anyone near to back away adds to his homeliness while also raising the score on his intimidation scale.

I throw a sideways glance at Vinn and she shakes her head slightly. We didn't expect to recognize him but there was always the chance. I flip the picture over to uncover the document below. It's an untitled, handwritten assortment of unorganized notes in what I presume is Leo's handwriting. Near the top is a list of aliases, mostly variations of the name "Hector Alvarez," a gruesome grouping of his preferred ways to kill people, his favorite types of places to stay when on the job, and a single name with a smudged phone number. No explanation who that name belongs to, friend or foe, or why it's there. If Leo wanted us to know, he would have told us.

"I assume this is who put Leo in the state he's in. He's leaving it to us to figure out who he is and why he's after Leo on our own, only giving us the bare bones. If he made it too easy, someone would trace us back to him."

"Seems that way," Vinn agrees. "Also safer for him to disassociate from us. But that doesn't make it any less frustrating that he has the information we need to help him and isn't parting with it. Only one more sheet of paper? Shit. Flip the page there, Superspy."

I do. All we see is a series of eight or nine dates, the oldest of which is back in the 1970s and the most recent in 2015. Again, no indication as to their significance. Leo had better be damn good at staying alive for the time being, as it's going to take some time to figure this out.

Vinn and I both stare at the pile lying before us as if it'll eventually transform into something that actually provides answers. "You know we can't outsource this," I tell her. "Not only because of the danger factor that eliminates the use of students, but it's clear that Leo wants to keep this in the family. No one else can have the slightest hint as to his past."

"Yeah, I know." Vinn doesn't sound happy about it. "Let's hope that at least one of us still has access to a database or two. Maybe governmental inefficiency will work in our favor for once and we haven't been scrubbed from the system. I think my group was still paying a guy who'd been killed six years before."

"Yep. But for now, we need to toss a coin. We still have several hours before dinner, assuming I ever want to eat again after all of that popcorn. Leo or Rebecca?" I pull a dime out of my pocket. "You call it."

It took seven flips of the coin before Rebecca came out on top, 4 to 3, but by that point we had to concede that with Leo's life on the line, we owe it to him to stop procrastinating on diving into his issue as well. We reluctantly set aside a block of time after dinner to see what we can find on his nemesis and to start formulating a plan.

As we get comfortable on the couch, the stark reality that we don't have much of a plan to resolve Rebecca's woes either hits home. "At least we have more information to process than what can be found on three sheets of grease-stained paper," Vinn admits, trying to stay positive. "But let's not limit ourselves to only her. When it comes to both Rebecca and Chase, all roads seem to lead to spiritualists. Chase's situation is clear cut, although I'll fill in a few gaps with educated assumption. One of the Roma picks Chase as a vulnerable target and starts the series of harassing incidents. They later send in the bridge player who casually mentions the benefits of a fortune teller. The fortune teller gains her confidence, then uses their relationship and Chase's desperation and naiveté to rob her place right under her nose. Rebecca isn't quite so straightforward."

"Agreed. But it's not too great a leap to connect Rebecca to fortune tellers as well. Her ex believes in a lot of the more fringe aspects of spirituality, landing her in the middle of the occult. She states plainly that she knows someone that can put a curse on Rebecca, then immediately afterward the incidents similar to what Chase suffered begin. That clearly isn't coincidence and, unless you believe in the power of sorcery, an actual human being is making those things happen. It's possible that Sara herself or friends of hers are behind it, but is she the kind of person that's willing to get her hands dirty? My impression is no, but we need to ask Rebecca. And if she's as smart as she supposedly is, she'll want to put distance between herself and the mini crime spree, especially as her connection to Rebecca would make her the number one suspect. I think her friends are out for the same reason. That leaves a third party, so why not a fortune teller who claims she can cast curses and already has no problem running afoul of the law?"

"Pretty big jump at the end there, Winters," Vinn replies, "but I'm not sure I disagree. It's at least a starting point, which is more than we had a few minutes ago. Remind me of the name of that shop Angela mentioned, and let's see if they have a website."

Two or three clicks later, and we're staring at the main

page for Lucky Hoodoo Products, which prominently features a sketch of a black cat with its back arched and hair raised. This shop seems to be a little less mainstream than the bookstore we visited, selling amulets, talismans, ritual supplies, and even a mojo bag to ward off evil. They also offer pricey monthly rituals that promise better health, wealth, and the cleansing of one's soul. "Can you click on the link to see what other rituals they offer?" I ask Vinn.

What we discover is more than a little disturbing. Along with ceremonies to bring money your way or help with relationships, there are a number of offerings for much darker purposes. Vinn giggles as she reads about the "Black Penis" ritual, which promises to bestow power over a man's sexual performance, used mainly to inhibit the ability to cheat with other women.

"Can we move on from that one?" I ask Vinn when she seems to linger too long. She complies, although it doesn't escape my notice that she bookmarked the page. "There, click on the 'black arts' link."

According to the text before us, this ritual can give the conjurer powers over the black arts to do their bidding, which apparently is often used to influence court cases. Other links bring us to love potions, a ritual to destroy a marriage, and one that promises to instill passionate yearning and desire in a lost love. With each link, we each grow increasingly uncomfortable with what we're seeing, but none of it appears relevant. It's when Vinn brings us to the "dume curse" that we strike gold.

"My god, Mal, look at this," Vinn says with bewilderment and maybe a little fear. "By offering up tobacco and liquor, burning incense, and consecrating the alter, you can 'create failure, unhappiness, crossed conditions, upsets and havoc on your enemies.' The only limit is that they don't allow you to wish for someone's death."

"No wonder Angela led us to this place. Remember that she did say that she doesn't believe that anyone from the shop itself would be involved in the strikes against Rebecca, so unless you believe that Sara paid for this ritual curse and that it works unaided by real people, someone else is involved."

"Right. And as long as we're allowing ourselves to hypothesize based on no real evidence," Vinn gives me a look, "what if Sara asked about this, or even bought it, and then her desires were leaked to a third party? Someone who, as Angela suggested, approached her on the street promising to deliver services far in excess of what $95.00 could bring?"

"Exactly what I was thinking," I tell her, and for once it's true. "So are you saying that we need to pose as true believers, purchase the dume curse, create somebody we want to target, and hope that someone approaches us?"

"Almost, cowboy, but I don't think it's a good idea for you or I to do this ourselves," Vinn says with a touch of pity at the lost opportunity. "Word might already be out that we talked to Angela and why. And if these people are as sophisticated as we think they are, we can't make up a fake target. You know where I'm leading. We need to send in someone with a legitimate complaint, someone who doesn't need to pretend to be upset at circumstances. Someone, say, who wants to counteract a curse placed against her."

It takes me a moment, but then my mouth drops open as Vinn smiles when her meaning hits home. Worse, she's absolutely correct. I reach for my phone.

"Let me get this straight." Rebecca was at my door almost before I hung up the phone asking her to take the flight up and must have rushed to put something on, as the floral pattern of her blouse clashes dreadfully with the stripes of her leggings. On the other hand, that's pretty much her style. She sits patiently and listens to us as we lay out our idea, which sounds even more ridiculous stating it out loud to her, without interrupting once. "You say there's an actual curse that's been levied against me and you want me to counter it by hiring my own witch doctor to shake bones or burn pig ears or something?"

"Well, um..." I begin.

"Cool! When do we start?"

"It's not quite that simple, Rebecca," Vinn chimes in. "First of all, let's be clear that neither of us believes that a curse is the cause of your problems; our working theory is that there's some very real human intervention involved. Conversely, no counter-curse is going to solve anything. We're essentially using you as bait to draw out the same kind of person that we assume Sara met as our inroad into that world. Up front, we have to admit that we're not at all sure what we're getting you into or how dangerous it may be."

"There's danger involved? Even better." Rebecca's enthusiasm for her role in this is making me uneasy, but she's shown on past occasions that she can handle herself. "So what do I do?"

"We need you to call to arrange an appointment for one of these rituals, and explain why in detail," I tell her. "We don't expect anything to happen right away other than maybe some bizarre entertainment and you'll have a story to share with your friends next time you're out for cocktails. But if our theory is correct, someone will approach you later. Maybe just after you leave the shop, or possibly sometime later. Vinn and I will be hidden somewhere outside in case they contact you immediately after you leave. If it's later, don't agree to make contact with anyone before you talk with us."

"Simple enough," Rebecca coos. "I wonder what one wears to a satanic ritual? Toodles!"

With that she flounces to and out my door. Vinn and I remain silent, both thinking the same thing. What in the world have we gotten ourselves into?

THIRTEEN

The dinner dishes are cleared and Vinn and I relax on the couch, each of us catching up on emails and browsing through social media. When I've run out of correspondence to answer or delete and lose interest in cats playing the piano on YouTube, I pull myself up, retrieve a key hidden in a can of baking powder in the kitchen, and move on to the bedroom. The dresser drawer stuffed with socks itself isn't locked, but the fake bottom is, and soon I'm carrying an old, scarred laptop back out to the living room where I plop down in my just-vacated spot.

Vinn stares at the computer as if it carries a disease, sighs, then turns to me. "Do you think you're still active?"

"One way to find out," I reply, part of me hoping that I'm not. It takes a few minutes for the old thing to power up, then another minute for me to concentrate hard enough to remember the precise sequence of letters, numbers, and symbols that make up my eighteen-digit password. One facial-recognition test later and I'm on the search page of a highly-secretive governmental agency that keeps track of every known domestic and international individual—good, bad, and everyone in between—that is of interest to whomever makes that kind of decision. Politicians, activists, terrorists, even the local schoolteacher who once made a derogatory statement about someone in the White House on Twitter. Tens of millions of profiles, maybe more, containing various amounts of detail, some running several pages while most only a sentence or two. The question now is whether Leo's stalker is among them.

I use proprietary software to scan in the photos from

Leo's file then type in "Hector Alvarez" and the other known variations under the "alias" section. About ninety percent of the requested information I leave blank, which isn't that unusual. The program is designed to search effectively with even less.

Never lightning fast, the blinking "retrieving" message begins to get on my nerves after the first two minutes. "Patience, Mal," Vinn says softly, but I notice that her foot is tapping at a furious pace under the coffee table. Finally, after what seems like three days, a bell tone sounds to let us know that the search has been completed. I click to open the file.

"Wow," Vinn whistles, "this guy must be one bad dude." And it's true. Virtually everything about him, including where he's from, his true identity, whatever he's done to get on the governments' radar, is blacked out. Any normal person would think that the more dangerous a person is the greater the interest in supplying agents with the most information possible, but that's not how government thinks. Knowledge is capital, so the best stuff is limited to the few who may want to use it for some purpose other than simply staying alive.

"Is there anything here we can use?" I ask myself out loud as I scroll down. "Well, at least it lists his most likely methods of offing someone, all of which seem to show that he prefers to do his killing up close and personal and tracks with Leo's notes. The variety on this page, though, suggests that his victims number in the double digits, probably higher. As far as any habits that'll clue us in on where he might be hanging out or how to find him....nada. Dammit."

Vinn utters a word that is a bit more creative than "dammit," but the gist is the same. We're really nowhere that we weren't ten minutes ago. I move to close out the website but Vinn puts her hand over mine.

"Mal, do you think we should maybe, well, that it might be useful, or at least would satisfy our curiosity if..." she hesitates to finish but I see where she's going.

"No Vinn. Leo and I have an understanding that neither of us will pry into the other's background. Besides, if he ever found out I ran him through the system, Hector Alvarez would be the least of our problems."

Vinn nods, seemingly relieved that I made the decision for us both. I close the top of the laptop and pull Vinn up off the couch, leading her to the room that has other purposes than the storage of contraband computers.

It's pitch dark when I wake up, instantly alert. It may have been a faint odor or the scraping of a key or an instinctual sensing of motion that set internal alarm bells ringing loud enough to wake me. I slowly rise up in bed to find Vinn already sitting up, dead still, her fingers to her lips. I have no fondness for weapons of any kind and rarely carry them, but my apartment has well over a hundred different guns, knives, sprays, poisons, and other items capable of rendering an unwelcome guest incapable of harm, possibly permanently. I grab two handguns and a heavy club. Vinn has her own preferences which tend toward knives and other sharp objects that she can throw with deadly accuracy.

We creep stealthily out of the bedroom, giving quick but thorough glances at the bathroom as we pass, then pass into the kitchen. By now my eyes have adjusted and I point toward the door, which once again despite my elaborate system of top-grade locks is slowly being pushed open. We station ourselves on either side of the door, barely breathing so as not to give the slightest clue that we're there.

The door is opening a fraction of an inch at a time, forcing us to wait. When the gap reaches about ten inches Vinn pulls it open wide from behind while I grab the front of whoever is entering, pulling them down to the floor while in the same motion twisting their arm behind their back and pointing the barrel of my gun to their face where they couldn't help but see it. Vinn checks for a second intruder and, seeing none, slams the door shut and reengages the locks before flipping on the light.

I find myself sitting on the back of a man, though his face is still pressed down hard onto my floor. I stay still while Vinn takes her time searching the prone figure for weapons. She finds more than a few and sets them aside out of reach.

"I'm going to ease off of you now," I tell the stranger, "and then you can slowly turn over and pull up to a sitting position. Keep your hands where we can see them. The slightest suspicious movement will be the last one you'll ever make."

I stand slowly, my gun trained at his midsection, while Vinn has a blade ready to toss or slash. The intruder puts his arms above his head as he flips onto his back, using his legs to push himself to a sitting position. I almost drop my weapon in shock.

"Simmons?" I squeak out, not believing it myself. "Is that really you?"

The face of a man about my age, dark hair matted with sweat, looks up at me, his eyes blinking in the light and squinting before revealing their surprise. "Griffin? What the hell are you doing here? I thought you left the game."

"I did. You just broke into my home. Uh, not yet. We

need to do a more thorough search." Simmons rises slowly, keeping his hands aloft, allowing me to pat him down and find one small pistol in an area Vinn wouldn't have been able to reach earlier. "Okay, move to the couch. I apologize if we're not ready to put these down just yet. We need an explanation."

"Old home week, I presume?" Vinn says, annoyance in her voice, as we direct Simmons to a chair while Vinn and I take positions on either side and to his front.

"We shared a couple of assignments near the end," I inform her. "Simmons was okay, but that doesn't explain what he's doing here. And Simmons, my name is Malcom Winters now."

"Okay, sure," he responds, glancing uneasily at the knives Vinn is keeping at the ready. "Look, I didn't know you lived here. All I was told is that someone at this location accessed a confidential file from an unknown source. It ruffled somebody's feathers. I was in the area, so I got the call."

"That was me," I admitted. "I didn't know that anyone would be monitoring who accesses the database."

"They don't, not usually," Simmons tells us. "The file you pulled must have had an alarm of some sort attached to it, sent an alert. Not that many files that get that honor. What in the world were you looking at?"

"Does the name Hector Alvarez mean anything to you?" Vinn asks, still not relaxing her grip on the knives.

"Alvarez? Are you kidding? Old guy, eyes that look like they'd kill you if you look at them too long? That Alvarez?'

Vinn and I exchange worried looks. "Sounds like one and the same," I say. "Why?"

Simmons casts a sideways glance at Vinn as he lowers

his arms, being careful to keep his hands in view. "I had an assignment a few years back. Five or six maybe? He wasn't my target but he was involved. Cruel, heartless son-of-a-bitch. I'm surprised he's still alive because there's an awful lot of nasty people that want him dead and have the resources to make it happen. A lot of governments wouldn't mind seeing him gone either. What did you want with him? You'd be better off steering clear."

I look to Vinn, who nods as she lowers her weapons. I avoid using Leo's name but fill Simmons in on the pertinent details of why we need to find Alvarez. "Is there anything you can tell us that would help?"

Simmons whistles low between his teeth. "As long as you don't blame me when his face is the last thing you see on this planet and understand that you didn't hear this from me. He takes his time, gets the feel of a place, waits until he doesn't stand out as an outsider. If what you say is true, he's probably been in Chicago for at least a month or more. He'll stay off the grid in a Spanish-speaking area, most likely renting a room. Eats in small local places, sticks with food from south of the border. Cuban, Guatemalan, Mexican in a pinch. Weakness is strip clubs but never goes to a private room with the ladies. Oh, and he's almost never without his hat. Sounds cliché, but he likes a Panama.

"That's as much as I can give you. Even if I did know more—which I don't—you know that I couldn't pass it on to a civilian. Now, can I get out of here and go back to my bed?"

"One last thing. How are you going to report tonight? We don't want a repeat, and the next guy might not get as cordial a greeting."

"Don't worry. All I do is enter a code. 'Problem

resolved.' The higher ups don't want to know any more than that—deniability you know. Could mean anything, even a termination. One suggestion, though. Don't go back online. The next guy could be better than me."

The next guy might also not be welcomed with as much restraint, but I leave that unsaid. Vinn and I watch Simmons go, I check my locks as I again contemplate how to make them more secure, then we crawl back into bed. Vinn's asleep in about seven seconds. She could be in a brutal knife fight and be bathed in blood and she'd take a shower and be out of it as soon as she got under the covers. Me, I stare at the ceiling where I see a man in a Panama hat lurking in the shadows while I wait for the sun to rise.

FOURTEEN

The earliest Rebecca could arrange an appointment with a spiritualist at the Lucky Hoodoo while working around the demands of her job was Monday night, which forces Vinn and I to focus on moving forward with Leo's matter whether we're ready or not. We immediately hit a roadblock.

"Neither of us speaks Spanish," Vinn notes glumly. "Which along with our pasty white faces will immediately make us stand out in the back alleys of Logan Square or Pilsen or any other predominantly Hispanic area of the city. Then once we start inquiring about finding a mystery man without providing context, assuming whomever we encounter speaks English, suspicions will be raised about the gringos looking for one of their compatriots. We'll be outed within minutes, won't get the information we seek, and most certainly word will eventually get to Alvarez and we'll have a target on our backs. Did I miss anything?"

"That sums it up neatly," I reply. "Which means that we need someone other than ourselves to do the dirty work, at least at first, and we swore not to draw anyone else into the investigation due to the high risk factor. Unless you see another way, we don't have much of a choice but to break that vow."

Vinn has always been less conservative than I am when it comes to using outsiders, but even she isn't thrilled at the prospect. "We at least have to draw a few lines," she finally admits. "For one, no students, even peripherally. I have a feeling that if this guy discovers he's being tracked no one involved, no matter how minor the role, will be spared from whatever he would do to shut down interference with his goal. And that wouldn't be pretty. Second, to protect Leo we'll only tell whoever this unlucky soul is what they need to know in order to locate Alvarez, little as it is, we'll give them free reign as to methods they use with the understanding that we don't want to hear the details, and they must accept the fact that his or her life could be on the line with a misstep. And third, I want to be clear that I don't like this one bit."

"Agreed," I sigh, "but I'll add a fourth rule. If our spy wants to back out at any time, they can do so no questions asked. And when it comes to confronting Alvarez, that's on us. Their role is for tracking purposes only. I guess that's two more rules."

"All right," Vinn says with a grim determination. "So the next question is who. I confess that the only Spanish or Latino people I know are from the university, so they're out. They'd probably look too academic anyway. We need someone that screams 'street.' Someone who wouldn't raise eyebrows walking in the areas where no one from outside the neighborhood would normally venture because that's where Alvarez will be."

"I have the perfect woman in mind," I think out loud, "but she's still working for my old employer and we don't want to dip our toes in that pool again. Besides, it needs to be someone local. I don't know anyone either, but I have an idea of a source who may. Remember Chuck?" Vinn doesn't immediately veto the idea and appears to be considering. We first met Chuck when he put together an odd, eclectic group of amateur but highly competent sleuths as part of a prior investigation.

"It's not the worst idea you've ever had," she admits.

"Maybe feel him out first, and definitely don't provide any details other than the basics, which has to include the 'risking their life' part. The fewer people that hear the name 'Alvarez' the better."

Chuck is one of the few contacts I keep in my phone, more due to our shared passion for tea than for any quasi-professional reasons. I get his voicemail and leave a message only asking that he call me back.

When he does, we're in the middle of a late breakfast of a caramelized apple and cheddar cheese omelet with toast made from a multi-seed bread from the farmers' market. Vinn takes the opportunity of my having to answer the phone to steal a bite of my eggs.

"Yeah, I know, it's been awhile," I tell him as we make small talk. "Good choice, if you're going with a white tea. Yellow Bud is one of my favorites too. How would you like to earn another sampling of a rare leaf from my private stash? No, nothing like that. All we need is a referral and we know you have a lot of, shall we say, unconventional connections. And once again, we're looking for someone that knows how to blend in."

I go on to provide a generalized and sanitized version of what we need, making sure to mention the "risk of life" part but excluding any piece of information that would allow Chuck to connect the dots as to the exact nature of the job. He expresses disappointment that he doesn't qualify himself but says he has a few ideas and that he'll have someone get back to me.

So now, with all we have to do on two different fronts and the time element beginning to press on our minds, all we can do is wait. A short delay is fine, though, as it'll give me the chance to make another omelet. Mine seems to be gone.

No phone call was forthcoming for the entire afternoon. Vinn is just packing up her bag to go back to her place when there's a knock on the door. Immediately suspicious due to Simmons' visit and the nature of the issues we're involved in, she once again stations herself behind the door while I cautiously pull it open a crack.

"Mr. Winters?" The voice is high and squeaky and heavily accented. Its source is a small, unnaturally thin, bronze-skinned man of about forty years old, but I need to get a better look at him to make sure. "A mutual friend suggested that you may require my services. May I come in please?"

I swing the door open just wide enough for him to pass through, stepping back a safe distance. He barely glances at Vinn but seems nonplussed by the sharp armament she holds in each hand. His eyes dart quickly around the room and I get the impression that in a short, single glance he has every detail committed to memory.

I remember my manners, sort of. "I'm Malcom Winters and this is my friend Vinn. I apologize, but before we get better acquainted, I'm going to have to search you. It's nothing against you, just a precaution based on recent history."

He shrugs his shoulders and allows me to pat him down without complaint, as if it's a normal part of his daily routine. His clothes smell of tobacco and his breath of mints. Upon closer inspection, I may have underestimated his age by at least ten years. "Thank you," I finally tell him, "and may I ask who we have the pleasure of meeting?"

I motion him to the seats in the living room, but he

declines and remains standing where he is. Vinn grabs a seat on a kitchen stool directly behind the man, keeping her weapons at the ready.

"You can call me Rafael, although my mother would not recognize me by that name. It's best we leave it at that. I understand that you are looking for assistance with a task. Explain, and I will tell you if I can be of help."

Since Vinn is out of his line of sight, I take the lead. "We're looking for a man who doesn't want to be found, and it's essential that he doesn't know that we're trying to find him. For your own safety as well, as we believe him to be extremely dangerous. We know very little else about him other than he'll most likely be found in a Spanish neighborhood, perhaps renting a room, and we have several names that he's used in the past and a photo." I pause, not wanting to continue unless I see some form of commitment. Rafael nods.

"That is what I was told as well. I can help you. I've been told that I have the kind of face that if described portrays an image of a million men, and a presence that's forgotten once I leave the room. If he's in this city, I will find him. My fee is simple." Rafael reaches inside his pocket, putting Vinn on alert. He pulls out a sheaf of crumpled papers. "These are my bills. I live a simple life so there are not many and they're not large, but before I begin I need you to pay these for me."

I take hold of the stack and look at a few random pages. A phone bill of $18.29, an electric bill of even less. There are maybe six or seven bills in total. "We can do that," I tell him. "Vinn will copy the man's pictures while I tell you what else we know about him. It won't take long."

And it didn't, but the paucity of information doesn't seem to bother our guest. He could be a complete fraud just wanting to get his bills paid, but I didn't think so, and I trust that Chuck's connections are valid. Worst case scenario, we may be out less than $100.00.

"I won't give you a phone number and won't call you," Rafael says as he readies to leave. "Just a precaution, so there is nothing to connect me to you. I will find you when I have something to tell you but not before."

"Notice that he said 'when' he finds something, not 'if'?" Vinn says as I close the door behind him. "I wish I shared his confidence."

"It bothers me that we know nothing about him nor how to reach him," I add. "Alvarez could kill him tomorrow and we'd never know. I guess for now, we're at the mercy of this character we don't even know and Rebecca. I know I'll sleep better at night."

Vinn grimaces but says nothing, which is fine. There's really nothing to say.

FIFTEEN

By the time Monday rolls around, I've had too much time to think with too little information for my brain to process, which invariably leads to my filling the gap by creating wild and improbable scenarios where something goes wrong and someone gets hurt. My nerves, already on edge, are frayed so badly that they may never revert to normal.

Sunday night Vinn and I held a prep session with Rebecca, most of which consisted of a debate as to whether she should visit the spiritualist as Rebecca or as Ted. Ultimately we couldn't think of a reason why it mattered— my mind overthinking again—and let Rebecca choose. Never one to pass up a chance to express herself through fashion, she chose the side of herself that allows her to try out her new embroidered Bohemian caftan, which in her mind is appropriate for all things occult. Her decision works out well, as it'll require her to come home from work to change, which gives us a chance to fit her with a device that'll let Vinn and I listen in on what's happening within the inner sanctum. Rebecca has worn a wire before and isn't happy about it as she thinks it makes her bra sag, but we let her know that this is non-negotiable.

Beyond that, Vinn and I weren't sure in what direction to have her steer the conversation with the medium or even whether we should create a plausible back story, and now, sitting in my apartment waiting for Rebecca on Monday afternoon, we still aren't. The passage of time hasn't helped.

"Let's face it," Vinn remarks to break an extended silence, "our main problem is that we're totally clueless as to how this session works or if there's any room for improvisation anyway. My guess is that it's a canned, by-the-numbers kind of harmless con job that's long on ceremony and short on substance. I don't think anything Rebecca says will make a difference. What actually happens in that session may be totally irrelevant."

"You're probably right," I admit. "And Rebecca's never been one to stick to the script anyway. Our main goal is to draw the interest of whoever outside that room makes the decision as to whether she's ripe for further pickings. The best way to do that is for her to present the type of situation the solution to which calls for the skill set of a fortune teller. She'll need to show enough passion about what's happened to her that she appears vulnerable to someone else preying on those emotions. In other words, we should just have her tell the truth and let her genuine feelings come out."

"God help us," Vinn mutters under her breath. "There are just too many unknowns here for comfort. Who is she meeting with? How long will the thing last? Has anyone already been tipped off about her session and will they be waiting outside for her tonight or will they contact her later? Is there any danger that we're not seeing? Do we need to be careful about being spotted? Will the wire work well enough for us to hear? I don't know, Mal, I'm just antsy on this one. Tell me I'm wrong."

"Wish I could, but at least we're on the same wavelength." I take odd solace in the fact that I'm not the only one obsessing over the unknown here. Before I can say something else stupid to add to our angst, Rebecca's familiar rhythmic knock announces her arrival.

The wildly colorful caftan lives up to its billing. "Rebecca, you look great," I tell her, and for once I mean it.

"Do you really think so?" she answers. "I almost changed my mind and went with my paisley shift dress. You know the one—I wore it to Joyce's baby shower. The tramp."

I have no idea who Joyce is nor why she ruffles Rebecca's feathers, but we need to get her focused. "No, this is perfect. And the flow of it makes it easier to hide the electronics. Let's get to it so that we're not late."

Vinn has the honors of bugging Rebecca since she has more experience concealing a wire in women's undergarments, which also saves the certainty of caustic comments from Rebecca should I fumble under her dress. It takes ninety seconds to install and the same amount of time for us to view her from all angles to make sure it doesn't show. I walk into my bedroom to test it, successfully, and it's finally go time.

We agreed in advance not to travel together just in case there are eyes already outside the shop. Rebecca will go in her own car and we'll follow not long after in a Zipcar. At this stage our main fear, among many, is that we won't be able to find a parking space close enough for the wire's signal to reach us but not so close as to stick out. Sound only travels so far when it has to go through walls. The bug only works one way so there's nothing we can do to call off the visit if parking is an issue.

To our great relief, it isn't. As we approach we see Rebecca's car parked in front of the next storefront, so we hang back and glide into a spot behind a van that will help hide our presence. I turn on the transmitter just in time to hear a car door slam shut, which is quickly followed by Rebecca's voice whispering "testing, one, two..." I make a mental note to strangle her later.

Woman's voice: "Hello and welcome. You must be Rebecca, yes? Please, so as not to waste time. Follow me." The woman's voice is slightly deep and husky, as if she's been sucking on sandpaper. The accent is an indeterminable Eastern European, maybe a cross between Hungarian and Italian, but most likely fake.

Woman: "Please, sit. I sense sadness, fear, maybe betrayal? And anger, much anger. Let me take your hand. No, other one. Relax, close eyes. Mmm. This line here is broken, it shows a lost love that returns, but not in love. There is much spite in this woman. I'm getting a name, Samantha, no Sienna, no. Sara. A woman you once loved but no more. She is the cause of your anger, yes?"

"I assume she could get all of this from Rebecca's Facebook page?" Vinn asks. I nod. "Gotta give it to her, she did her research."

Woman: "She feels hurt and in return offers hurt. Not once, many times. You want to stop the hurt, yes?" Rebecca hasn't said a word so I assume she's nodding. So much for wanting to steer the conversation. The medium did our work for us and Rebecca is uncharacteristically mum.

Woman: "The anger runs very deep. Much work to be done. Please, take this scarf. Rub forehead, now hold in right hand and say these words." Whatever Rebecca is saying is too faint to hear clearly but sounds like nonsensical syllables. "Now I present it to this alter, let me light five, no six, candles. Quiet please while I make offering." The woman mutters her own nonsense for a few minutes then the room is quiet for a few more.

Woman: "Very powerful, one time not enough. Rub this ointment on temples before bed, burn two candles for six minutes, no more. Do for a week then return. Done, now go."

The total elapsed time was only about fifteen minutes, apparently not long enough to lift a curse without subsequent sessions and, of course, additional fees. I didn't expect much but still find myself disappointed. Granted I wasn't inside for the visuals, but I was hoping for more of a circus.

The van hiding us pulled away during the session, allowing us to follow Rebecca's progress as she exits the shop and heads to her car. As she pulls away, we decide to wait a few minutes before following. Twenty seconds later, a dark sedan parked across the street makes a u-turn and speeds after Rebecca. Change of plan. We leave our spot and fall in line, at a distance, behind the sedan. Vinn grabs her phone and calls Rebecca.

"Rebecca, dear, do us a favor. First of all, do not, and I repeat, do not turn around and look behind you. You may have a tail. I know it's tempting, dear, but please do as I say. Now obey the speed limit and take a long way home so that we can beat you there, do you understand? Nothing ridiculous, just let us get there a minute or two before you do. No, please don't stop for tacos. Okay, thanks. Eyes straight ahead, Rebecca."

I floor it and head for home.

We park a block away so that whoever is following Rebecca doesn't recognize a distinctive blue Zipcar out front, then sprint to get closer to my three-flat. Vinn takes up position behind a large oak tree one house down while I crouch between parked cars across the street and further down the block. We barely make it before Rebecca turns the corner.

Rebecca's shadow waits until she's had ample time to park and exit the car before arriving on the scene, driving slowly at first then accelerating once Rebecca makes clear which building and unit she lives in. I get a clear but brief glimpse of the license plate number and repeat it out loud until I have time to grab a pen from my pocket and write it down on my left arm, gaining an odd stare from the neighbor walking his Labrador.

I join Vinn behind the tree where we wait several minutes until our guest would have had sufficient time to park and make their way back to Rebecca's door if that's their plan, but they're a no-show. Whoever it is must have accomplished what they set out to do.

"I got the plate number," I tell Vinn. "But that's about it. Too hard to see anything else from that position."

"I took a series of pictures as the car went by," she replies, one-upping me. "We'll have to see if any of them turned out, but I did get a quick look at the driver. Male, white, 40s, short shaggy hair. I doubt I'd recognize him if I saw him again, though. Only saw a profile for a second."

Rebecca's waiting for us on the landing outside her front door. She's protective of her space and rarely allows me inside her apartment, whether because she's put holes in the walls and doesn't want her landlord to see or has unmentionables lying around the living room I don't know. She follows us up to my place. We're barely seated before she starts in.

"Were you able to hear? If so, then you know I didn't even get a word in. The space was exactly what you'd expect, dim and smelling of incense, with a beaded entrance door, and a crystal ball that glows on a table in the corner. Tre' cliché. The woman too. Straight out of central casting for a gypsy movie. Once she took my money she seemed only too eager to get the reading done and get me out of there, although she made sure to leave enough time to let me know that I'll need multiple sessions to solve my problem. Are there really people that believe that shit?"

"Sounds like you got the one-size-fits-all treatment, Rebecca," I tell her. "If you become a regular visitor I'll bet that the reader would do a little more research and present herself as much more mystical. Hopefully that won't be necessary though. As Vinn told you, you were followed here. The next person who reaches out to you, if they do, will be on a whole different level."

"We're not sure how this works," Vinn adds. "Since they took the trouble to tail you but didn't make immediate contact, my guess is that they're going to check you out first. They can get your name and credit card information from the shop and they have your address, so they could look into your financial status to see if you'd make a good mark. Depending on how close the occult community is, they may even discover that you've been cursed by one of their confederates and that would open up a world of possibilities in their minds. They could play you and Sara off against each other until you're both drained of funds."

"Don't worry, we won't let it go that far," I insert in response to Rebecca's frown. "But if they do make contact, you will need to meet with the new person at least once, maybe more. At that point we'll have to re-strategize since we don't have enough data right now to make long-term plans. Unfortunately, all we can do now is wait. We've done all we can and the next move has to be theirs."

"And if they don't contact me?" Rebecca asks, expressing the very thought that we were hoping she wouldn't raise.

"Then we think of something else," Vinn says quickly. "Now, who's hungry?"

SIXTEEN

"I may have found her!" Malika practically screams into the phone. My mind has been so muddled and pulled in so many directions lately that my first thought was "found who?" After all, we're searching for any number of people at the moment. Fortunately it only takes an instant before the name "Ruby Phillips" rises from wherever it's been buried in my brain and I can answer with an equal if not as sincere level of excitement.

"That's great, Malika, I'm impressed." I deliberately don't ask her how she did it for the purposes of deniability later, but it's impossible to hold back an artist who insists on displaying just how difficult a task was and how brilliant they were to pull it off.

"I identified her from a single W-9 form that was recently filed on her behalf by some greasy diner where she must have just taken a job. It had to have been a mistake because there's no evidence from tax records that she's being paid, so an arrangement to pay her in cash must have been reached shortly after she started. Oh, and her full first name is Rubella. What mother would give that name to a child and why didn't someone stop her? I guess that's beside the point."

Now that she's revealed the extent of her genius and provided an address in Little Italy that is almost guaranteed to be fake, Malika seems to have run out of things to say. A little prodding is necessary. "And by chance do you have the name of that diner? An address would be great as well."

"Oh, sorry. I have it here somewhere. Yep. 'The Kuban Kabana.' Two Ks. Stupid name, but it gets five stars on Yelp. Sounds vaguely familiar too. Food must be great. It's not that far from campus—I'll text you the address. I'll have to try it sometime."

"Yeah, you do that Malika. Tell me what you think." I resist telling her to make sure to bring a purgative or that she recently worked with the owner of the place on a matter completely unrelated to his business. My mind is reeling and I need to get her off the phone. "Look, great job, make sure to send us a bill for your services. I need to run." I hang up before she can prolong the conversation or remember why the diner's name rings a bell. My phone is still warm as I place my next call.

"It can't be a coincidence, there's just no way." Vinn's been repeating that mantra ever since she walked through my door. "But even conjuring up the wildest theories I can think of, I can't create a connection between Leo and the fortune tellers or how that might be related to this killer who has him in his sights. It doesn't make sense."

"Nothing about Leo has ever made sense," I remind her. "But I agree. Right now we assume that there has to be the most convoluted or improbable connection imaginable, but once we figure it out we'll probably wonder how we ever missed it. Our problem is that we simply don't have enough facts."

"Well I think it's time that we got some," she snorts. "That man has been holding back on us. We need to pay him a visit. And this time," she adds, "we stay sober."

Leo may be in isolation and in the throes of distress, but his radar for when guests are on their way remains intact. We're one step from his landing when the door opens wide.

We hustle inside and immediately feel it close behind us while I count the locks Leo's bolting shut to see if he's added even more since the last time. Without saying a word we move to the kitchen and settle into our usual spots. Leo's face remains impassive but his left pinky finger makes tight circles on the arm of his chair, an unprecedented display of tension.

"Ruby Phillips," I begin. "First, we need to hear how you met her, then everything you can tell us about her, and finally we need to talk with her. And you don't get to choose what you think is relevant. Spill."

It might be my imagination, but Leo seems to relax and there's the slightest upturn at one corner of his mouth, his idea of a smile. Whatever the reason he thought we were here, this isn't it, which raises a whole lot more questions but I'm not sure which ones. Vinn looks increasingly angry.

Leo raises one finger as if to put us on pause and brings his cell phone out of one of his unlimited number of pockets. He pushes one button, holds his phone to his mouth, and says "Come," hanging up without waiting for a response. He then proceeds to close his eyes to make us temporarily disappear. Vinn and I look at each other, unsure how to respond or how long we're expected to wait. Seconds later, Leo rises and flings open the door. If Vinn and I were irritated and confused before, those emotions just increased tenfold.

"Well don't just sit there," Rebecca instructs. "Grab the lady a chair."

"When the incidents were reaching their peak, before I talked to you, I sought help online. That's where I met her, in a support group for victims of crimes and we hit it off instantly. I mean, she was the target of a series of petty thefts, and other little bullshit kinds of things just like I was. And like me, she reported it to the cops and they did nothing. So after repeating to each other what happened to us several times and me wishing Sara would go to hell and her saying the same thing about whoever did this to her, our conversation morphed into normal bitching and moaning about how unfair life is. That's when she mentioned that she lost her job and needed work. I suggested Leo."

There's a tingle at the base of my spine that won't go away until I'm either sure of my hunch or can put it to rest. "Rebecca, a couple questions. First, do you remember if Ruby was already in the chat room when you entered or did she come in later? And did she mention anything about herself that would lead you to suggest she work in a diner?"

"How would I remember that?" Rebecca responds in a huff, drawing glares from Vinn and I. "Fine, let me think." She closes her eyes and drapes her arm dramatically over her forehead, always the drama queen. "I think I was there first. No, I'm sure of it because the other couple women there had just been mugged or pickpocketed or mundane stuff like that, and I was on the verge of leaving when she popped in. As for your other question, she may have mentioned that she was a line cook but the place she worked closed. She needed funds fast to feed her kids."

Vinn's eyes are bright and she's moved to the edge of her seat. She feels it too. "Did she make any suggestions as to how you might stop your string of bad luck?"

"No, what could she say? Wait, that's not true. Now I remember but she only mentioned it in passing, that's why I didn't remember at first. When I quoted Sara telling me that she had someone put a curse on me, I thought she'd laugh it off but she casually told me that if I was interested she knew someone that could counteract the curse. You know I don't believe in that crap, so I—" Rebecca stops mid-sentence, her mouth dropping open. "Don't tell me. No, she's not involved in any of that occult nonsense. Remember, she's a victim just like me."

"I'm sure that's true," Vinn says softly, not meaning a word of it. "After you gave her Leo's contact information, have you seen her online anymore?"

"No, but I'm sure there's a good reason for it. Look, you and Malcom have a very skewed view of real people. You think everyone is a crook or evil in some way. Ruby has someone out to get her and is one of the good guys, just like me."

Rebecca's characterization of how Vinn and I see people isn't far off, but that doesn't mean that we're wrong. I turn to face Leo. "Your turn, big guy. When and how did Ruby approach you?"

"'Bout ten days ago, came to the diner. No call first. Said she was lookin' for job and Rebecca sent her to me. Not sure why, don't really need help." His eyes shift to Rebecca, who visibly shrinks into her chair. "But she put on apron, made bean dish. Better than mine."

"So you hired her?" I ask. Leo nods. "Can you describe her? Be as specific as you can."

"Fifty-six, fifty-seven. 1.6, 1.7 meters. Sixty-five kilos. Light brown skin, maybe South American. Accent sounds Venezuelan but not sure. Dark hair, above shoulders. Much work on her teeth. Small reptile tattoo on neck, mole to side of left eye. Short nails, she chews."

Rebecca stares at Leo in disbelief, but the other two of us in the room know that he could accurately tell us how long

Ruby's eyelashes are if we needed that information, which we don't. Not yet, anyway.

"Leo, is she still working for you? Is there any way we can get a picture of her?" I ask.

"No. Five days. Gone. No call, no note." Leo began to sound increasingly disturbed as he gave Ruby's physical description, and his anger continues to build even with these few words.

Vinn suddenly sits up straight, meeting Leo's eyes with a steely gaze. "You knew. That's why you filed the—"

I cough to interrupt her and give what I hope is a discrete nod in Rebecca's direction. Vinn opens her mouth as she thinks about continuing but bites her lip and stops talking.

Leo takes advantage of the pause to pull out a bottle and four glasses. Vinn and I pass, but Rebecca takes up the challenge, ending our ability to continue our conversation with Leo without her present. As we move toward the door, Vinn looks back at Leo in disgust.

"He knew!" she hisses as soon as we're out of hearing range. "That's why he filed the W-9. It didn't make sense because it would be completely out of character for Leo not to pay wages under the table, or to file any government form for that matter. I'll bet he hasn't paid taxes in decades. He wanted to leave a bread crumb for us to find and to put us on to Ruby."

"Just to be clear," I respond as we ascend the stairs. "let me see if we're on the same page because it sounds too fantastic to be true. This Alvarez character puts Leo in his sights, reason unknown. He calls on Ruby, which certainly isn't her real name and whose connection to him we don't know, since she's already in Chicago, and asks her to do some scouting and to gather intelligence. She reports that he can't ambush Leo at home because she correctly sees Leo's apartment as a fortress where Leo would have the home field advantage. By finding the apartment, she also sees Leo and Rebecca together. So far, this all could have happened weeks or months ago for all we know."

We move inside my unit and settle in on the couch while I continue my summary. "Ruby keeps watch on Leo which leads her to discover the diner, but she can't approach Leo directly without looking suspicious. She already has some sort of connection with the occult community because we think it was her that set Chase up for them to rob—she was the bridge player that suggested a medium. For some unknown reason she decides to use spiritualism as a part of her plan. She reports herself as a victim to the cops in order to have something in common with Rebecca, who she intends to use to get to Leo. She tries to get Rebecca to use a fortune teller which will somehow get her into Leo's orbit but is rebuffed. She changes tactics and mentions that she needs a job, which results in Rebecca sending her right into Leo's lap. She leads Alvarez to him, he tries to kill Leo and fails. Leo suspects Ruby had something to do with it, files the W-9, Ruby stops going to the diner. Then after all of that we in our ignorance manage to place Rebecca into the spiritualist's grasp all on our own, which gives Ruby the opportunity she was looking for to use Rebecca to get to Leo, however that's meant to play out."

"That's pretty much how I see it," Vinn admits. "And we can even take it a step further and consider if Ruby put Sara up to the mischief she initiated with Rebecca as part of this mystery plan to bring Leo to Alvarez, which would mean that we played right into her hands by encouraging Rebecca to meet with the fortune teller. Wild if even a portion of this is true, but the fact that we both ended up there says something. And if we're right, we just did exactly what we promised ourselves we wouldn't do."

My face must look blank, as she gives an exasperated sigh before explaining.

"We vowed to limit everyone we use as help solely to the fortune teller investigation and to keep them sheltered away from Alvarez because we didn't want them anywhere near a cold-blooded killer. So if the investigations aren't separate but one and the same, we just exposed Malika, Chase, and everyone else to a murderer."

SEVENTEEN

"You gotta be shittin' me." Officer Mendez doesn't sound happy to hear from me, but then again he never does. I have a hard time figuring him out, more specifically his attitude toward Vinn and myself. He seemed appreciative of the role we played in solving a few murder cases recently and practically delivering the killer to his feet, which had to have given him a boost within his department, but then every time I reach out he sounds like I'm as welcome as something nasty he stepped in on his way to work.

"Dead serious. This woman appears to be at the hub of a series of crimes and may be setting up Leo, who you've met, for a hit. All we're asking is the use of your sketch artist for a little while."

"'Appears,' 'may be,' in other words you ain't got squat as usual. I gotta be frank, Winters, if I bring this through channels you're never gonna get the okay, especially if I mention your name, which I'd have to do." He's probably right on that point. I'm not the most popular person among the CPD brass. "But maybe Petra will do it freelance. Last name's Musgrave. She works a beat but is training to draw. Might want the practice. You'll either get a call or you won't."

Mendez hangs up before I have time to consider if his response deserves a thank you or not. We now have a working theory, crazy as it is, and that means that we also have about a thousand different actions we need to take. All of this hinges, of course, on our assumption that Ruby is the catalyst tying all three of our investigations together. As much as both Vinn and I want to get back out on the street to look for her and then to use her to find Alvarez, after much debate we agreed that it would all be a waste of time if she truly is a victim and has no connection to him, which would torpedo our whole theory. Which means that at a minimum we need to see if Chase can identify her. Which means that we need to show her a likeness of Ruby which we don't have. Ergo, the sketch artist request.

I'm relaxing with a glass of iced tea made from rare echinacea root leaves infused with citrus, an experiment my taste buds are determining if it's a pass or fail when the phone call comes.

"I understand you're in need of my services," comes a youthful voice through my phone, with no prelude such as her name. "I have time tomorrow afternoon but I need to come to you, can't do it in the station. $200.00 unless your witness is an idiot and keeps changing their mind or can't remember anything, then it's double and no guarantees as to results."

"That works," I tell her, not mentioning my name either. Maybe this is hush-hush super spy stuff so that no one wants their identities revealed. Or its her youthful exuberance simply forgetting the basics. I give her my address and we settle on a time. Leo hasn't been to the restaurant in a week, so I assume he's available. He's just not going to like it. I frown at my tea, decide that it's something I don't like either, and pour it down the drain.

Leo's attention to detail and the skills of the sketch artist produce a remarkable portrait of a woman reminiscent of a pencil sketch in the Art Institute that is so lifelike you'd swear it's a photograph except for the fact it was made centuries before cameras existed. The last fifteen minutes are spent with Leo quibbling over a hair here or a skin tone there. When he's satisfied, I have no doubt that we're looking at the woman going by the name of Ruby Phillips.

I insist that Vinn tag along when we go visit Chase, partly to get her take on whether the old woman's reaction is genuine and partly because Vinn was the client's pet detective last time we were there. Even though this time we've been there before and should be recognizable, it still takes just as much effort to get upstairs to the hallway outside of Chase's unit.

"What the hell do you want?" she screams at us as she opens the door. Must be her standard greeting.

"Mrs. Horowitz, it's Vinn and Mal," Vinn tells her soothingly while still keeping her distance. "Remember? We're investigating the loss of your jewelry. May we come in? We have something to show you."

"As long as you're better than the last two morons who came here," she grumbles before turning and leading us back to the kitchen table. Vinn pulls a copy of the sketch out of a manila folder and sets it before our host.

"Is this the woman who referred you to a fortune teller?" she asks.

"Where'd you get this?" Chase sounds confrontational. "That's my bridge partner. Couldn't play worth a damn. Remember when she bid two no trump? Don't know who she is, must be new here. Why do you have her picture? Did she say something about me? What does she want? Who are you again?"

Vinn looks a question at me and I nod furtively. We got what we came for and don't need to pester Chase any further, as it seems like she's having an off day and we now have a lot to do. We express our gratitude and make our way to the door.

The "lot to do" turns out to be more wishful thinking than actuality. Two days have passed since we met with Mrs. Horowitz and we seem to be stuck. Our number one goal is to locate Alverson and neutralize the threat he poses to Leo, whatever form that may take, but we haven't heard from Rafael and don't even know if he's alive or still working the case. Rebecca hasn't been contacted by a band of gypsies so for now that's going nowhere. We have a stack of copies of a remarkable likeness of Ruby but aren't sure how to use them to find her without tipping her off that we're looking for her. Vinn conveniently forgot about the danger of using outside sources now that Alvarez' presence hovers everywhere and had me use a connection to run the license plate number of Rebecca's tail through the DMV for a name and address, but so far no response. So this man and woman of action are sitting in my living room instead of beating the streets.

"The weak link may be Sara," Vinn postulates as she munches on raisin nut cookies. "We've kind of pushed her off to the side but if we're right, she was used by Ruby to get to Rebecca, who in turn was being used to get to Leo. She may still be in touch with Ruby or know how to reach out to her, and from what we've seen she isn't shy about talking about her occult connections. At the very least we can fill in some gaps as to who she used to place this supposed curse on Rebecca and how it was implemented. Might be able to reach some of the smaller fish who were doing the devil's work and if we're lucky, one of them will give us what we need to move up the chain."

"That might at least give Rebecca some peace for now," I admit. "Although the plan as you just stated will take some time. I'm not sure how much of that Leo has. Which raises another question. Ruby had Leo alone for the time she worked at the diner with him. She could have easily disposed of him while his back was turned. Why didn't she?"

Vinn gives it some thought. "Could simply be that she isn't a killer, that her job was to locate Leo and stay close until Alvarez could do it himself. Remember that Leo wouldn't have filed the W-9 if he wasn't suspicious. She found Leo all right but probably sensed he was on to her. And if he was, there's no way she could get the jump on him."

"Possible. I'm still uncomfortable with the slow routes through Sara and the fortune teller's minions, but it's better than sitting here waiting for something to happen. Let's pop down to Rebecca's and ask about where we can find her ex and what approach would work best on her."

We're just rising to do exactly that when there's a loud pounding on my door. Not Rebecca's usual rhythmic knock and too forceful for the meek Rafael. Leo hasn't left his apartment in days. Puzzled as to who it may be, I cautiously swing it open and am stunned to see Mendez standing beside an officer in uniform, who upon second glance is Petra Musgrave, the aspiring sketch artist. Against my better judgment but curious as to why they're here, I motion them inside.

"Good, you're both here. You remember Musgrave. I have a few questions about that sketch you had her prepare, and I need the truth. Understand that I came here as a courtesy but we can take this down to the station if necessary."

"What's this about, Mendez?" I'm not happy with his attitude and decide not to offer him coffee or tea. His loss. "I told you why we wanted to get her likeness and you practically hung up on me."

"Yeah," he replies, not contrite. "But things are different

now. At 3:14 this morning, the mutilated body of a woman was found in an alley down in Pilsen. At roll call this morning a photo was distributed—not routine but this one was especially brutal so it's all hands on deck. Musgrave happened to be on shift today and thought she recognized her, then recalled the sketch she made for you. The woman's face was pretty beat up but she thinks it's the same person. I agree."

Mendez leans over and places a series of 8 x 10s on the coffee table between us. I spread them out while Vinn retrieves one of the sketch copies from the kitchen island. The condition of the body is as gruesome as Mendez indicated, but the face is still recognizable despite the bruising. We spend several minutes comparing, hoping to convince ourselves this isn't Ruby, but the longer we study the more certain the conclusion. We just lost our best lead.

"Yeah, she sure looks like the woman in the sketch," I admit. "Remember, though, neither one of us saw her in person. And we're not sure that the name we have for her is real."

"That's the other reason I'm here," Mendez says, obviously not relishing the fact. "Her prints are in the system. Small-time grifter named Maria Mariola, splits time between here and South America. As far as we know, no family in the States. We need Leo to go to the morgue to identify her as the woman he hired."

"We'll get him there, but we'll need to take precautions. We believe that whoever killed Ruby—um, Mariola—has his sights on Leo as well. I told you this."

Mendez sits back and motions Musgrave to take notes. "Tell me again."

With substantial input from Vinn, who has a better recall of detail than I do, it takes us about half an hour to fill Mendez in on what we know and our theories of the case. His frown deepens as he becomes aware that we're still short on facts and long on speculation, but he listens intently without interrupting.

When we're done, he sits silently for several moments. "Shit," he finally says, which summarizes where we are perfectly. "Okay, you've heard the speech before. Leave Alvarez or whoever that guy really is to the professionals. With what you have you won't find him anyway and would only draw yourselves into his path if you get further involved. I can't formally give the okay to keep looking into these gypsies, but frankly as to that I don't give a damn."

He rises to go. "Get Leo to the morgue within the next twenty-four hours. Today would be better. And if you hear anything useful you know how to reach me." With four long strides he's at the door, Musgrave scrambling to catch up.

"Damn it to hell," I mutter as soon as the door closes and I attend to my locks, although my curse is drowned out by Vinn's much more extensive and creative string of profanities. "If nothing else we just confirmed that Alvarez is still in Chicago."

I no sooner finish turning the last deadbolt when there's another knock on the door. Assuming it's Mendez coming back to ask something he forgot, I reverse my process with the locks and pull the door open wide. For the second time this morning, I don't see who I expect.

Standing before me with hat in hand and shifting nervously from foot to foot, stands Rafael.

EIGHTEEN

"I apologize that it took so long," Rafael says meekly, "but that can happen when someone doesn't want to be found. And I'm afraid that my information may already be out of date. He moves every week or so, sometimes after only a few days. But the good news is that he stays in the same general vicinity."

"Did he catch on that you were looking for him?" Vinn asks.

"I don't think so. Another reason for the delay—I tried to vet anyone I needed to talk to before I approached them. As you know, word spreads fast in any ethnic community when suspicions are aroused about almost anything. There aren't a lot of Bolivians in Chicago and along with his frequent moving a few tongues were already wagging. Still, I was discreet. I also have a high interest in self-preservation." I glance at Vinn, who raises an eyebrow at me. Neither of us interrupts to ask why Rafael thinks Alvarez is from Bolivia.

"It came down to a combination of picking up his preferences from the neighborhood gossip—as a stranger his presence and behavior raised the very awareness I was careful to avoid—and a stroke of luck. I learned from a bartender in Humboldt Park that he has a fondness for saltenas..." he sees our blank stares and shifts gears... "which are a baked pastry filled with meats, cheese, potatoes, sometimes olives and mixed with a slightly spicy sauce. Often they're fried but then they're called tucumanas. They're similar to empanadas and usually eaten as a snack rather than a meal." Rafael frowns at his own digression before continuing.

"The point is that while they're available in much of

South America, they're especially popular in Bolivia, and as you might expect each region of the country has its own variations and it's a matter of pride whose is better. Which means that Alvarez would eventually find a variation he preferred and stick with it. I asked locals about restaurants and bars that offer them and which ones served them with llajua, a habanero-based sauce very popular in Boliva but not so much in other South American countries. That narrowed it to about five places, and I tried them all." Rafael looks sheepish, as if this was an unnecessary indulgence.

He pauses and his eyes take on a sort of dreaminess, perhaps nostalgia for his culinary expedition. I'm not patient. "And then?"

Rafael snaps out of it. "Sorry. And then I made a mental ranking of which ones I thought were best and spent a couple of afternoons in the top location, a nondescript bar on 18th near Racine. It was also the only one in Pilsen, a neighborhood more conducive to blending in or even hiding than those near the other eateries, which made it a more likely choice. He showed up on the second day. I left a few minutes after he arrived and staked out the door from an alley across the street, then followed him when he left to a room behind a laundry a few blocks away. I stuck with him for a few days, enough to know that he doesn't go out much except to eat and then to move. As of yesterday he was in a boarding house above a Spanish grocery just off Paulina. By that time I decided I had as much useful information as I would ever get and figured you'd be impatient by now."

"I suppose once he was in for the night, you went home and picked him up the next morning?" I asked. I knew the answer but had to make sure.

Rafael nods. "I quit after he returned from dinner about 7:30 last night. Why, did something happen?"

Vinn is quick to jump in after giving me a warning look with her eyes. "No, nothing," she lies. "And we appreciate your help. The information you collected will be invaluable." She stands as she finishes talking and Rafael takes the cue, rising a beat later. I tell him that I already paid the bills he left on his first visit but that if he received any more in the interim to send them my way and that we'd reimburse him for the salt-enas as well.

"I guess that's useful," Vinn sighs, though her tone says otherwise. "We already knew he's in Chicago or Ruby wouldn't be in the morgue, but this narrows it down a bit. The question now is what do we do with that information?"

I stare at Vinn waiting for her to follow up with a brilliant idea, but none is forthcoming. Asking the questions is always easier than coming up with the answers. I'm opening my mouth to prod some sort of a response from her when there again is a knock on my door. I may have to install a turnstile at this rate. At least this time I know who it is from the fact that the rhythm of the knock matches the chorus of a song from "Kinky Boots" that's been traveling up through my floor from the unit below all week. And this time it saves me a trip downstairs.

Rebecca flows all aflutter into my apartment, face flushed and arms waving as she heads directly to her chair in the living room before she even says a word. Four seconds of silence upon entering sets some sort of a record for her, but sadly she quickly more than makes up for it.

"I was just on my way out to see Claire, you know Claire, she was at the nail salon where the tamale joint used to be, but that was before she moved over to that dreadful space on Ashland next to the bank, but I still prefer her over anyone else because she has such a talent for knowing just what color matches my mood, don't you know? I mean I tried Melanie but…"

"Rebecca, is there something more pertinent that you want to tell us? Does it have something to do with the bouquet of flowers you're holding or were you bringing those to Claire to match colors?" Rebecca frowns. She's never liked being rushed in getting to the point, which often requires the listener to virtually meet many of her personal attendants or to sit patiently while she describes all of the fashion faux pax she observed while eating at the latest trendy pop-up, but today I have no tolerance for irrelevance.

Rebecca looks down at the dozen or so flowers she's clenching tightly in her left hand as if she wonders how they got there, clearly thrown off track by my cutting off her preamble. It only takes a few seconds for her to fast forward to where she eventually was going to get. "Oh, these. Yes, it's about these. Vinn, dear, would you be a darling and put them in some water?"

Vinn glares at her but Rebecca's too engrossed in examining a fingernail to notice. "They were attached with a rubber band to my doorknob along with this note." She leans forward to hand me a wrinkled piece of lined paper that was at one time part of a pocket-sized spiral notebook. On one side, printed in dark green ink in script as cluttered as the paper it's written on, is a simple "I can help" with a local phone number. I pass it to Vinn as she returns and sets a water glass containing the flowers on my coffee table.

"So, it's probably them, right? The fortune tellers? Or

one of them? So what do you do now? You're going to take fingerprints, right? Or maybe trace all the pens with that color ink that have been sold in the last few months and then find out who bought them?" Rebecca's voice rises in excitement as she speaks.

"Or," Vinn chimes in, not even trying to mask the irritation in her voice, "you could call the number and see if someone answers."

"Before you do that, though, did you notice that there are actually thirteen flowers, not twelve? And," I continue as I look at the information that just popped up from a website that identifies flowers from a photo, "they appear to be anemones."

"You would think that would be a message wishing you bad luck," Vinn interjects, stealing my moment as she reads off the screen of her own phone, "but an even number of any-thing, including flowers, is a symbol of death and are thought to usher in bad luck. Superstitions also state that anemones, along with marigolds, are thought to offer protection against witchcraft and bad luck."

"So it seems like someone is offering you their services to help with your curse," I tell Rebecca, who's been shrinking back deeper into her chair as we speak. "Vinn's right. You need to call this person—it's what we've been waiting for. No time like the present."

"Wait, not so fast," Rebecca objects softly, an obvious quiver in her voice. "You didn't look up the colors. All of the reds, yellow, and purples. They must mean something."

"Oh, you're right, Rebecca," Vinn replies in a grim, solemn tone, a slight upturn at one corner of her mouth as she watches Rebecca pull her knees up to her chest, holding them tight with white knuckles. "It means that they're the colors the flower shop happened to have in stock when the mystery person bought them. Man up, woman. Make the call."

Vinn's taunt has the desired effect of snapping Rebecca's mind out of a superstitious cloud as she digs in her purse for her phone. Putting it on speaker is quickly rejected as being too obvious that others are listening, so I ask her to move to the center of the couch and to turn up the volume, then to talk with the top portion of the phone held away from her ear. Vinn moves up close to Rebecca on one side while I squeeze in on the other. One big happy trio.

The phone rings five, six, seven times. Just before Rebecca's finger reaches the red button to hang up, a woman's voice responds, eerie music playing behind her. "Tomorrow night, 11:00 p.m. 6705 North Clark. Come alone."

"Well that was certainly theatrical," Vinn says as the line disconnects. "She might as well have been auditioning for the role of one of the crones from Macbeth. Hard to believe that people believe in that hoodoo."

"Sara certainly does, or maybe she sees through it but uses the occult community as a way to fulfill her wishes as to Rebecca, which allowed Ruby to take advantage of her," I respond, keeping one eye on Rebecca, who despite her bravado seems to be two shades paler than she was before the phone call. "But we know better, right, Rebecca?"

It takes her a second, but she recovers her nerve. "Naturally. This girl isn't going to fall for that mumbo jumbo. Now, I need to go shopping. I've already been seen in that caftan."

"Before you go, we need to ask for your help," I quickly say as Rebecca rises to leave. "Vinn and I need to have a word with Sara. How would you suggest that we set that up?"

Rebecca begins to lower herself back down to the couch before pausing and straightening back up. She looks both troubled and thoughtful and is eyeing the door as if she wants nothing more than to be done with this conversation.

"Well for one thing you can't approach her as friends or associates of mine," she finally responds firmly. "She'll paint you with the same brush and won't give you the time of day. Much better if you leave my name out of it entirely. I assume you want the name of her psychic source, correct? You'll have to get that out of her through casual conversation, maybe as someone in need. You have her social media links, yes? It shouldn't be hard to arrange to run into her. She never misses a chance to be seen somewhere and always posts where she'll be, uploads pictures and tweets while she's there, and then talks about what a glorious time she had afterwards. Now, toodles. Poshmark awaits."

Without another word, Rebecca glides away, closing the door gently behind her. Both Vinn and I stare at the direction of the door, waiting to hear another knock, but our efforts are met with a welcome silence.

"I guess we've run out of visitors for the morning," Vinn finally says. "What do you have for lunch?"

NINETEEN

"I don't think a bar would be the best venue for our accidental meeting," Vinn notes as we scour Sara's postings, Vinn on her laptop and I on mine. "Too much noise, too many distractions, and it looks like she mainly goes there to troll for men. Not conducive to raising the subject of fortune tellers. Rebecca was right on point, she never misses an opportunity to promote herself. This will take a while to sort through."

"Maybe not," I tell her. "Our mistake might be starting out with Facebook, Twitter, and the like. I just pulled up her LinkedIn profile. She's savvy enough to leave off all of her more personal forays into the social scene on here and confines her posts to events that make her look good professionally. Charity fundraisers, business conferences, and so forth. And bingo, here we are. She and a few other members of her firm, including several higher-ups, are attending a ball whose purpose is to raise awareness of the plight of the homeless. Whoa, that's tonight at Navy Pier's Grand Ballroom."

"Tickets still available though," Vinn notes as she types furiously on her keys. "Before we go any further, let's see what Miss All-About-Me has to say about it outside of a site where her professional contacts will see her comments." I watch as Vinn reads, then types, then reads some more. Her eyes suddenly brighten. "Here we go, buried in her private postings. Don't give me that look, it's Hacking 101. Honestly, nothing is really private online. So on LinkedIn she's all about how important it is to support efforts to help the homeless and attending this event is the least she can do, yadda

yadda. Looks good to her bosses and business associates. But to her friends six weeks ago when she was asked to go to the ball by her company, she's whining about the bad food, interminable speeches, and how boring the evening will be."

"She's not completely off base. Good cause, but that doesn't mean those events are fun. And it sounds perfect, like she'll be more than happy to find an interesting stranger to talk to about something other than the homeless. Maybe someone who is having trouble with a relationship with a man and who doesn't know what to do about it. Someone who will be absolutely intrigued to hear about how the dark side of spirituality helped her, and if she plays her cards right, might even get a name and number."

"Dammit, not exactly my kind of thing either. Okay, you get tickets while I go home and look for something to wear and to try to make myself presentable. Yes, tickets plural. If you think I'm going to descend into hell alone, you don't know me. I need someone to share the misery. Let's plan to get there close to the starting time so that we're among the first people there. We can browse the silent auction items while keeping an eye on the door. With almost a thousand people there, we need to make sure we tag Sara and find out which table she's at so that I can find her later. And Mal, dress up."

As Vinn uses her phone to hail an Uber, I reserve two bronze-level tickets at $150.00 each, which will get us a table in the back with the rest of the cheapskates. We don't even get a complementary key chain at that price, which I'm sure will break Vinn's heart. As she heads out the door, I go to shave and shower and, yes, dress up.

Navy Pier is exactly what it sounds like, a pier jutting out over 3,000 feet into Lake Michigan that was commissioned by the Navy over a century ago. Eventually deserted by the military, it fell into disrepair until revitalized as a tourist destination with shops, boat rides, a children's museum, an enormous Ferris wheel, and spectacular views of the city. Highly popular with tourists, it's generally avoided by locals because, well, it's highly popular with tourists. This will be my first visit despite having lived here now for a few years.

I can count the number of times I've seen Vinn in makeup, much less dressed for show, on about half a hand. She's one of the few women I know who can make whatever she's wearing, in her case usually jeans and a hooded sweatshirt or t-shirt, look like it was made to accentuate her beauty. She'll never believe me, but tonight, in a shimmering red dress with just the right amount of plunge and a pair of heels, and a minimum of makeup to highlight her eyes, she is stunning beyond belief. It's enough to make me glad that I'm accompanying her after all, so that wandering eyes among the city's elite don't tempt her to look for greener pastures.

It's a bit incongruous, then, to arrive at the pier in a rusty yellow Pontiac Aztec which is only being held together by the numerous and varied bumper stickers on all four sides of the car and the strategic placement of duct tape. Fortunately the entrance to the ballroom itself requires a walk of around half a mile, by which time no one who saw us exit the monstrosity will continue to make the association. It's a beautiful summer evening so we choose to stroll on the outside walk portion of the pier, thus also avoiding the countless kiosks selling cheap Chicago refrigerator magnets.

Nearing the end of the pier, the number of suited and bedazzled men and women increases as the quantity of the shorts and camera set falls off. Despite the temptation to linger outside to enjoy the view, we have a mission to accomplish and head inside. We both stop just as we enter to gaze at the opulence of the setting, accentuated by the eighty-foot domed ceiling. As expected, there are only a handful of guests so far, and none of them are Sara. We grab drinks from the already-harried bar staff then loiter off to the side with a clear view of the door, pretending that we belong.

It's nearly an hour before Vinn elbows me. "There she is, in the silver sequins taking a selfie. Go." I stroll to the far side of the entrance while Vinn stays put so that one of us will be in whichever direction Sara heads. Chimes signal that dinner will be served shortly, so I blend in with the crowd looking for our table with one eye and watching Sara and her crew with the other. I note the location of their table near the front before finding Vinn standing on a chair waving at me from the rear near the kitchen. She may look as refined as hell, but you can't take the farm out of that girl.

Vinn has claimed seats that have us facing in the general direction of Sara's table, but with no actual view of her. "We've got at least forty-five minutes or so for dinner, and they'll be speeches that will go beyond that," I whisper. "It's poor taste to leave during the inevitable slide show or their plea for cash."

"I have a feeling that won't stop her," Vinn says out of the side of her mouth as she smiles in greeting to a few other wanderers banished to the kiddie table. "Keep an eye out.

She'll want pictures of herself in these surroundings without other guests photobombing her, so I guarantee she'll get up to go to the bathroom during dinner."

She was right. The plates of rewarmed chicken are barely being served at our table before sparkly movement catches my eye. A glance toward Vinn shows that she sees it as well. "If you'll excuse me," she tells the table, "I'll be right back." Her hand presses down firmly on my shoulder as she rises, a signal to stay put.

The dessert dishes have been cleared and the gala organizer is well into her speech extolling how generous gifts such as ours can help save unfortunate people such as the uncomfortable, rumpled man standing awkwardly beside her when Vinn returns. A slight nod as she sits tells me she scored, which all of a sudden makes this whole evening worthwhile. Having tasted the chicken I offered no resistance when the wait staff took Vinn's entrée plate away uneaten, but I did save my chocolate cake for her, which is quickly disposed of along with her own.

"Dear, would you like to view the silent auction items with me before they get too crowded?" she coos at me. "I think I saw a weekend in Monaco that looks absolutely smashing."

We rise to the glares of our tablemates, wander slowly to the auction tables, then make a sideways dash for the door.

"I offered to take her picture for poses that didn't lend themselves to selfies," Vinn tells me from the bathroom as she removes her makeup. "That allowed her to climb to areas that presented fabulous backdrops of the city, and also to use both hands to hold props. I have to confess, she can be creative, which I guess comes from taking tens of thousands of photos of yourself. Not that my assistance was enough to encourage her to engage in conversation. If anything, her attitude seemed to be that I was the privileged one to be allowed to take her picture.

"So it was on to Plan B. When we retreated to the women's bathroom, I let a few tears flow and confessed that I didn't want to go back into the ballroom. Even as a woman I'm baffled by whatever it is about being in a bathroom together than seems to form a sort of bond, but she seemed genuinely sympathetic. When I mentioned your infidelity and how I felt betrayed, and just wanted to do something, anything, to get back at you, her eyes lit up and she was hooked. We moved back out and sat by the window while I spilled my guts. I'm afraid you didn't come off very well."

Vinn comes out to join me on her couch, looking much more comfortable in a pair of cotton shorts and a t-shirt sporting the periodic table. "From there, it didn't take any prompting," she continues. "She texted me Madame Sophia's contact information and raved about how the spells she cast helped her take revenge on an ex-lover. Didn't supply a name but I assume she was referring to Rebecca. She was well versed in Rebecca's suffering but from what I could tell has no clue as to how it was carried out. For all I know she actually believes in curses."

"It's a start," I confess, not showing my disappointment in the lack of detail. "So now we have one name and if all goes well with Rebecca tomorrow, will have a second. Or maybe even the same name. Then what?"

"Good question," Vinn responds. "With Rebecca, we expect that whoever reached out to her will be more than willing to offer a way to counter the curse, for a price. We'll have to wait to see the nature of the countermeasures to determine how to proceed. If it involves the use of henchmen, we watch and learn, maybe even intercept one of them. Otherwise, if it's burning candles or sacrificing a cat, we're exactly where we are with Sara's psychic."

"Right. Nowhere. Ideally, I'd like to send someone in with a problem that would require the use of associates to trigger a series of misdemeanors, but with Alvarez involved we can't take the risk. I'm thinking we might have to do a little snooping to see if these women keep records, then see where we go from there."

Vinn smiles. "Always like the opportunity to use my lock picks. So unless you have any other brilliant ideas, I think we've accomplished enough for today. Tomorrow night we'll be with Rebecca when she meets her mystery woman. What do you say we spend the first part of the day in Pilsen checking out the saltenas?"

"Great," I say out loud, while inside my head my inner voice cries "not on your life." Stepping into Alvarez' territory isn't the best way to start any day, cheese-filled pastries or not.

TWENTY

"At least it's not the middle of winter," Vinn tells me, trying to find a bright spot to our casual stakeout of the grocery on the ground floor below the apartment in which Alvarez is crashing, or at least was as of two days ago. We finished off the breakfast pastries we bought at a local Mexican bakery an hour ago even though we had purchased enough for our breakfasts for the next three days, and are eyeing the pan dolce we've been saving for an afternoon snack. We're sitting on a bus stop bench down the block with a clear view of the front of the grocery, which includes a door to the boarding house upstairs. In our reconnaissance in the early hours this morning we realized that there was no inconspicuous place from which to observe the rear stairs, but hope that the fact that the back area is fenced and locked would encourage Alvarez to leave by the front way. If he leaves. If he's still staying there.

"Remind me again why we're here at all," I retort, rekindling a debate we'd had last night. "If we get lucky and he shows his face, we can follow him, but to what end? To find out where he's indulging in fried cheese today or what his preferred beverage is? The odds that today's the day he's going after Leo are small, and if those are his plans for the day we'd be much better off if we were already at my place when he gets there."

"As I said," Vinn replies with more than a little irritation in her voice, "I want to see his face so that I'll recognize it even in disguise. I want to see how he walks, if possible what his voice sounds like, to smell him, to feel his presence. I know it sounds crazy, but I like to get a sense of the aura of anyone I'm going to have to confront someday. In a weird subconscious way, it helps my brain anticipate how they act and react and enable me to make split-second decisions that may save my life. Or yours."

It's the same discussion that ended in a stalemate last night and I choose not to prolong it any further. I've learned to trust Vinn's instincts and if she thinks getting up close and personal with her prey makes a difference, I need to also learn not to argue. I just don't want to waste a good chunk of time when we could be doing something more productive.

Just as I'm crafting a response that will both save face and smooth things over with Vinn, she elbows me in the ribs. "Binoculars, now," she whispers, even though we're half a block away from the grocery. Having already conceded that this is her show, I pass them over. Four seconds later, I'm hurrying to catch up to her.

The mid-morning streets aren't close to being busy and there are few stores around in which to window shop or other reasons for two gringos to be casually strolling this part of Pilsen, so we're forced to keep our distance from our prey. The way he changes pace for no apparent reason isn't a good sign.

"Vinn, slow down. I think we've been made. We need to call this off."

She ignores me and continues on. In the time it took to glance her way and urge her to discontinue and then look back up, Alvarez has disappeared from view. "Do you still have him?" I ask her nervously. "Vinn, do you know where he is? If not we need to stop. Now."

"We're fine," she mutters angrily between her teeth as she continues forward. As we approach a narrow alley to our right, the slightest movement of a shadow causes me to instinctively throw my arm out and pull Vinn back. At the same time, a flash of metal appears and slashes in our direction followed immediately by Alvarez himself. Vinn stoops slightly to retrieve the blade she keeps around her ankle while I move forward, weaponless, to try to buy us some time. At that very moment, a woman with her young child emerges from a doorway between us before freezing stock still in fear. Before I can yell at her to go back inside, Alvarez disappears back down the alley.

"Are you all right?" I gasp at Vinn, who's still holding her knife as the woman lifts her child and runs down the street.

"Fine, no damage," she tells me, her voice strained. "Dammit. Another second and I would have had him." She turns to me and I watch as all color drains from her face. "Shit, Mal. I'm sorry."

I follow her gaze downward and see blood spilling from a deep slice in my right arm. I don't feel it and wonder if I'm in shock. I slide slowly to the ground as my vision blurs, and the last thing I remember seeing is Vinn pulling her shirt over her head and ripping it into pieces.

"It's my fault," Vinn tells Leo bitterly as he once again works his magic with his sewing kit, this time favoring a neon yellow ointment he stores in an old mason jar. "I should have listened, but I was irritated with Mal, let my personal feelings about what this man wants to do to you get in the way, and ignored both Mal and my better judgment."

Leo grunts in response, whether an affirmation as to the situation or his acknowledgment that I can elicit irrational behavior in otherwise rational people I don't know, and frankly don't want to know. I concentrate on not passing out mid-stitch.

"I was able to throw him into the back of an Uber before the cops came calling," she continues. "If they were summoned at all. Gave a hefty tip to the driver to keep quiet and to clean the blood off the seat. The worst part is, our involvement is no longer a secret." I look up at Vinn, squinting through my pain. That's the worst part?

"He already knew," Leo mumbles, a needle protruding from his mouth.

"I'm not sure it makes a difference either way," I contribute as Leo adds a dark magenta salve over my cut before wrapping it in gauze. "We didn't have a plan in place that requires secrecy anyway. Come to think of it, we didn't have any semblance of a plan at all. But now that he knows us, we need to come up with a way to use that to our advantage."

Vinn looks thoughtful. Leo looks inebriated. I look ahead. In all of the excitement, I almost forgot about Rebecca. We need to get ready for her nocturnal meeting with a woman of the dark.

The 6700 block of North Clark Street borders on the seedy, with a used car lot, liquor store, strip mall, and other low rent street-level businesses with cheap apartments on the upper levels. The address given to Rebecca is a tattoo parlor, which is closed with darkened windows, so presumably she's to enter the door to the apartments above. The late hour and dim street lighting are ideal for Vinn and I to park one store down and remain unseen in the shadows. Rebecca, once again, is wired. We watch as she pauses at the door to read a note, which she tears off and stuffs into her purse before proceeding inside.

"Apartment 2B," she whispers as we listen to her climb the stairs, slow going in her three-inch heels. Her knock lacks her usual flair and several long seconds pass before we hear the creak of hinges indicating the door is opening. If there's a greeting from inside, it's too soft to be picked up by the sensitive mic.

"I'm Rebecca, I have an appointment?" Rebecca ventures tentatively, making it sound more like a question. "Am I in the right place?" Again her host is silent, and several minutes pass with the only sound being that of Rebecca rifling through her purse. Eventually we do make out sounds of feet traveling on a wooden floor, which we assume means that they're moving to another room inside the apartment. We'd asked Rebecca to drop hints as to where she is if she could do so without making it obvious that she's leaving a trail for others to find, but that apparently isn't possible at the moment. Not a big deal, as with a small apartment there are only so many rooms anyway.

"In here? The door with the dried flowers?" Thank you, Rebecca. The door closes with a firm click. Show time.

"You are Rebecca," an old woman's voice sounds, as if telling our friend something she doesn't know. The voice quivers and is halting, a perfect imitation of piped-in witch dialog from haunted houses everywhere. I glance at Vinn, who's rolling her eyes. "Sit. Extend your arms, palms up. Close your eyes, please, I need quiet."

We also stay silent in the car, listening intently for clues as to what's going on in the room. They're subtle, barely audible, but we do discern creaking and moaning and a continuous playing of music that can only be described as creepy. Rebecca's mic is more sensitive than the human ear and my guess is that she isn't consciously aware of the sounds, that they're meant to be subliminal. If it weren't for the gravity of the reason she's there, they would be laughable.

"Seriously?" Vinn can finally take no more without comment. "When do Scooby-Doo and Shaggy appear? If she tells Rebecca to light a candle and swing a dead cat in the graveyard at midnight to make all her troubles disappear, I'm going in there to hurt somebody."

"Remember, Rebecca aside, most people who are willing to pay for the services of a fortune teller already believe this crap. To us, it's theater. To them, it's an expectation."

Vinn nods her head but still appears ready to charge out of the car. I make a mental note to check if there are childproof locks on the next Zipcar we rent. Several more moments pass and Vinn's impatience becomes contagious. Finally, we hear the creaking of a chair as if someone is straightening up.

"You had a love that ended badly. Feelings hurt, bad karma created. It has stayed with you, dormant, for many years. Now your partner—I see a woman, very beautiful woman—has returned to seek retribution. She has had a curse placed upon you by one of my kind. It has attached to your aura, to follow you and to bring misery at every turn."

The woman pauses, and as time extends even I grow tense wondering what solution she will propose. Rebecca also apparently loses patience.

"Is there a way that you can remove the curse and to protect me from its return?" she asks anxiously. I realize then that the old woman was waiting to be asked, to lure her prey into a position where it's Rebecca, not her, that insists on what is probably a pricey cure.

"Very difficult, much harder to dispel than to cast," the woman tells Rebecca, clearly setting her up for a big payday.

"But possible, yes. Only I, Madame Adria, and a few others can do." Vinn and I move forward in our seats. Come on, Rebecca, you know what to say.

"It's not enough just to get rid of the curse. I want my ex to suffer some of the same things I did. Like, a counter-curse?" Vinn and I relax. Good job, girl. We decided in advance that the only way to bring out the thugs who key a car, or the hackers who wreak havoc online, would be to go on the offensive.

"Ah," the woman responds. "Can be done, yes. But need much preparation. Cannot do today. Must meditate, find the curse, gather materials. You must return. Maybe many times. You will hear from me."

"Clever," Vinn says. "What do you want to bet that the first call she makes will be to the woman who Sara used to initiate the curse. Madame Sophia, I think? Sophia will agree to call off the dogs haunting Rebecca, for a price, then down the road will probably bring Sara back in to pay to take off her curse. A never-ending cycle and influx of cash. Adria here needs to discuss terms with Sophia before she knows what to charge Rebecca, thus the stall tactic."

"And every time Rebecca comes back, an additional fee," I agree. "I wouldn't be surprised if they actually have a common fee sheet that they consult. 'Remove curse, $1,000.00. Counter-curse, $500.00' Then they split the proceeds. My guess is that they all even use the same set of low-lifes to do their bidding. A one-stop shop."

As we talk, we can tell that the session for now is over. A chair slides back, a door opens, and footsteps sound. About thirty seconds later, we watch as Rebecca awkwardly ambles to her car. We wait a few minutes to see if she's being followed then start for home to debrief.

As before, Rebecca is waiting for us on the landing outside my door. We're still on the stairs when she starts chattering. "A girl answered the door and took my money," she begins. "Maybe twelve years old? She only spoke to let me know how much and then counted it twice. $100.00 by the way. Cheaper than I expected but I know that's just the bait."

We move inside and I decide to just let Rebecca keep going. I'll ask questions at the end. "The room I was taken to was everything you'd expect. Dim bluish lights, heavy flowered curtains, beads, a crystal ball on a table in the corner. And this woman. It's as if there's a dress code. Very similar to the first one, but much finer materials, and more layers. Heavily jeweled, rings on every finger. She looked like she could have been eighty, but I think she made herself up that way. My guess is forty, maybe a few years either way.

"You heard what was said, right? I said I could get her to offer the chance for me to put a counter-curse on Sara and I did."

"You did fine," I respond to her fishing for complements. "I think you set the bait perfectly. Now all we do is wait."

Rebecca leaves while Vinn and I remain on the couch as she changes the dressing on my arm. "You did have your source set up the phone tap, right?" she asks.

"Yep. Ouch, careful! Any conversation on the phone number Madame Adria gave to Rebecca will be recorded and sent to my email, so as long as she uses that number to conduct her occult business, we'll know her next step."

Her nursing duties done, Vinn heads to the bedroom. My energy drained, I decide to give myself five minutes to recover before following. It's the last thought I remember having.

TWENTY ONE

"We lucked out for once," I tell Vinn as she emerges, bleary-eyed, from the bedroom. I flip the switch on the coffee machine I had all ready to go. "It looks like the number Adria gave to Rebecca is the same one that she uses for her personal calls, or at least any of them that relate to her occult activities. She didn't waste any time, ringing up Sophia at 7:42 this morning. She didn't identify herself as Adria, but I assume it's her based on their conversation and the fact that it's her phone."

"Mmphrg," Vinn mumbles, which I've learned in Vinn-speak means not to discuss anything that requires the use of more than a single-digit number of brain cells until she's on her second cup of coffee and has some food in her stomach. I allow olive oil to heat in a large skillet as I chop bacon and asparagus into small pieces, then throw them into the pan to crisp up while I beat eggs and freshly-grated Parmesan cheese together with just a dash of salt and a generous amount of pepper. Vinn is just refilling her mug when I slide the omelet onto her plate. Two minutes later, half of it already gone, she nods at me to continue.

"You might as well just listen to it yourself," I tell her as I press a couple of keys on my laptop. Instantly the voice of the woman we listened to at Rebecca's session last night is projected out into the room, much more clear and less witchy than we heard through the mic.

"Margaret, it's Carla." Vinn raises an eyebrow at me and I pause the recording. "What, you think that they use their real names when they put on the mystical show to con people out of their money?" She makes a face then signals me to play on.

"I need to talk to you about one of your marks, some chick named Sara," Carla/Adria continues without a trace of the accent she used with Rebecca. "It looks like she had you throw some pretty serious shade at a guy that came to see me last night and he's looking for—"

"Wait," Vinn interrupts, showing she's making it into the land of the living. "I get that she's referring to Rebecca as 'he,' but how does she know that this Margaret woman, who I agree has to be Madam Sophia, was the one who helped out Sara?"

"I wondered the same thing myself," I reply. "It's possible that this is a small, tight-knit community so they all know what the others are up to, but I don't think that's it. Notice how Adria used the phrase 'it looks like.' That indicates to me that she consulted something to obtain that information. My guess? That the less honest section of the fortune telling/psychic community keeps a database accessible to all of them in order to avoid stepping on each other's toes, in other words screwing up someone else's con."

"Much more sophisticated than I would expect, but possible," Vinn admits. "If true, it would be nice to get ahold of that. Could blow the whole crooked enterprise wide open. Nothing we need to focus on at the moment though. Okay, continue."

I scroll back a few seconds. "—to see me last night and he's looking for me to get rid of a curse you put on him for Sara last month and then to throw one back on her. How do things stand there?"

A few papers rustle before Sophia responds, perhaps consulting her notes. "Yeah, I remember her. Nasty piece of work, her. She's nearing the end for what she paid me for anyway, so I'll call off the guys. When are you meeting up with him again? I'll have them do one last thing, maybe break a window or something, so he'll be even more desperate when he comes back in. Give you a chance to up your fee a couple Cs. After that you can tell the boys to switch it around depending on what package he goes for. Give it a little time, maybe we can flip her back again."

Adria chuckles, or maybe under the circumstances it's a cackle. "Sounds good. Let's see how long we can keep it going. Say hi to Marv and the twins. Later."

"That's it, and so far no more calls that are at all relevant" I tell Vinn as she stares at my laptop as if it has the answers to whatever questions are running through her mind.

"Okay," she finally says. "That was enlightening in one sense, but really only confirmed what we already suspected. That at least some of these grifters work together, or are at least cooperative, and that Rebecca can expect to have a pretty high number thrown at her next time. If they want to keep this back-and-forth going between she and Sara, though, she probably has some leverage to negotiate."

Vinn opens my refrigerator door, peering inside to look for something to complement the omelet she's digesting. "But let's talk big picture. What do you think we need to do to stop them from harassing Rebecca permanently, and when do we make a move? As much of a bitch as Sara is, I don't think I want to be a part of allowing these people to do to her what they're doing to Rebecca, and worse yet to have Rebecca fund it. And how does any of this help Leo? It's great that we made a connection between these occult people and Alvarez through Ruby, but so what? Where does that get us? And what's our next step there?"

Ninety minutes ago, each one of those questions were rattling through my brain with no answers miraculously popping out. It's disconcerting to hear Vinn express them because I was hoping that her scientific mind would sort through all of the disparate data we've accumulated, which isn't much, and see the logical path to a solution. Or at the very least, to know what information we need to get to formulate that plan.

Fortunately, my own non-scientific brain came up with an activity that, if nothing else, will give the illusion that we're doing something useful while we wait for one of us to come up with something better.

"Vinn," I tell her. "I think it's time to commit a crime."

The cops have almost certainly pinned down Ruby's last known address as part of their murder investigation, but it's unlikely that Mendez would provide us that information without asking why we need it. Even if he felt generous and did give it to us, or even if he turned us down flat, if a neighbor reports suspicious activity or an actual break-in at Ruby's place shortly after our request we could expect an uncomfortable stretch answering questions in a precinct somewhere in the city. Our scruples have already been compromised beyond recognition as a part of this investigation, so Vinn has no issues asking for one more task from Malika. It says something disturbing about the security system of our men and women in blue that she emails Vinn back with what we need less than ten minutes later. Surprisingly, it matches the address from the W-9 that Ruby filled out for Leo. Maybe she's not the sophisticated criminal we thought her to be.

"Garden apartment in a two-story frame," Vinn tells me after pulling the house up on Google Maps. "Won't win any awards for best-maintained home on the block. Probably an illegal third unit so it might not have a back entrance. It would be a mistake to underestimate the woman, but my guess is that the lock on the door won't be a challenge so if we do have to go in the front way it won't take long."

"That's good to hear," I tell her. "Although I'm a little uncomfortable going in without our usual precautions. I know it's my idea and time is an issue with Leo's life on the line, but skipping surveillance entirely is a bad idea. We can't be sure that she lived alone."

"Which is why we watch the place for an hour or so before making our move," Vinn replies impatiently as she packs her kit of lock picks. She's always been more willing to take risks than I am and seems to have already forgotten what happened the last time she ignored my plea for caution. "And once inside, what we find should quickly indicate if more than one person lives there. It could be as simple as counting toothbrushes in the bathroom."

The Little Italy neighborhood overlaps with University Village, where we work, and is just north of the Pilsen area where we had our confrontation with Alvarez. Other than a myriad of Italian restaurants and Italian ice shops along Taylor Street, the main commercial drag, there's not much there to remind a traveler of their trip to Rome. The side streets are similar to those in many other parts of the city, with a mix of renovated homes and houses in dire need of a hammer and nails or a coat of paint, with a couple of apartment buildings thrown in for good measure. Ruby's apartment is in the 1300 block of Fillmore, just far enough away from the crowds to give us some privacy.

The bad news is that there's no place to stay in one place

for any length of time without raising eyebrows among the neighbors. We walk the block back and forth slowly a couple of times, making me wonder for future reference if renting dogs for an evening is a thing, before Vinn has had enough.

"Screw this," she says, substituting a more colorful and physically impossible verb for the word "screw," as we approach the building for the third time. "Stay here." She turns off the sidewalk and scurries down the gap between our target building and its neighbor to the east, disappearing when she reaches the back yard, only to reappear a few moments later from the opposite side.

"No lights in the windows, only a single car in the garage and none parked on the slab
next to it, no movement or noise that I could tell," she whispers breathlessly. "Riskier to keep drawing attention to ourselves with our pacing. Oh, and of course no back entrance."

She grabs my sleeve and pulls me toward the three steps that lead down to the front door, where she utters another naughty word under her breath. "A little more sophisticated than I would expect for the area," she tells me as she examines the lock, "but not impenetrable. Keep watch."

For Vinn, anything over two minutes is unusual, and we're just approaching that amount of time when she turns the knob and pushes the door open. We step inside and move quickly and quietly through the rooms to confirm that we're alone, then a second time to verify that Ruby lived alone. Satisfied that we shouldn't be interrupted, we relax. I hand one roll of light blocking window covering to Vinn while I take the other. It's much more efficient and ultimately faster to be able to turn on room lights than to use flashlights, but we need to make sure that the light isn't observed from the outside. The apartment is small with few windows and it doesn't take us long.

There's no office, so the next most likely room in which to find anything useful, in whatever form that might take, is the bedroom. Vinn moves there while I take the rest of the apartment. The cabinets and drawers in the kitchen are sparsely filled, but it does take some time to check underneath drawers and to look for false bottoms. I complete my search of the bathroom in three minutes. The small living room has few places to hide documents but I take precautions by running my hand through cushions, looking at the underside of the coffee and end tables, and lifting the couch. The last items to check before joining Vinn are the multiple picture frames, a common place to store secret papers behind a family photo. In the course of taking off the backs, though, my attention is drawn to the photos themselves. Including some montages, there are probably about twenty pictures in total in various frames on the tables and walls. I pull out seven of them and look at them carefully. I have a hard time believing what I'm seeing, so I bring them to Vinn.

She's got papers strewn all over the bed, so I arrange the photos on the nightstand. She stares at them for several moments, her face growing pale, then turns to the bed to draw a bound photo album out from under a pile of papers. Together we turn the pages, neither of us uttering a word. With each page, what was a terrible possibility becomes a near certainty. The second to last yellowed photo in the book is of two young men and a girl of about four or five. The girl is presumably Ruby and one of the men resembles exactly what we imagine a younger Leo would look like. The other man, presumably Alvarez, has a rifle slung over his shoulder. The last picture far more recent, a candid shot of a camera-shy man who's a dead ringer for Alvarez. The final proof of what we're seeing, if it's even necessary, is probably sitting among the mess of documents on the bed. We sink together to the floor, our backs resting against the side of the bed.

"My god," Vinn finally manages to say, clearly shaken. "Are you thinking what I'm thinking? Ruby and Alvarez were siblings. He killed his own sister."

"The resemblance is too close to ignore," I respond. "And even worse, if we're right, Leo is their brother."

Our discovery has both of us wanting to leave this place as fast as possible, to get back to a familiar space to digest the meaning and tragedy of what we found. I grab a large garbage bag from the kitchen and without sorting push all of the papers on the bed into the bag while Vinn rifles quickly through the remaining drawers and closet shelf, throwing whatever she uncovers into the bag as well. We strip the windows, adding the coverings to our now-bulging bag, and make a quick exit. Whatever this means, we'll figure it out at home, but both of us know that it will be something awful and something we'll wish we never knew.

TWENTY TWO

The plastic bag sits on my living room floor in the same spot it was an hour ago and remains undisturbed. Vinn and I have been staring at it the entire time, neither of us wanting to be the first to pour out its contents. I'm the first one to break.

"You know we need to have a long and uncomfortable talk with Leo," I finally say, the first words either of us has spoken since we entered my apartment. "But before we do we need to be well-armed with as much information as possible. I'm not happy that he's been holding out on us, nor are you. It's one thing to be secretive when the facts you withhold are strictly private and irrelevant, but another thing altogether when the information could be helpful in stopping a psychotic killer from killing him. Or us."

"How could he not recognize his own sister?" Vinn answers, although apparently to a question at the forefront of her brain and not to my own comments. "And why not tell us that these are his siblings? He doesn't impress me as someone who would be embarrassed by family. Especially under these circumstances. I don't know, Mal, I agree that we have to go through the documents in that bag but I'm reluctant to do it and I'm not sure why. Maybe for the same reason that Leo has been holding back. It's like pawing through a friend's dirty laundry."

Instead of prolonging the conversation, which is cathartic but getting us nowhere, I pull the bag close and pour its contents onto my coffee table, creating a lopsided mound that spills onto the floor. I notice Vinn suppressing a yawn and only then realize how late it is, but there's no way we're going to bed without reviewing every single document in front of us. I step over a small pile as I go to the kitchen to make coffee and tea while Vinn starts sorting.

"All I've been doing is scanning for dates to try to put these in a rough chronological order," she tells me ten minutes later when I return with warm caffeinated beverages in two of the largest mugs I own. "It's not precise by any means and the papers and photos in this pile over here will need closer inspection to date them, but it'll at least get us started. If it's okay with you, let's look at everything together. It's slower but I think in this case two sets of eyes and two very different sets of brains are necessary to make sure we don't miss anything."

I ponder her last statement to decide if I've been insulted but decide not to take umbrage. I'm the first to admit that Vinn is more intelligent than me by a factor of ten, but she would say the same thing about my street savvy. Besides, our anger at this point is directed at Leo, so there's no point in fracturing our unity.

Vinn's first stack is far smaller than the rest. We quickly recognize that these date from Ruby's childhood. "Birth certificate," I cry out and grab it before Vinn can claim the glory for herself. "Not Rubella after all. 'Rubinettia Viola Soliz.' Born January 22, 1967 in Camiri, Bolivia. So Leo's Bolivian?"

"Well we damn sure know he isn't Cuban," Vinn replies with a faint smile, presumably referencing Leo's lack of skill at preparing Cuban cuisine. "And that tracks with what Rafael told us about Alvarez' culinary preferences. Ruby must have had a sentimental side, saving a few memories from various stages of her life. I think we can safely pass over some of these childhood mementos. Let's move on."

The first sheets of paper we pull off Vinn's next stack are

jarring, jumping from the innocence of a child to the political anger of a young woman. There are numerous flyers of various sizes, colors, and fonts, but all with a similar goal, spreading dissent against the government of President Juan Jose Torres. Calls for his overthrow, support for alternative leaders, notices of rallies.

I look at Vinn with a blank stare. She apparently reads my mind. "Sorry, honcho. Wasn't my part of the world either and none of it rings a bell from history class." She pulls open her laptop, types, bookmarks three or four sites, and proceeds to read silently, summarizing as she goes.

"Looks like Bolivia was politically unstable in the late sixties, early seventies," she tells me. "The military overthrew the government in 1969 and installed a general to lead the country. Torres took his place as the commander in chief of the armed forces. Then less than a year later he was made to resign by right-wing army leaders, but when that same group forced the general serving as President to resign, Torres ended up taking his place with the support of a national labor groups."

Vinn pauses as she skims. "He immediately cancelled American interests in zinc mines and oil reserves, expelled the Peace Corp, and instituted what this source calls 'leftist' policies. He convened an assembly of miners, teachers, students, and peasants to show that he represented the voice of the people. None of this made the U.S. happy—much too populist. He also started making nice with the Soviet Union. Do you remember who our President was at the time?"

It takes me a minute. "Oh god, it was Nixon. Let me guess. He didn't just sit still and let Torres go unpunished."

"Good guess," Vinn replies. "Recent documents confirm that the Nixon Administration, with the knowledge of the State Department, sent half a million dollars to supporters of yet another general, Hugo Banzer, who led a bloody coup against Torres. Over a hundred people died and Banzer became President. For the next seven years he led a military dictatorship that was known for repressing dissent, torture, and the disappearance of opponents. He closed the universities. Ninety percent of the population ended up in extreme poverty."

"Good for us," I say wryly. "But bring this back on point. What does this have to do with Ruby? She would have been three or four years old when all of this was going on."

"Then I guess the flyers she saved were from her brothers, one or both." Vinn sounds uncertain as she speculates. She picks up another paper. "She could have just been interested in history, but I don't think so. My Spanish is poor, but these appear to be notes for a speech and they're plenty incendiary. Anti-Torres. And it's handwritten, so again, this points to the involvement of at least one of her brothers. She probably looked up to him and saved these things. Again, maybe a little sentiment on her part."

"If that picture is truly of the three siblings," I add, "then both of them would have been old enough to actively participate in any sort of action for or against the regime around 1970. You know who's got these answers, but let's keep going first."

The next of Vinn's piles is a large assortment of notes, some of them neatly transcribed on printer paper and others hastily handwritten on envelopes and scraps of paper with dates, locations, and plenty of explanation marks. All of them are in Spanish, so Vinn hands me a handful without having to explain that we're sharing the burden of inserting the language of each note into Google translate.

It takes about twenty minutes. It became clear halfway through my stack that we were looking at her efforts to find someone, and only a few more notes to be obvious that that person was Leo. Vinn quickly reached the same conclusion but we still take the time to combine our efforts into a single collection just to make sure.

"So she started looking for Leo almost fifteen years ago and moved to Chicago after she found him," Vinn states. "And her frequent use of the word "hermano" removes any doubts about their relationship. It would've been too easy to let us know why. Apparently not out of sentiment because she never reached out to him for as long as she's been here. If on Alvarez's behalf, why the delay in taking action? Or did she just decide if Chicago were good enough for him, she'd move here as well?"

"Interesting to speculate, but in the end irrelevant," I reply. "It's getting late. Let's continue."

The last pile is larger and more diverse than either of the first two. And, as it turns out, intriguing and informative. Vinn lets out a low whistle. "I assume you didn't find a laptop either, but I'm not sure we need to go back to look for one. Ruby seems to have kept very detailed paper records, starting with this notebook."

By this time, our mugs are empty so I get up to refill them while Vinn starts paging through. I hurry back, not wanting to miss anything.

"We struck gold here," she tells me with a renewed energy as I slide down to snuggle close. "There're about twenty names here of women, both what I assume are their real names and then their occult aliases. See, look: 'Corina Albu, Madam Mystique. Tacky. It lists their specialties such as Tarot cards or palm reading, and limitations."

"There also appear to be some that have asterisks next to their names," I note. "Maybe half? Could mean almost anything. Any familiar names?"

"All three. Chase's Isadora is here, as are Sara's Sophia and Rebecca's Adria. Stars next to the last two, but not Isadora. Frustrating that Ruby doesn't provide more details next to each name."

Vinn flips through several blank pages and we're about ready to toss the notebook back on the pile when one more short list appears, this time six men's names and phone numbers. As with the women, two have asterisks and the rest do not.

"No notations at all this time, dammit," I mutter. "But it isn't too great a leap to think that maybe these are the guys who do the dirty work. The asterisk may mean something different for them. Maybe for both groups, though, it identifies individuals who are willing to go further than the others. More extreme."

"I like it as a theory" Vinn admits. "But we may never know and I'm not sure it's relevant anyway. Let's see what else we can find."

We pile through a lot of paperwork that is clearly unrelated, such as car repair receipts and to-do lists, which upon brief glance do not contain an item such as "set up old lady to be ripped off." I set aside a ledger while Vinn finds a desk calendar and a checkbook. We pause to look at both of them before continuing our digging.

"The ledger covers the last eight years plus," I observe. "It lists the women's names down the left column and then monthly figures to the right. Can't be anything but income from each fortune teller, probably kickbacks for tips or Ruby's share of a job they work together. Some of these women were much more active than others. It seems pretty clear that Ruby has been living here and working with these women for almost a decade, throwing them business in return for a share of the score. A sort of symbiotic relationship."

"A couple of these numbers are really high," Vinn says with a slight whistle. "Hold on just a minute." She pulls out the notebook listing the gypsy women. "The women with the highest numbers on your ledger, and they're substantially higher than the rest, all have asterisks next to their name. I'm on board with your theory now. These are the high rollers."

Vinn grabs the checkbook. "Considering the dive she was living in, she certainly didn't spend all that cash on rent or nice furniture. Let's see where it went."

Beyond regular payments to her landlord, utility bills, and food, the only things that stand out are periodic amounts to "CASR," BRA," and similar initials. Most of Ruby's income from the ring of gypsies seems to have gone to these recipients. Vinn's fingers are already flying.

"'CASR' was a revolutionary group in Bolivia but it doesn't seem to have been active for almost a decade," she tells me. "Putting 'BRA' in gets the anticipated links to lingerie stores, even in South America. The others don't pop up at all."

"A research project for another day," I suggest, stifling a yawn. "The calendar? Then maybe call it a night."

"Agreed," she responds with sleepy eyes. "Lots of color-coded notations next to specific times over the course of this year. Do you remember the date of Chase's bridge game?" I didn't, with my memory this late at night having to strain just to remember what bridge game Vinn's referring to. I need to look it up before passing on the date. "Yes, here it is. It matches. Not that we really needed the confirmation at this point, but no question that Ruby was the partner at cards that led Chase to Madam Isadora. Chase was probably just one of a long string of many cons they worked together over that eight-year period."

I struggle to stand up and then pull Vinn to her feet. In the process, though, my eyes catch a large number of identical half-sheets of paper with yellow and orange trim in the remaining pile. Out of curiosity, I pull one up, read it, then a second and a third.

"Vinn," I stop her as she's dragging her feet to the bedroom. "You should see these. They're receipts for wire transfers, all to accounts in Bolivia, with those same initials on them as references. Ruby's profits from her partnership with the con artist fortune tellers and psychics were used to fund revolutionary groups in Bolivia."

"Pretty big jump and a wild theory there, Winters. Next you'll be telling me that Alvarez kept tabs on his sister, knew she was in Chicago and of her association with the Roma, and forced her to use them to get to Leo." As her voice trails off, Vinn's eyes grow wide. "Oh, shit. We need to talk to Leo." She looks at the clock. "Except it's 4:00 a.m. He'll be asleep."

I shake my head. "You know him almost as well as I do, Vinn. He's not only awake, I'll bet he's waiting for us."

Which may not have been hyperbole. We arrive at his door with a grocery bag containing the photos and a selection of documentation just in case Leo requests proof of our accusations or just wants to see what we have. My knuckles are halfway to the door when it swings open to a view of my tenant's backside as he makes his way to his usual spot in the kitchen. I'm curious whether he still considers this nighttime so that a bottle of potent hooch will be offered or if we'll see bowls of Froot Loops on the table.

Neither is the case, which indicates how disheveled Leo's mind must be. Or perhaps he's simply scared. Or it's 4:00 in the morning and all he wants is for us to say our piece and go away. I'm happy to oblige.

"Leo, we've made progress in our investigation of Rebecca's problems with her ex and the fortune teller," I begin, "and in the process have found that her issues have a substantial overlap with yours. Prior to her death Ruby, the woman you hired as a cook, had a long association with a criminal gang of a number of Roma women who essentially used their supposed skills as fortune tellers and psychics to con their marks out of substantial sums of money and other valuables."

So far he appears impassive, but I expect that to change after my next few sentences. "We believe that she used the profits from this enterprise to fund radical groups in Bolivia. And has been doing so for quite some time. We also think that Alvarez took advantage of her connection to these groups and worked with her in some capacity, or at least used her for certain tasks. That would explain why she approached you for employment, to verify that it was you so that Alvarez could fulfill his mission and kill you. We're still not sure how, but the gypsies are involved in some way. Either Ruby objected to his use of them or was no longer needed for whatever plan he has, so he killed her."

Leo's formerly sleepy eyes have sharpened and his jaw his working. He still hasn't said a word but there's no question his mind is in overdrive, estimating how much we know and calculating what he can say and what he can keep to himself. Vinn decides to be the one to push him over the edge.

"Leo," she says softly as she leans forward. "We know that Alvarez' real last name is Soliz, and we know that he's your brother. And we know that you know this. But we also may have discovered something that you don't know." Vinn pauses, glances at me, then looks Leo directly in the eyes.

"Leo, Ruby's true name was Rubinettia Viola Soliz. She was your sister."

Leo's face turns pale, his eyes widen, and his mouth quivers. If there was any doubt that he was ignorant of her relationship to him, it's been answered. Still silent, he moves deeper into the kitchen, dragging his chair, then stands on it to gain access to a locked cabinet above the refrigerator. With some difficulty he produces a key from a chain around his neck and manages to grab a dusty bottle from the back of the cabinet, which he places with care on the table before wrangling three shot glasses. No one speaks as he uncaps the bottle and pours a vile-looking violet liquid into them. He raises his glass in a silent toast and we all down the contents in a single swallow. Belying its appearance, this stuff is remarkable.

Leo refills our glasses but makes no move to offer a second toast, instead taking a small sip. His gruff voice is soft in the predawn hour. "Was told she was dead," he begins. "I left home when she was four, five. Never saw her again. Didn't know it was her."

We wait for more, but Leo shuts down. "Leo, my friend," I finally say, "we need the whole story. It's time."

Leo's nod is barely noticeable but enough that we wait while he gathers his thoughts. He stares off at some unknown point in the air but after an interminable two or three minutes begins to speak.

"We were poor, hungry. My brother is older by three years. Always angry, wanted change. He called for revolt, was a leader of others against government. Active. Speeches, violence. If there was a rally against Torres, he was there. Wanted me to join but I was a kid, maybe 24? Didn't have his spirit, his energy. Stayed with family while he left to join revolt. This made him angrier. We fought."

Leo pauses but ignores his drink. His eyes seem to be looking at a long-ago memory and their corners are damp. "He had big role in coup, joined military people. Says he killed, maybe true. Never forgave me. When General Banzer took control, many people who supported old regime killed or tortured. I was one."

A small gasp comes from Vinn's direction. I'm too mesmerized to move. Leo still avoids looking at us, if he even remembers that we're there listening. "My brother had me arrested, told lie that I opposed coup. Was in jail for two maybe three years, beaten most days. Finally escaped. Left the country, went to Mexico, Cuba. Then here. Never tried to find my brother, never wanted to. He probably thought I died in jail. But he must have found me, maybe through sister. His memory is long and anger is deep. He wants me dead."

Whether Ruby tracked him down on Alvarez' behalf, for her own unknown reasons, or her presence in the city was a total coincidence we may never know. The same for my next question, but I have to ask.

"Leo, do you have any idea why he would kill your sister?"

He shrugs but looks troubled. "Jus' like you said. Could be she didn't know he meant to kill, tried to talk him out. Or didn't want loose end. Don't know. Too late now. Doesn't matter."

Vinn motions toward the door with her head and we both rise to leave Leo alone in his thoughts. As we head upstairs the sun begins to peek above the horizon but a dark cloud soon blocks its rays. A fitting metaphor for the past twenty-four hours. Vinn turns toward the bedroom but I take her elbow and guide her back to our laptops in the living room.

"We need to do one more thing before we can rest. A thought popped into my head during our talk with Leo and it would be just like me to forget it if we don't follow up now. Those dates on that piece of paper in Leo's folder. You take the first five, I'll take the last four. Compare them to assassinations, other killings, or the like in Bolivia or other South American countries. I have a hunch."

It takes us way too long given our sleep-deprived state, but within an hour we have matches for each date. Political figures killed or mass bombings of government or opposition offices. No one ever held responsible on any of them.

Vinn can barely stop yawning but her mind is clearly functioning at full capacity. "Good call, Mal, it fills in a gap. So you think that Leo had a deal with the U.S. government to keep tabs on and report his brother's activities in exchange for being set up here under a new identity. And that partial phone number was probably his source in the CIA or wherever. Alvarez already hated his brother and wanted him dead, but maybe he found out about this recently and that's what finally motivated him to come after Leo. With a vengeance."

"Something like that," I admit. "Cooperating with the government doesn't sound like something Leo would do, but it was a different time back then and if it was the only way to save his skin he might not have had a choice. Knowing Leo, though, I doubt he ended up giving them any accurate or useful information, but Alvarez wouldn't know that. It would explain a lot."

Without another word, we close our laptops and move to the bedroom. We crawl under the sheets, exhausted, but sleep won't come and we lie still, once more staring at the ghosts on the ceiling.

TWENTY THREE

I'm floating somewhere between semi-wakefulness and sleep when an insistent pounding intrudes upon what little peacefulness I've experienced in the past twenty-four hours. Vinn reacts by giving me a firm push before rolling away from the source of the noise and covering her head with a pillow. Groggily I stumble out to the living room where I can now hear Rebecca's voice adding to the cacophony. I hesitate but know I have no choice but to let her in.

It's Ted who pushes himself in before the door is fully open, meaning that this must be a workday and it must be early, as he's usually off to his job by 7:00 a.m.

"Well?" he demands in a tone that must work on his subordinates but only acts to annoy me.

"'Well' what, Rebecca?" I respond casually, which only seems to infuriate him further.

"When are you going to put a stop to this so-called curse? My taillight was broken this morning. I thought you were good at this kind of thing."

I don't move aside to let him into the living room, as I want this conversation to be short and him on his way quickly. "Assuming that was related to Sara and the fortune teller and not a Lexus driver in a hurry, that was the last one, as least for now." I describe the conversation between Adria and Sophia. "You can expect her to reach out to you soon now that she sees you as a ripe source of income. Set up a meeting as soon as you can. Things are accelerating on a couple different fronts and we need to push this."

He wants details but I demur and manage to push him out the door in a flurry of panic by looking at the imaginary

watch on my wrist and commenting on the time. His footsteps are still sounding on the stairs when Vinn emerges from
the bedroom demanding pancakes.

Rebecca's call wasn't long in coming. Her voice echoes
through the phone from Ted's cavernous office.

"Nine o'clock tonight, same location," she says hurriedly.
"And you were right about her greed. She wanted fifteen hundred dollars as a deposit with more due later. I managed to
talk her down to five hundred, which gets me what she calls a
'sample' of what her powers can do. I hope that's okay."

"I hope so too," I admit. "I'm guessing she'll make her
first action dramatic enough to hook you, which in my mind
would mean something physical that she can document, not
hacking emails or anything like that. If we can catch the goon
she hires in the act, that'll be enough and you won't need to go
back again."

Either that was all Rebecca wanted to hear or someone
entered Ted's office, as the connection was cut without any
further comment on her end. What I didn't say was that the
odds of knowing which associate Adria planned to use and
then being at the right place at the right time to intercept him,
not to mention getting him to open up about his activities,
weren't something I would bet the farm on.

I check my email and am disappointed at the lack of
any culpatory phone conversations coming from Adria's cell
until Vinn reminds me that it's only been about twenty-four
hours since her call with Sophia and that it's unlikely she'll
reach out to anyone until she has Rebecca's cash in hand. She
helps me set up notifications of any further emails so that I
can get updates immediately upon receipt and avoid constant
phone checking. If Adria does call one of the henchmen to

give instructions on what to do to Sara, we may not have much time to be on the scene when it happens, and it only takes a matter of seconds to break a taillight or to key a car.

As the day wears on, we wear down and alternate taking naps so that one of us can check Adria's phone conversations each time a notification bell chimes. By 4:00 we're satisfied that nothing will happen today and are mostly rested, giving us the opportunity to debate questions that have been bothering both of us.

Vinn goes straight to the point. "What's Alvarez waiting for? And again, why kill Ruby? I understand eliminating anyone that could point a finger at you for a murder, but isn't that usually done after the person is killed, not before?"

I nod. "And he used her to tell him where Leo lived and where he worked. Leo actually hired her to work at the diner. He could have also used her to set him up. Or asked her to slash his throat when his back was turned while making tortillas. And where do the Roma fit in? It doesn't make sense."

"We don't really know his preferred methodology," Vinn responds, "but I get the feeling that he likes to do his killing himself, up close and personal. And considering this is his brother, it's very personal. Maybe he intends to do it in a particular way."

"I thought of that too. Could be he's been dreaming of killing Leo for so many years that he's created a particular scenario in his mind that he feels the need to follow to the letter. That would explain the delay, that everything has to be just right. And as we discussed before, maybe Ruby had second thoughts or tried to talk Alvarez out of harming her brother."

"Which leaves us guessing," Vinn sighs in frustration. "But here's something else to think about. Was Ruby Alvarez's only connection to the Roma? Could he have been using the women or their associates himself? Are they a part of his plan when it comes to Leo?"

"Interesting," I admit, and it is. "It's possible that Ruby found out that he went behind her back with them, perhaps his actions threatened her cash flow, and she objected. We both think the Roma could still be in play here, but how?" A sudden horrifying thought occurs to me. "Do you think he, or they, might be using Rebecca to get to Leo? Or does he plan to take aim at Rebecca first as a signal to Leo that he's next? And he's using the gypsy women to lure in Rebecca?"

Vinn's eyes go wide and I detect a slight shudder. "I hope it's just the way our minds work based on our past histories that are pointing us in this direction," she says. "But now that we've raised these possibilities, based on virtually nothing but our imaginations, we can't dismiss them. Dammit, Mal, I don't like this. Not one bit."

I hold her closer and for a long time we say nothing. Eventually Vinn reaches for her phone to order pizza, and we shift our thoughts to Rebecca's upcoming session with Adria.

It's déjà vu as Vinn and I sit our same positions in the same borrowed car in the same parking space as the last time Rebecca visited Madam Adria in her apartment above the tattoo parlor. True to form, though, Rebecca is wearing a different dress for this session. Can't have anyone see her wearing the same thing twice.

There's no pausing once she's inside the door this time around, suggesting that when it comes to the bigger sums,

Adria wants to handle those herself. A slightly squeaky door opens and closes before we hear the first spoken words.

"Welcome back, Miss. Did you bring the payment?" Vinn rolls her eyes at the complete lack of effort to hide that this is above all a business transaction. Rebecca remains silent as Adria presumably counts the cash before continuing. "You must understand that this will cover removing the curse that surrounds you, and a small taste of what I can do to exact your revenge upon the one who arranged it. But my skills are vast and require payment in kind. Once you see what your money can buy, you must come back and bring the rest."

"What exactly will this 'small taste' be?" Rebecca asks, following our script.

"It is not for me to decide," Adria answers. "I am only the medium to the spirit world. I place the request and let them know the severity for which you paid, that is all. You come to me because few have such skills to speak to the other world. But it is they who decide the penalty, not I."

"What a crock of shit," Vinn mutters angrily. "So the more money Rebecca pays, the harsher the spirit world's actions against Sara? What do the spirits need with money? Does she light a bigger candle for each hundred you pay her?"

I assume these are rhetorical questions and let Vinn blow off steam without responding. I keep my attention on the exchange going on inside. All I hear, though, are some barely audible chanting and stifled coughs from Rebecca.

"She hates incense," I remark to Vinn, "because it means whatever she's wearing will need to go to the dry cleaner."

The next thing we hear is the squeak of the door and the whispering of a child. She's hard to hear, and both of us instinctively lean closer to the speaker as if that will actually help. Before long Rebecca emerges from the door and heads for her car. Only a few seconds pass after she pulls away before my phone rings.

"I assume you agree that there's no need to debrief tonight," she tells us. "After she took my money and told me about her connection to the spirits who will be visiting Sara, she lit a few candles, burned some godawful incense that smelled like a locker room, and closed her eyes while she mumbled. The girl came to tell me that the woman was in a trance and that she could be like that for many hours. I'll bet as soon as she heard the apartment door close she was in the kitchen eating ice cream."

"Thanks, Rebecca, great job again," I say. "We'll let you know if we hear anything and please do the same." I hang up without waiting to hear Rebecca's complaints about our passive approach to the investigation, as my own mind is plenty loud enough on that same topic.

I drop Vinn off at her condo before returning the Zipcar to its rightful spot and walk home. My brain is too overloaded to think straight and it's not quite late enough to go to bed, so I spend the next half hour browsing Netflix looking for a mindless show that doesn't involve superheroes, aliens, or serial killers. Failing in my quest, I open my laptop on the off chance that Adria reached out to someone after Rebecca's session. To my surprise, she didn't disappoint. The number she calls reaches voice mail.

"Josef, I need you for a job. I'll send you the woman's info. Nothing serious, just something small but dramatic for show. Need to reel this guy in before we raise the bar. Wait until tomorrow night to give me a chance to commune with the spirits..." she laughs to herself... "and let me know what you do and when. Usual rates."

I copy down the number she called and match it against one of the names we already have from Ruby's notebook. We've got less than a day to get Josef's address and a physical description and to figure out how to set up a tail so that we can follow him, observe what he does to make Sara's life just a little more miserable, and then grab him for questions. Piece of cake. To show how important getting that information is, I make an executive decision to put it off until tomorrow.

TWENTY FOUR

"Just a thought before you reach out to Malika and add to the list of felonies she's committed on our behalf," Vinn lectures me when she calls the next morning. "Did we ever get a response from your source that you sent that license plate number to? The one I risked life and limb to get after Rebecca's initial psychic consultation? Maybe, just maybe, we'll get lucky for once and it was Josef driving that car."

"Um," I respond, the most appropriate answer I can produce on the spot considering following up on my request for a trace hasn't once crossed my mind since I sent it off to my source with access to the computer systems of Secretaries of State across the country. "We're never that lucky, but it doesn't hurt to look. Give me a second while I check my emails." I conveniently leave out the fact that it took me half a day to remember the name and email address of my source the first time and I don't have any better recall now.

Six minutes later, just when Vinn's patience was about to morph into a litany of profanity, I find Janet's email. I'm tempted to pretend that she said that she needs more time to look into it or that the car was stolen the day before Rebecca's session, because once I relay what it really says Vinn will be insufferable for months. Instead, I take a deep breath and decide to be truthful. "Good news, and very astute on your part," I begin shamelessly, hoping high praise will prevent her from rubbing it in later. "The car does, in fact, belong to a Josef Codona. Was this the driver you saw?" I forward Vinn the email so that she can look at the driver's license photo of Josef.

I can almost hear her shrug. "Could be. You know I didn't get much of a look. Doesn't really matter at this point since we know he's the thug being called upon to start giving Sara hell. Looks like he lives up in Jefferson Park, so not too far. Have you thought about what we'll do about surveillance?"

"Give me a minute." Before I call Chuck, my fellow tea aficionado and go-to for this kind of job, I look up the address on Google Maps. The house is a brick ranch in need of a little maintenance on a block of mostly single-family homes, which could pose an issue in finding a place to establish a stakeout.

Chuck agrees when he hears the address. "Not easy, that's for sure. It's a working-class area with neighborhood watch groups making sure the riffraff passes through without stopping, so it's difficult to loiter around any one spot for very long. Unfamiliar cars will draw attention and there are people up there, mostly retirees with time on their hands and chips on their shoulders, who live to stop anyone they don't recognize and give them the third degree. But it can be done."

"I don't expect it to go on for very long," I tell him, trying to stay positive. "In fact, I'd be surprised if the guy doesn't do the job tonight. We need you to be mobile and follow him until we can catch up and take over."

"No problem. One spotter will probably be enough since we only need to keep watch over his car, not the man himself, although if we need to hide in a tree or something a second person nearby with wheels would be ideal. I'll have someone there within an hour or two. Keep your phone on, and make sure to answer a call even if you don't recognize the number."

With what I spend renting Zipcars, it would probably be cheaper to actually buy one. They really need to have a frequent driver program. I set it up, tell Vinn I'll be by to pick her up, and head off to get the car.

"What exactly do we expect to get out of this guy once we capture him?" I ask her as she settles into the passenger seat. "I can't imagine he knows much about the workings of the fortune teller group. It's more likely he gets a call naming a target, the parameters of what he can and should do, and then gets paid when the job is done."

"I admit it's grasping for the proverbial straw," Vinn responds. "But first, don't forget that this was your idea. Beyond that, grilling him could be useful to understand the extent of what these people do and how often they do it. Get an overview of the operation at the bottom level. And who knows, he could be a cousin to one of these women and hears the stories around the table at Thanksgiving."

"At best, though," I continue in my role as Debbie Downer, "we'd gather enough information to turn over to the cops to take these women down, if they're even interested in doing so. And my guess is that there are more cells just like it operating around the city. Finding the connection to Alvarez, or anything useful in preventing him from getting to Leo, won't be something that we're likely to get out of Josef. I assume that if Alvarez needs his services, the request would only come through the Roma women."

"I agree we'll have to work up the chain of command," Vinn admits. "Instead of calling on the cops, at least initially, we'll use the threat of arrest to get Josef to give us something on Adria or Sophia, then the threat of exposure against them to trade for whatever information they have about Alvarez. Someone somewhere has to know something."

We spend the afternoon looking again through all of the

contents of the bag that we took from Ruby's place, consider going back to look for a laptop, and toss ideas back and forth as far as how best to protect Leo. What remains unspoken but hangs heavily in the room is the certainty that in order to remove any threat to Leo, Alvarez has to be removed from the picture and that there's only one way to do that.

We're clearing the dinner dishes, scraping the remnants of stuffed peppers into the trash, when my phone rings from across the room. My initial impulse in seeing an unfamiliar number is to ignore the call before remembering Chuck's admonition. The female voice on the other end is vaguely familiar, so she's probably an associate of Chuck's I've worked with before. She doesn't introduce herself.

"The target is on the move," she says breathlessly. "Chevy Impala, either blue or black. Plate begins CL6. Heading east on Sunnydale toward Milwaukee. Closing distance."

Vinn and I are out the door in a flash and within five minutes are in the rental car moving east toward Milwaukee Avenue. If Josef continues down that way, we have plenty of time to intercept him. Sara lives in the DePaul area, so we assume that he's heading in that direction. We drive north and continue slightly east, then pull over to wait for an update. It's not long in coming.

"Turning east on Fullerton," the voice tells us, confirming our suspicion as to his destination. "Dammit," she says moments later in a panic. Semi blocking me at the underpass. Can't make the turn. I've lost him. Will try to pick him up from another direction."

We don't wait for another call and hurry in the direction of Sara's condo, which is on a quiet block on Seminary south of the campus. "Remember, Adria asked Josef to do something 'small but dramatic,'" Vinn reminds me as I cruise through a stop sign. "I guess we should have found out if Sara has a car, because something on the order of a smashed windshield would fit the bill. Otherwise, what? A dead cat on her doorstep? Throwing a rock through her windshield?"

"Hopefully we'll get there before he does to witness whatever it is firsthand," I answer. "But this traffic is brutal. Even if we don't see what he actually does, as long as we find him we can fake it. Should we camp out or cruise the neighborhood?"

"Let's drive around a perimeter of her place," Vinn suggests. You look down streets on your side and I'll do mine, and any glimpse of his car and we give chase." She looks at the clock on the dashboard. "But I'm not sure we beat him here. Let's give it once or twice around and then get out of the car and watch over her building. I don't want to miss this chance."

We're on our second time driving two blocks in all directions of Sara's unit when Chuck calls to tell us that his tail wasn't able to relocate Joseph. I cut off his apology and tell him we'll get back to him later, trying not to sound peeved. It could've happened to anyone.

After seven or eight minutes, I pull over next to a hydrant down the block from Sara's building. We agree to split up and Vinn heads to the alley to see if she can find a car with damage in the rear. I'm on my second stroll down the block, peering into gangways and looking for the Impala when my phone sounds, the ringtone telling me it's Vinn. She sounds distraught.

"What's the matter? Are you okay? Did you find something?" I ask, words spilling out of my mouth.

"Yes I found something and no, I'm not okay. I think

you'd better come look for yourself. I'll meet you at the south end of the alley."

Vinn's expression is dark as I near, but without a word she turns and proceeds up the alley, forcing me to scramble to catch up. A few garages break up parking lots filled with cars and garbage and recycling bins line the way. The spaced out streetlights behind the rows of homes do little to brighten the area, their dim glow casting eerie shadows. Vinn slows as we approach the back of Sara's building, where five cars are parked on a concrete slab. Vinn stops to face me, halting my progress as she places her left palm on my chest.

"Don't get close and don't touch anything," she whispers. "Take a look and then we need to leave. Quickly."

She points to a space between a gray SUV and a Prius. I stop at the back end of the cars, waiting for my eyes to adjust to the darkness. Soon a twisted leg enters my vision, extending out from under the SUV. I crouch down and can only make out the dark form of the rest of what appears to be a woman.

"I had to check first to see if that's Sara and second to see if I should call for an ambulance," Vinn says quietly. "It's 'yes' to the first and 'no' to the second. Her head has a large dent and there's a deep slash across her neck. I felt that was enough and didn't feel for a pulse. I don't think it would be a good idea to leave any trace of ourselves, don't you agree? Now let's get out of here."

We walk quickly the opposite way of where we came in, keeping in the shadows as much as possible. Other than a man walking his dog on the next block, we encounter no one on our way to the car. My hands are trembling as I place them on the steering wheel. "That son-of-a-bitch," I curse angrily.

"Agreed," Vinn responds. "But no time to talk. Drive, Mal. Now."

And I do.

"I don't know, Vinn, it just doesn't make sense," I tell her once we're safely back in my living room, as much talking out loud to myself as to her. Without asking, Vinn pours two generous glasses of my best aged bourbon in lieu of our usual tea and coffee, and she isn't wrong. "I mean, this guy didn't have a record and there's no indication that he's done anything more than nuisance crimes on behalf of the Roma women. Killing doesn't exactly fit the description of 'minor but dramatic.'"

"Maybe she resisted, or got a good look at his face and he panicked," she answers as she sips. "Which I might believe if she only had a knock on the head, or even if she was strangled. But a slashed throat? That indicates that Josef would have brought a knife along with him and it's also an especially angry way to kill. I agree it doesn't fit but then again, it's too big a coincidence to ignore."

"There's another angle we have to be concerned about totally apart from why Josef killed Sara, if he did." Vinn throws a puzzled look my way and I'm surprised she hasn't seen it. "When the cops start investigating the murder, one of the first things they do is look at the exes. Granted, Rebecca broke it off with Sara several years ago, but it was a nasty break and it's only a matter of time before detectives find out about their confrontation at the bar. And there's most likely some sort of record at Sara's place that'll bring them to Madam Sophia. If she admits to being behind all of the incidents Rebecca endured, that will put Rebecca right near the top of the list of suspects. And if they find out about Adria..."

"They'll know that Rebecca hired her to seek revenge on Sara," Vinn finishes for me. "Even if she has an alibi for tonight, it'll look like she hired Josef through Adria to kill Sara. And I expect that Adria will put all of this on Rebecca, telling the cops how upset Rebecca was and how she wanted to get back at Sara, but she never expected her to take it this far... Shit."

"It gets worse," I say. "The only way that Rebecca can provide a plausible defense is to tell the truth. And that gets you and I on the map. Even if one or both of us don't end up in jail, we'll spend a lot of time at the station answering questions and will be under constant watch. That will leave Leo completely exposed."

We both stay silent for several long moments, as every time one of us opens our mouths to speak it becomes more clear how bleak our situation is. If I know Vinn, her mind is travelling in the same direction as mine, albeit faster and evaluating more permutations, and she'll come to the same conclusion that I have. She doesn't disappoint.

"As I see it," she states flatly. "Our first step is to warn Rebecca what lies ahead for her. Then you and I need to go to ground. We can't risk being taken off course and have to finish what we started before we see a single cop." She sees me nod in agreement. "How long do you think we have?"

"A couple of days at best. Sara's body probably won't be discovered until morning, then they'll need to process the scene. Tracing her to Rebecca will take some time and then going through her to find us even longer. It could stretch to a week or two before our names come up."

"Agreed, but we can't take chances. Get Rebecca up

here, then pack your stuff. We'll stop by my place so that I can do the same. Let's plan to be out of sight by morning."

"What are you saying?" Rebecca stammers, understandably in shock. "I asked you to get her off my back, not kill her."

"Rebecca listen to me closely," I reply, trying to keep the annoyance out of my voice. "We didn't touch Sara. We never even spoke with her. It wasn't us, and don't even try to blame us because we put the fortune teller's actions in motion. We're not even sure her guy is the killer."

She doesn't look convinced but doesn't reply. Vinn has always been more persuasive as the calm voice of reason, and she instinctively takes over. "Rebecca, we'll eventually find out who did this to her and you'll see that whatever guilt you're feeling now is misplaced. But there are some more immediate ramifications to her death that we have to discuss and you need to focus. Pull up your big girl panties and listen closely."

Rebecca's eyes take on more of a sharpness, probably resentful over Vinn's pandering or her subtle implication that Rebecca should assume partial responsibility for what happened. Eventually her head moves up and down an almost imperceptible half-inch, which Vinn takes as a good enough acknowledgement to continue.

"As Sara's ex-boyfriend, it won't take long for the police to come calling." Vinn tries to sound reassuring. "They may or may not suspect you, but once they find out about your visit to Madam Adria and its purpose, and they will, you'll shoot up their list as a person of interest. Now hear what I'm about to say. It's critical that you be completely open and honest about your activities, and that includes asking Mal and I to intervene. If you try to fib or leave something out to protect yourself or us, they're going to wonder why."

My turn. "Vinn and I are going to disappear for a while but we're not going away. Do us a favor and tell Leo that we're devoting all of our time to the job he asked us to do but we need to keep a low profile to avoid both Alvarez and the cops. I expect we'll be able to wrap this up soon and everything will be back to normal. Now go, we have things to do."

Rebecca has the look of someone with a million questions but allows Vinn to take her elbow and escort her out the door. As soon as she's out, Vinn leans back against the door and loudly exhales before turning her attention to me.

"'Wrap this up soon?' If you have a secret plan I'd appreciate it if you'd let me in on it. In the meantime, get a move on and start packing, and I suggest you throw in enough clothes for more than a few days. I need to make a call."

I pull a large duffle out of the back of my closet and get to work. We have to assume that starting in the near future, both of our places will be closely watched by the authorities, so I have to make decisions quickly but efficiently as the most essential items required to meet every contingency that may arise in the days or weeks ahead. Ten minutes later, I zip up the bag and we're out the door.

TWENTY FIVE

"You mean to tell me that half of your bag is filled with tea?" Vinn practically screams. Probably not a good time to tell her that her nose wrinkles in a cute way when she's incredulous. And no, it's not half of my bag. Close, though.

"You said to pack the essentials," I tell her in my defense. "Clothes and toothpaste I can get anywhere without drawing attention to myself. But not any tea worth drinking." I think she's just jealous, having failed to bring her favorite blend of artisanal coffee beans.

We're settling into a luxury condo on the fifty-first floor overlooking Lake Michigan courtesy of friends of Vinn's who she called to confirm that they're out of town for the summer. "Courtesy of" might not be quite accurate, and that phone call probably didn't involve asking permission to house sit, as the fact that Vinn brought us into the building through the service entrance and then used her lock picks to gain entry to the unit is what we in the profession call a clue that maybe the owners don't know that we're here. In a way it's brilliant, as it's about as atypical of the traditional hideout as possible and no one will think to look for us in this type of environment, as long as we don't draw the attention of a sharp-eyed concierge.

It takes us about four minutes to find the password to the wifi and soon our new command center is up and running. The first thing I do is go online to see if there's been any communication between Adria and Josef. I'm surprised to find one from the middle of the night. Vinn settles in next to me on a couch that probably cost more than my first three cars combined and I press a key.

"Josef, do you know what time it is? You'd better have a damn good reason for waking me up."

"It's you that has some explaining to do." Josef sounds angry, his voice rising with every word. *"What did you get me involved in? Did you know she was dead? Were you trying to set me up?"*

"Dead? What in the hell are you talking about?" Adria is shrieking into the phone. I lower the volume. *"I didn't tell you to kill her. I never authorized that and didn't give you the code word. What did you do?"*

"Me? I was going to snatch her purse if I found her or break a window if I couldn't. I found her all right. Under a car. Did you send one of the other guys out there?"

"Calm down. Stop yelling." Adria is regaining her composure, taking control. *"You're sure she's dead?"*

"I'm not an idiot, Carla. I didn't stick around to ask her if she's alive if that's what you mean."

"Wasn't one of us, Josef, I'd have been informed. It might have been—no, never mind. You didn't touch her, leave any trace of yourself there?"

"I'm no amateur. There's nothing to link that woman to us."

There's a long silence before Adria—Carla—continues the conversation. *"Not so sure about that, Josef. I may need you for another job, this time a k-level for real. I'll get back to you."*

The lines disconnect and there are no more links to transcripts in my inbox. I'm still processing what we heard when Vinn speaks up.

"Two immediate takeaways. First, unless he's a damn good liar, Josef didn't kill Sara and doesn't know who did. That being said, it doesn't take much reading between the lines to hear Adria admit that they've used him to kill before."

"Take those thoughts a step further," I tell her, thinking aloud. "Josef may not know who killed Sara but I think Adria might. Did you hear her catch herself with her 'might have been' thought? You know what I'm thinking. We've been chasing a connection between Alvarez and the Roma. Worth considering if he did this one. Fits the profile, the slashed throat is much more personal than what you find with the usual mugging. Which, if true, gives support to the idea that Alvarez is working his way in to Leo by first killing everyone that he cares about. This may be his way of teasing Leo. By going after Sara, he's signaling that he can get to anyone, and that Rebecca may be next.

"But it gets worse, if that's possible," I continue. "You heard Adria. Rebecca is the sole living connection between Sara and the gypsies. It sounds like she wants to take care of that. So even if I'm reading this wrong and Alvarez' hands aren't in this or he has no interest in Rebecca, it's clear that Adria does. Rebecca's life is in danger."

I'm hoping that Vinn tells me I'm full of crap and being too alarmist, but no such words come from her mouth. Instead, she turns to me, her eyes full of both anxiety and determination. "I think," she says slowly, "we need to pay a visit to Madam Adria."

"At some point soon, and the sooner the better, yes," I agree, "but not until we're armed with information that we can hang over her head. We need her to confide in us fully as to her link to Alvarez, if any, and to agree to leave Rebecca alone. I have the feeling that threats of violence are an occupational hazard to her and won't in themselves have the desired effect. We need more."

Vinn considers this. "Okay, granted," she grudgingly

admits. "But if we're going to take valuable time digging into her activities, just getting her to agree to leave Rebecca alone won't be enough. If, and yes it's a big 'if,' she and the Roma are working with Alvarez, we can use that to our advantage."

I'm a bit slow on the uptake but then see where she's going. "In other words," I say, more a question than a statement, "turn them against him, use them to set him up so that we can take Alvarez and these women out of our lives once and for all."

Vinn smiles patronizingly at me as if I were one of her slower students finally catching on to a scientific concept. "Yes, but more than that. If we're the ones to actually take Alvarez out, they would have something on us and don't think they wouldn't use that to their advantage. We need to orchestrate this so that the exact opposite is true. Mal, we need to put Adria and her cohorts in a position where they have no choice but to kill him, or at the very least participate to an extent that they won't rat us out to the cops. That not only prevents them from having information on us they can use for blackmail, it gives us what we need to make sure they never get near any of us again."

We've always known that the only way to keep Leo safe now and in the future is to put Alvarez in the ground, but to hear Vinn speak the words out loud is a grim reminder of the task that lies ahead and of how the lives we lead with our former employers will never be completely left behind. We're both quiet, staring at the floor, as we consider what comes next.

After a few long moments, I break the silence. "I'm not so sure that I trust them to do what needs to be done, and a part of me demands that I look into Alvarez's eyes as he lay dying, for Leo's sake. We can discuss that further later. For now, I think you'll agree that we don't have the time to gather and sort through police reports of unsolved crimes to establish the connections to the Roma to hold over Adria's head. We need to start acting fast and do whatever it takes to get what we need quickly. That means before we go see Adria, we pay a rather unpleasant visit to Joseph."

"Speaking of unpleasant," Vinn replies dourly. "I think we need to make use of Malika one more time. We'll save it until there are no other options, but the most reliable way to get a parent to do something they wouldn't otherwise do is to threaten their child. I know we won't act on it, but Adria won't know that. Mal, we're entering a dark world here. We need to act accordingly."

I don't respond but of course she's right. While Vinn reaches for her cell phone, I sort through the clothes I brought. First impressions are important, and for our visit to Josef, we need to look like people we're not.

Vinn has a practical foresight that I seem to lack, so while I packed my emergency bag with tea and underwear, she thought to include a variety of serious weaponry in hers. We each choose the bulkiest handguns in her collection more for the impression they make and their obvious presence beneath our jackets, but then supplement them with our weapons of choice. For Vinn this means strapping sharp blades to her forearm and ankle while for myself it's still a handgun, just smaller and more accurate at close distances. We're dressed to look not like actual detectives but closer to those stereotypes people see on television and will perceive as real.

Uber obviously isn't an option here, so it's Zipcar once again. If that company ever discovers the various reasons we rent from them we'll probably be banned for life. We know from Chuck's earlier research and observations that Joseph either works from home or uses it as his base of operations, so we agree that it's worth the chance to show up at his door unannounced and hope that he's there. Catching someone totally off-guard can be an important first step if we can keep him off balance enough to say something he'll regret later and never would have uttered if given time to prepare.

We circle his block a couple of times to make sure that activity by his neighbors is limited and to give a dog walker time to move on. We score a parking space immediately across the street from his home but before exiting the car wait a few minutes to see if there's movement behind the curtains.

"Too conspicuous just sitting here," Vinn notes after about five minutes of inactivity. "Let's get this done before one of his nosy neighbors calls a real cop."

We walk briskly to Josef's front door, where I knock loudly and long. We hear footsteps from within and try to put on our official-looking faces. I feel ridiculous.

The door opens about ten inches to reveal the unshaven face of a man in his fifties, his eyes darting nervously between the two of us. His voice is unsteady and suspicious as he utters a single word. "Yes?"

"Josef Codona?"

No sooner does he begin to nod than I forcibly push the door open with my shoulder as Vinn follows immediately behind, quickly closing it. Josef is still processing what's happening as I pull his arms behind him and push him up against the wall. "We have some questions for you."

"Do you have a warrant?" he manages to squeak out despite the fact that I have his mouth firmly squashed against the floral wallpaper.

I try to sound sarcastic. "He thinks we need to show a warrant," I tell Vinn. "How quaint. Mr. Codova, that would mean there's a record that we're here and we don't want that. Just in case."

I swear I hear Vinn snicker at my poor acting job but hope it's my imagination. I also hear movement from elsewhere in the house. "Why don't we bring this conversation somewhere a little more private?" I tell him.

I continue holding his arms tight behind him as he leads us through the kitchen to a small room in the rear of the house that appears to serve as an office. A desk faces the far wall and the only seating is a tattered chair pushed up against the desk. I push hard and hopefully painfully on Josef's shoulders to force him into the chair then swivel him around to allow Vinn to place a pair of handcuffs around his wrists. I recognize the cuffs as a pair she used on me for an entirely different purpose a few weeks ago and have to work to refocus on the task at hand.

I swing Josef around. Both Vinn and I have our jackets pulled back far enough to display our weapons, which causes our victim's eyes to grow wide. I begin to wonder whether the cowed individual in front of me is the same man who supposedly has killed on behalf of the Roma women. Each of us steps closer to him so that he has to crane his neck to look into our eyes. Vinn takes the lead.

"We've had our eyes on a certain organization for some time," she begins in her best imitation of bad cop. "Fortune tellers. Psychics. Mediums. Con men. Actually," she bends down inches from his face, "con women and the men who do their bidding. What are we looking at here, Cal?"

Cal? I almost don't catch on that she's throwing the

conversation to me. "Some petty crime," I begin. "Vandal-ism, cyber stalking, theft. But also grand larceny, assault, and murder. Last one pissed our bosses off enough to send us here, Josef, with no warrant and with no paper trail. Pretty girl, young. Slashed throat. Anything you want to tell us about that, Josef Codona?"

I'm relieved to see the panic in his eyes and the sweat beads forming at the edge of his forehead, although it's also continuing to give me pause about whether he's actually killed before, as we suspect. He's not acting the part of a seasoned criminal.

"That wasn't me, I swear!" He's practically crying.

"Ah," Vinn says smugly as she lowers herself to his eye level. "But you clearly know about it. Just happened overnight. Hasn't made the news. So we'll ask you again, Josef, anything you want to tell us?"

His mouth opens but no words come out as he looks first to Vinn, then to me, his mind reeling, looking for an out. The slap comes so quickly that it takes me by surprise. Don't let it be said that a woman doesn't have the strength to inflict pain. Significant pain, judging from the look of agony on Jo-sef's face.

"You have two choices, Josef," Vinn tells him softly as she pulls her sleeve back to reveal the knife, which gleams from the light overhead. "You can tell us all, and I mean everything. Or we'll leave here and go to one of the others. Let's see." Vinn pulls out the list of the other henchmen used by the women and starts reading. When she gets to the third name I loudly clear my throat. Vinn looks up at me and I shake my head. "I see," she says, taking out a marker to cross off his name. Josef begins shaking.

Over the next hour, he outlines the work he's done for the Roma, ranging from keying cars to physical assault, but when it comes to killing he balks. Only upon being pressed, slapped twice more, and not-so subtly threatened with unspecified harm does he admit that maybe a few others on our list have gone that far, and he gives up two names of the victims and approximate dates. When it comes to supplying information about the organization's workings, he pleads ignorance and I unfortunately believe him.

Only when we feel that we've drained him of any and all useful information do I pull out my cell phone to show that he's been recorded. The look of disappointment on his face confirms that he was planning on denying everything later. Vinn removes the cuffs, but before we leave gives him one word of warning.

"Josef, if we get word that you've told anyone—and I mean anyone—'bout our visit today we won't be so nice the next time around. In fact, I doubt we'll even bother to knock. Got it?"

He nods enthusiastically, I tell him to count to one hundred before leaving the room, and we slip out quickly. Within a minute we're back in the car and moving as fast as we can away from the house.

"Do you think he'll talk?" I ask Vinn once we're a couple of blocks away.

"Fifty-fifty," she shrugs. "But I think he'd be more worried about would happen to him if he admits his confession about their activities to the Roma than what we'd do to him if he talks. That being said, let's not give him time to think about it. We need to get to Adria. First, though, lunch."

TWENTY SIX

"I don't think our posing as rogue cops will work with Adria," I tell Vinn as I sop up the remnants of melitzanes off my plate with the last piece of bread from the Greektown restaurant we stopped at on the way back. "We were lucky with Josef that he's not as seasoned as we expected and also that he's the nervous type. I don't think we'll be as fortunate with her. We need to straight out lay our cards on the table and threaten to expose her."

"Our tarot cards, you mean?" Vinn replies with a slight smile, always the calmer of the two of us. "I agree, but before we do that we need to beef up our blackmail material. You check to see if Josef ratted us out yet to Adria and I'll search the cops' database to match up those names he gave us with a dead body."

I'm relieved to find that Adria has neither made nor received any calls from Josef or anyone else even peripherally connected to the matter at hand. I'm not sure how long that will last given Josef's nerves, reinforcing the need for quick action. I pass this information on to Vinn, who nods in acknowledgment as she continues to peer at her screen, her fingers periodically flying across the keyboard. Five minutes pass and I find it increasingly difficult to keep quiet and to prevent my toe from tapping. Vinn notices and holds one finger up to indicate she's almost done with whatever she's doing.

"Surprisingly, the information provided by Josef checks out," she finally tells me. "I tracked down the two killings, one from last year and one from three years ago. Both remain unsolved. The reports the police released are as usual devoid of any useful facts but there were a couple of blurbs in newspapers and some social media talk that filled in how and where the victims died and some background about who they were. A few of the assaults lined up as well. I don't think we have the time for me to research any more of the crimes he mentioned. This should be sufficient, don't you think?"

"The murders alone should be enough," I tell her. "If not, we'll have to form a Plan B and I hate to think what that might entail. Plan A is bad enough."

We're heading to the door when my phone rings, the few bars from the chorus of Beyonce's "Diva" stopping both of us in our tracks. Vinn's expression mirrors my own concern.

"Yes, Rebecca?" I try to keep my voice level to disguise my stress.

"They were here, at my door." She makes no attempt to hide her distress. "Police. Two of them, one of them was that cop you know. Morales. No, Madina. No..."

"Mendez," I interrupt. She must be flustered, as she's worked with him in the past. "What did they want?"

"What do you think? To ask about Sara. You said they would come but I thought I'd have a few more days. They told me that they may want me to go to the station to make a formal statement but for now they were just gathering information. So I let them in and talked to them. That was okay, right?"

"It depends on what you told them, Rebecca," I respond as I move to the couch, Vinn at my heels. I put her on speakerphone.

"Just what you said. The truth. About how she harassed me in the bar, her hiring that fortune teller, all of the little crimes they committed against me." She pauses. "I let them know just what I thought of the police response to my complaints and their refusal to offer me personal protection." I wince but say nothing. "They were very interested in my meeting with Madam Adria and asked me to recreate the conversation with the exact words that were used. Oh, and I made sure to tell them that you and Vinn were listening in during my session and that it was your idea to meet with her because you wanted to flush out one of the guys that was making my life miserable and that you thought maybe they were connected to some guy who wants to kill Leo. Mendez went upstairs and knocked on your door then came back and asked if I knew where you were. He wants to talk to you."

No doubt he does. "Thank you for the update, Rebecca. I'll call you later to discuss this further. It may be from a different number than the one you have programmed for me. Check on Leo for me." I hang up to cries of "wait" from the other end. Vinn's already taking her sim card out of her phone and I begin to do the same.

"Dammit," she whines. "I love this phone. I don't suppose I can go throw it in my unit?"

I assume the question was rhetorical and don't answer, instead dropping my sim card to the floor and grinding it with the heel of my shoe. Vinn tosses hers to me to do the same. We exit the building and walk toward Michigan Avenue to throw them into an overflowing trash bin that should be collected later today. We cross the street behind a line of cars waiting for a red light, slipping the two phones through an open window in the back seat of a Honda Accord with Iowa plates.

"First stop, somewhere to grab a couple of burner phones," I state. "Then on our way to Adria. Hopefully we'll beat the cops to her place."

An hour later we're pulling into our accustomed parking space outside of Adria's apartment. It's the first time we've been here in the daylight hours and the area reveals itself to be dingy and dirty. We stay in the car for a few minutes looking for any unusual activity before exiting. Vinn takes the near side and I cross the street to examine the other parked cars for municipal license plates, police scanners on the dashboard, or other signs of a police presence. Seeing nothing, I take one step back into the street when I catch a slow-moving dark Ford Explorer moving up the block. I instinctively duck behind a car and see Vinn do the same. Sure enough, it pulls over two spots in front of our Zipcar. I watch as a familiar figure exits the passenger side, joined shortly by a uniformed driver. The cop moves to the back of the house as Mendez pushes the buzzer. After a verbal exchange I can't hear, he steps inside.

Vinn's in the middle of a string of creative profanities when we join up back at our car. "Could've been worse," I try to pacify her, "Imagine if we were already inside when Mendez showed up."

"Yeah, it's not that," she replies. "It's just that the cops seem to be moving uncharacteristically fast on this one. Mendez must be pushing it. If Alvarez is using the Roma in some way, this may accelerate his timetable. And it may not be long before Rebecca is arrested or that an alert is put out looking for us. We're running out of time, Mal."

"I know," I say glumly. "But as it stands we can't do anything based on what we know now that won't leave too many loose ends, and we're stuck in that position until we get the information we need from Adria. I was on the fence before about using an implied threat against her kid to pry her open. Not anymore. With any luck, though, that won't be necessary. Mendez is good and can be intimidating. We can use that once he leaves. If she's smart, and I think she is, she'll be open to an arrangement if we promise that we have a plan that makes everything go away."

"As long as she doesn't ask for details of this so-called plan," Vinn mutters.

We have plenty of time to come up with the so-called plan but are still left with "wing it" as the top choice when Mendez and his cohort emerge nearly ninety minutes later. As they pull away from the curb, Vinn receives a text which causes her to compress her lips and close her eyes. I wonder who she's shared her new number with but she makes no move to share the content of the text and I don't press. We wait until the cops turn at the next corner before hustling to the door to the right of the tattoo parlor to press the buzzer, hoping that Adria will assume it's the cops coming back to ask something they forgot and will just buzz us in. For once we get lucky and five seconds later arrive on the landing just as the door to an apartment opens up a crack. Without waiting to introduce ourselves, Vinn kicks the door open the rest of the way and we rush inside.

"Who...wha.." the woman sputters, backing away in fright. Vinn blocks her escape route to the back of the house as I pull a gun out of my jacket and use it to motion Adria to the couch. She glances back at Vinn, who now holds a knife in her hand, before silently complying. Vinn squeezes in next to her while I pull a chair up close enough that our knees nearly touch.

"Now that we have your attention, Madam Adria," I do

my best to sneer her name in contempt, "we need you to listen closely. We've been assigned to protect a couple of individuals presenting themselves as Leo and Rebecca. Their real identities are irrelevant. Who retained us is also unimportant, suffice it to say that they're not the kind of people that you want to disappoint. As a result we've learned quite a lot about you. Some very interesting information, I must say."

I can see Adria's mind churning as she begins to regain her composure. I need to keep her off-balance. Her lips part slightly as she thinks about mounting a defense. I quickly reach across and press three fingers over her mouth. "Hush. There will be plenty of time to talk in a few moments when we want you to talk. For now, just listen. We're not green, we do our research. We have a nice long list of your, shall we say, less than legal activity. You and your lady friends have been running lucrative cons for a long time, and if you want to continue you'll need to do what we ask of you. Except for the murder part, that you've got to stop. And you've got to give somebody up for Shannon three years ago and Perez last year. We know the role you played in those killings and would be happy to tell those cops who just left here all about it. Or not. We're reasonable people, just a little tit for tat. No strong-arm."

"Unless necessary," Vinn chimes in as she plays with the tip of her blade. "We're not above some physical persuasion or punishment. You wouldn't want us to have to visit you again or to, say, stop by the Lincoln Elementary School. Eva, is it?"

Adria's face drains of all color and her lip starts to quiver. I now have my answer as to the nature of the text. Our plan was for Vinn to convey the threat, which has suddenly morphed from implied to specific thanks to Maleka, since she's better at playing the bad guy than I am and much more convincing. I'm sure I'll get another thorough evaluation of my poor acting skills in the car on the way back. In the meantime, though, we need to get what we came for.

I put my hand under Adria's chin and pull her head back to face me. "It's very simple. We know that you were involved in some petty mischief against Rebecca and that she hired you to squash it and give Sara some of her own medicine. We also know that as a result you're now up at the top of the cop's list as a person of interest in her murder." The look of terror on Adria's face indicates that so far I'm on point. Time to take a chance with some educated speculation. "And we know that you've been working with Hector Alvarez to set Leo up to be killed. What we don't know is how you're involved in that or what his plan is. That's what you're going to tell us. Now you can talk."

The combination of fear and fury in her eyes proves that we scored with our hypothesis. A brief thought of revolt flashes through those same eyes, but a sideways glance at Vinn's knife and a furtive look at a picture of her daughter on the bookshelf behind me dampens any thoughts of resistance. Vinn decides to sweeten the pot.

"I know this is difficult for you," she says reassuringly. "Alvarez is a very bad man and you're wondering who's the lesser of two evils. If you decide to continue helping him, all you get in return is your life back, except then you still have us and the cops to worry about, and most likely years behind bars. If you cooperate with us, Alvarez and the cops go away and you have our gratitude. Not much of a choice in my book. But it's a choice we need you to make right now."

In truth, Adria had already decided before Vinn spoke. But now she releases the tight fists she had been making and seems to crumble within herself, burying her head in her hands. When she begins to talk, her voice is soft and wavering.

"It started with Maria. Maria Mariola. She approached one of the other ladies, said she could help us make more money. She was able to bring us rich people, she said. Old people, easy marks. We don't like to deal with outsiders, we keep everything in the family. But Madam Mystique—her name is Lavinia, my cousin—she was having a tough time, needed money. So she said yes, we try it one time. Ended up being a big score with a lady who wanted to ask her dead husband something. So now we all wanted a piece of this."

"When was that?" Vinn asks.

Adria pauses to think. "Long time. Ten years, maybe nine? This Maria, she would pretend to be a friend of a friend or a health care worker or something like that just to get into parties or events then would steer talk to areas that we can help with. Don't know how she did it, a smooth talker this woman. We all started to get more money, sometimes lots more. Maria took a percentage. It was good, until..."

Adria stops, her haunted eyes staring off into another part of the room. After a few long minutes where she seems to be lost in a memory, I decide to prompt.

"Until?"

As Adria comes back from wherever her mind had taken her, she looks almost surprised at our presence. "Until she told us we needed to help her with something else. Not ask, told. We refused. She insisted, got angry, but we said no. That's when she brought him.

"He was an old man but hard. Bad, bad aura, it frightened us before he said a word. But then he spoke and we were scared even more. He made threats, like you, but worse. Then he slashed my arm for no reason." Adria pulls her left sleeve up to reveal a three-inch scar, still red. "It was a warning. Cooperate or else. What choice did we have?"

"What did he want you to do?" I ask tentatively. It's what we came here to find out, but I'm not sure I want to hear it.

Adria takes in a deep breath and subconsciously glances at the door, probably trying to will us to leave. When that doesn't work, she goes on. "I don't know his reasons or what's in his mind. All I can say is what he told us he needs us to do. First thing, this Maria, she did to a girl what she had been doing to those rich people. Put in her brain that she needed to take revenge on an old boyfriend, and arranged for this girl to run into him, then to go to Madam Sophia to put a curse on him. Idea is to have him come to me to take it off."

I can't help but interrupt. "This 'girl,' you're referring to is Sara, correct? The woman who was killed last night?"

Adria's face pales and she nods. "Yes." She opens her mouth to say more but decides against it and tries to deflect. "Maria. She's the one you need to talk to."

Vinn and I exchange a look that must have been more revealing than we knew, as Adria blanches to a degree where all blood drains from her face. "Maria was also killed," Vinn tells her.

Adria pulls her knees up to her chest and begins rocking in place, mumbling to herself. We're losing her and need to get what we need quickly. Vinn forcibly grabs her by the arm, causing the woman to emit a small yelp. It gets her focused, at least for now.

"There's more," Vinn tells her, not kindly. "Tell us."

Adria nods slowly. "I don't know much more. He wants

us to get close to people close to some other man and bring them all together in one place, then he will take over from there. That's all I know, I swear."

"How do you plan to get those people together?" I ask.

"Don't know yet," she replies. "Still to be worked out."

Vinn and I rise simultaneously. "We need you to keep us informed," I tell Adria as I write the numbers of our burner phones on a scrap of paper. "We don't like what you've done or what you're planning to do. But we'll arrange for you to do it in such a way that you won't need to worry about Alvarez or the cops ever again. I know there's no reason to trust us, but your other option is far worse." I let the handgun show again while Vinn strolls over and picks up the picture frame containing the daughter's photo, tucking it under her arm.

We don't wait for a response and let ourselves out the door. Once inside the car, neither of us is in a hurry to move.

"At least we're now in familiar territory," Vinn finally states. "We know what Point A and Point B are and that we need to get from one to the other, but have absolutely no clue on how to do it." She smiles. "So all's good with the world. Now how do tacos sound?"

As we pull away from the curb, debating whether to go with our standby fish tacos from Antique Taco or to head down to Pilsen for some authentic birria or al pastor versions with unforgettable salsas, my eyes are drawn to a dark pickup truck pulling out of a space half a block behind us. Probably nothing, but I notice Vinn repeatedly glancing at the passenger side mirror.

"Glad to see I'm not the only one being paranoid," I tell her, trying to sound nonchalant.

"I'm sure that's it. Paranoia," she responds, not convincingly. "But the fact that both of us picked up on that truck may mean it's something more. How about we humor our cases of the jitters and you take the long way to dinner? You keep your eyes straight ahead. It'll be easier for me to track it without looking obvious."

Obedient to the core, I turn onto an obscure side street that probably never sees anyone but residents travel its path. Seconds later, Vinn tells me that the truck is still behind us.

"Dammit," she says along with a couple of other words I'll have to look up later. "But let's be absolutely sure. Head for Lake Shore Drive and let's go south for our dinner."

Difficult as it is, I refrain from looking into my rear view mirror even when I should in the normal course of driving so as not to spook our tail, if that's what it is. Vinn shows herself to be admirably skilled in keeping her head faced forward while still keeping track of the truck in her own mirror.

We're on the Drive passing the zoo before she speaks again. "Still there, about five cars back and one lane over to our right. Time for you to put on the gas and do a little maneuvering."

I immediately accelerate and weave to the left, pushing our rental up to near seventy in the forty-mile-per-hour zone. Vinn's curse tells me that our companions have given up any effort at stealth.

Traffic is almost always heavy on Lake Shore Drive, especially approaching the Loop exits. Tourists moving slowly in the left lanes as they take in the views of Lake Michigan beaches that line the road to the east mingle with locals who just want to get where they're going and drunken teenagers joy riding, all of whom make losing a tail virtually impossible for more than a few seconds. With no more reason to be secretive,

I glance in my mirror to see the truck gaining on us, with only a BMW between us.

"Keep your eyes on the road and try to get us away from them, but don't exit. Too much traffic if we get off and we'll be sitting ducks." Vinn pulls two handguns out of hiding, puts one in the console, and readies the other. No sooner does she do that than our back window shatters.

"Shit!" she shouts. "Keep moving!"

I have to assume that she wasn't hit and I don't feel any pain myself, so I concentrate on weaving into the other lanes and accelerating when possible. We're approaching Soldier Field when Vinn next speaks as she wedges herself into a tight position facing the back seat.

"Lower the back window on your side. When I tell you, I want you to swerve into the lane to our right and hit your brakes hard. Got it?"

"Ready when you are," I reply. No time to ask her game plan, I just need to have faith. I try to relax my white-knuckled grip on the steering wheel without success.

"Now!" Vinn shouts. I instantly without looking to see if it's clear move to the right and slam on my brakes. Six ear-splitting shots come in quick succession from Vinn's direction. Without being told, I immediately floor it. One quick glance in my side mirror is enough to see that Vinn's aim was true, as the truck tumbles across lanes toward the west shoulder. I don't stick around to see what happens next.

There's now no traffic behind us and I quickly move onto the ramp for Highway 55 toward St. Louis, then slide across lanes to exit as soon as possible after getting too many stares from other drivers due to our shattered window. We travel deserted residential side streets until we're within walking distance of Pilsen and, just beyond, our offices at UIC. I pull the car over in front of a boarded-up brick two-flat and we start our hike.

"You okay?" I finally ask after the first few blocks.

"Yeah," Vinn replies, not steadily. "You?"

There'll be time to discuss what just happened and what it means in terms of moving forward, but for now we're both content to just walk and stay quiet. I find myself on auto-pilot next to Vinn and am so lost in my thoughts that I'm surprised when I suddenly realize that there are other people around. I'm not so surprised when I see that we're nearing a hole-in-the-wall renowned for its tacos.

As we near the entrance, Vinn uncharacteristically loses her balance and bumps hard into a passing woman pushing a stroller. After the appropriate apologies, Vinn sheepishly hands me a phone.

"Couldn't use our own if we want to stay off the grid," she says with a shrug. "You call the cops and Zipcar to report the car as stolen. I'll go in to get food."

TWENTY SEVEN

"I see only two possibilities," Vinn says as she licks sauce off her fingers. We're back in what we hope is the safety of the high-rise apartment, although after what just happened I'm not as sure of anonymity as I was previously. "One, that the men in that truck were part of the Roma gang of swindlers and tried to kill us at the direction of one of the gypsy women. Two, that whoever they were, they were acting at the direction of Alvarez. But I have a problem."

"Way ahead of you," I interrupt, "if your problem is that neither scenario seems likely. There was no time for Adria to call anyone after our visit and for that person to get there in the few minutes it took us to leave her place, get into our car, and leave. Also, while you were finishing your tacos, I checked our phone tap and she hasn't made or received any calls since we left. As far as Alvarez, I guess that's possible, but how did he know we were there? And again, unless he or someone he hired was staking out Adria's place, how did they get there at the very time we were there? Our decision to go there was im-promptu, so we didn't know ourselves that we'd be there when we were. Unless he has a team working for him that we don't know about following our every move, cross him off too."

Vinn frowns. "I'm with you up to the point of cross-ing Alvarez off. It's got to be him, don't you think? We've been working on the theory that he wants to torture Leo by murdering everyone close to him before he goes after Leo himself, and I'm not ready to abandon that yet. And if we eliminate the fortune tellers, who does that leave? I know that you and I both have people out there that would love to see us gone, but this would be way too big a coincidence and I'm not ready to make that leap yet."

"Agreed," I admit reluctantly. "For now, let's assume Alvarez was behind the attack as a working theory. That still doesn't answer how he knew we were there or who those men were. From what little we know about the man, he prefers to do the dirty work himself, up close and personal. Why would he deviate from that?"

"Because he didn't have a choice," Vinn answers. "We're a wild card he didn't anticipate, and when we disappeared he wasn't equipped to find us on his own much less get close to two seasoned players to do the job himself. But you're right, that still leaves some questions that need answers. If he didn't find us, who did? And who could he get in an unfamiliar city to kill for him?"

"Both impossible to answer with what little we know, so let's brainstorm. Second question first. What if we're wrong to cast off the Roma network entirely? If it wasn't Adria, it could have been someone else. Or more likely, Alvarez knew or was given the names of those men with the asterisks next to their names and went to them directly, asking them to do a side job. We know he already met the women through Ruby, it isn't a giant leap to think that he also got the names of the men and went to them."

"Doubtful he asked," Vinn says solemnly, staring at the ceiling as she thinks. "I'm sure there was the threat of force behind his 'request,' if that's what happened. The other possibility is that he was able to tap into a network of bad guys for hire, which would require that he found a source he trusted to give him that information and probably help act as an intermediary. You know what would help, don't you?"

I do know, but was hoping she wouldn't ask. "Yeah, we need to know the names of those guys in the truck. I assume that they didn't survive, or if they did weren't in a condition where they could flee the scene. And even if they weren't carrying ID, their prints are probably in the system. The system that only cops have access to. Cops who are looking for us and that aren't happy we're in hiding."

"Details, details," Vinn replies with an uneasy smile. "Let's come back to that. As far as the other question, we shouldn't be that easy to find. The cops have the capability and the equipment and if they were really serious about bringing us in, they'd already be breathing down our necks. Anyone else? They'd need phenomenal luck or a source."

Vinn's analysis is producing an uncomfortable thought at the outskirts of my mind, one which I deliberately push away before continuing our discussion. "Let's first discuss the possibility the men in that truck were scouting Adria's apartment and we stumbled right into their path. We both agree that they wouldn't have been waiting for us, it's too long a shot and takes a lot of guesses on their part based on information the gypsies don't even have. And why would they be watching Adria? She's one of their own and hasn't done anything to cast suspicions on her as a traitor. And I don't believe that they saw us emerge and instantly changed over from watching her to trying to kill us. That leaves the other possibility."

"That we were followed there?" Vinn asks. "I don't know, Mal, that would mean that they know we're staying here, or..."

I watch as her eyes grow wide. "Yep," I tell her. "They knew about the Zipcar and where we would pick it up. Which they would only know if someone hacked into the Zipcar records, and forgive me if I don't think that's within Alvarez' skill set. So he had to have had someone do it for him. And if they found us through Zipcar, they either intercepted us at the car's location, or..."

"Or they put a tracer on the car." Vinn shifts in her seat. "As unlikely as that seems, if their goal was to kill us it would have made a lot more sense for them to ambush us when we picked up the car than to wait until we were driving on city streets. And there wouldn't have been time to get the chosen killers to the car fast enough to intercept us, but there was enough time for any mope to plant a tracer to give them time to pick up our location later. Person One tagged the car while Persons Two and Three were loading up their weapons and on their way."

"So the question is, who in Alvarez' circle has the sophistication to hack a company's records and also has access to that kind of equipment and connections to hired killers?"

"No one," Vinn sighs. "So he had outside help. Serious help."

I'm about to make the suggestion that has been bothering me when my burner phone buzzes. I recognize the number and grip Vinn's hand.

"It's Rebecca," I tell her. "I think things are about to get even worse."

Rebecca is many things. Temperamental, touchy, defensive, headstrong, and insecure come to mind. Even slightly excitable. One attribute I've never observed before, though, is hysterical. So as loath as I am to take her call, my nerves shoot into overdrive the minute I push the button to answer her call to hear her screaming into the phone in mid-sentence. She didn't even wait to start until the connection was made.

"...you do, Malcom? The cops have been at my door not once but twice demanding to know where you are. And not in a friendly way, especially the first one. Something about a shootout and a crash and bodies and I don't know what else.

What on earth did you get me in the middle of?"

There was no need to put her on speaker to be over-heard. Vinn sees the flash in my eyes and shakes her head. Now isn't the time to remind Rebecca that she's the one that got us into this mess, not the other way around.

"Rebecca," I begin in as calm a voice as I can muster, "I need to ask you some questions but first listen to me and follow my instructions. From now on until I tell you otherwise, you are not at home. Do you understand? Lock your doors, pull your shades, turn out the lights, and whenever you move around your unit, crawl on your hands and knees to avoid any movement observable from a window, and be as quiet as humanly possible. No more show tunes, no fiddling in the kitchen. In fact, remove the light in your fridge. Now put down your phone and go, then come back to me from a safe place."

Vinn nods her approval as we silently wait several agonizing minutes. We both let out the breath we were holding as soon as we hear Rebecca's voice.

"Malcom, you're scaring me," she says, her voice quieter but quivering. "What's going on?"

I decide it's time to spill. "Rebecca, the cops came because two men in a pickup shot at Vinn and I a couple of hours ago. We managed to get away unharmed, but I don't think I can say the same thing for them. I don't have time to go into too many details, but there's a very dangerous man out there who's trying to kill anyone close to Leo, which is the reason for the attack. It's also the reason that you're a target as well."

I hear a muffled gasp and Rebecca's breathing rate noticeably increases. Time for some false assurances. "Vinn and I know what we have to do, and we hope it won't be long before things can go back to normal. In the meantime, you don't leave your apartment and you don't go to work. Understand?"

I don't get a response but she's not a fool so I know she'll go along. "Now tell me about the visits from the police. You said you had two? Tell me about the first one."

"He was a brute," she begins quietly, although the memory of his visit appears to be giving her some of her old self-assurance back. "Pounding on the door like he wanted to bust in, then pushing it open with such force that he nearly knocked me over. Got into my face. Loud, abusive, a real asshole. Did you ever see Woody Harrelson in Rampart? You know the one, remember that scene..."

"Rebecca," I interrupt. "Focus. Tell me about the cop."

She pauses. "He grabbed me, hurt me, got about six inches away from me and growled. I'm not exaggerating, Malcom, it was a growl. He said that he knew that I know where you and Vinn are and if I didn't cooperate he would arrest me but not until he beat me within an inch of my life. And I think he would have, too, but he got distracted by some noise from outside. He looked out the curtain, came back and slapped me, and said he'd be back and I'd better have the information by then. Then he left."

"Did you get his name or badge number? What did he look like?" Vinn asks.

"It all happened so quickly. He was in uniform and had a badge. His name was Stevens or Simmons or some S word. Badge began with a 7 but that's all I know. He was so close I couldn't see it clearly but that wasn't exactly my top priority at the time, you know?"

"Can you describe him?" I ask to follow up on Vinn's unanswered question.

"White, dark features, brown hair cut short. About thirty maybe. No facial hair. Some sort of a mole or maybe a zit under his right, no left eye. Garlicky breath. Does that help?"

Not really. "Yes, very much, thank you Rebecca. How soon after that did the next group arrive?"

She doesn't have to think about it. "Almost immediately. Maybe two minutes, tops. And it wasn't a group, it was just your cop pal Mendez. He also thought I knew where you two were but he was nicer about it. Telling me that it's in your best interests to bring yourselves in, that you're not suspects, he just wants information, that kind of thing. When I told him I didn't know, though, he wasn't happy and didn't believe me. Started talking tough. So much for telling the truth."

"All right, Rebecca, thank you. If you think of anything else that will help, especially about that first officer, let us know immediately. Remember, you're in hiding. Your life depends on it."

I hang up before hearing her reaction. Vinn puts her head in her hands and lets out a loud sigh. "Great," she says angrily. "Is it really possible that Alvarez is using a dirty cop?"

I don't tell her that I had already considered that a possibility. "It would make sense. A cop would have the resources and equipment and that would explain a lot. Not a certainty, but I would put it at a strong probability."

"Wonderful. Somehow we need to tell Mendez without turning ourselves in or giving up our location. Requires some thought. In the meantime, why don't we discuss 'Vinn and I know what we have to do.' Wishful thinking, Winters, or do you have a plan?"

A little of each. We begin to plot out a way to save our lives.

TWENTY EIGHT

Paranoia is a valuable tool that's kept me alive more than once. Expecting the improbable, even the impossible, will at some point pay off when something that never should have happened occurs and you're prepared for it. Vinn knows this as well, so when I tell her that I'm travelling by el to a distant neighborhood to buy more burner phones, cash only, and then moving somewhere completely different to initiate my call to Mendez, with additional phones to call from a different location miles away to finish the call if it runs more than a few minutes, she doesn't look at me like I'm crazy. The odds that he would be set up to trace my call, much less be able to actually do it successfully, and then to dispatch someone to find me before I'm gone, are slim to none. But stranger things have happened.

I'm within the shadows of Guaranteed Rate field when I initiate the call. Mendez' reaction to my calling him at the station is always a sort of controlled fury. This time, I expect uncontrolled rage. In some ways I'm relieved when he isn't available.

"No, no one else can help me," I tell the woman who answers the phone. "But could you pass on an urgent message? Tell him Malcom Winters will be calling back in thirty minutes. Sorry, but trying isn't good enough. I know you can reach him and trust me he'll want to talk to me."

I hang up without waiting for more objections as to why what I'm asking for is unreasonable, then stare at my phone. On a call for less than a minute, no reason that my call would have been tracked, and I'll be leaving the vicinity now anyway. With a sigh I let experience prevail over parsimony and toss it in a nearby trash can, then head back to the el.

Thirty minutes later I'm in the South Loop outside of a bagel shop. I move into the opening of the alley next door to mute some of the traffic noise. This time, I'm connected without any further interrogation. Less than a second later, the screaming starts.

"Winters, what the hell is going on? Where are you? How soon can you and your friend get to the station? In fact, stay where you are. I'll be a nice guy and send someone to pick you up. Your own personal escort."

"Officer Mendez, is that any way to treat the victim of a crime?" I reply calmly. "I'm simply calling to ask if you've found out who stole my Zipcar and details on what happened to it. You know, something like the names of who was shooting at it. My insurance company wants to know."

"Winters, I swear when I do catch up with you you'd better hope it's in a public place. Stolen, my ass. Don't you think I've compared the time you reported it to the time of the incident? Still, I'd be happy to provide you with that information. Say, an hour here at the station?"

"Sorry, Mendez, no can do." Time to stop with the games. "Look, I'll make you a deal. I'll call back in two hours and you'll give me those names. In return, if they match up, I'll tell you who they are and how they're connected to the guy who's trying to kill us. And as a good faith gesture, I'll give you something right now. But first answer me this..."

Before I finish, I watch as a squad car turns the corner and heads up the street in my direction. I immediately hang up and step back further into the shadows of the alley until it slowly passes then hustle toward the train station on the next block. Fifteen minutes later, my pockets one burner phone lighter, I'm near the Merchandise Mart and call back.

It takes me a few seconds to interrupt Mendez' string of profanity the minute he hears my voice. I don't waste any time. "Answer me this. Did you send an officer out to speak with Rebecca before you went there yourself?"

"Of course not." Mendez' tone has gone from angry to annoyed. "Why would I do that? Against my better judgment, I've taken point on this thing and when I want a witness interviewed I do it myself."

"Then you've got a problem." I describe Rebecca's encounter with the cop. "I know it's not much to go one, but the killer is getting some help from one of your boys in blue. Find him, Mendez. It's bad enough we have to deal with a trained killer without having the odds further stacked against us."

I can feel the heat radiating off Mendez' face as if I were there in person and know that he doesn't want to believe me but has to consider that I'm telling the truth. I glance at the time on my phone. "Gotta go. An hour and thirty-five minutes." I hang up and toss the phone beneath the tire of an idling delivery truck.

Ninety-eight minutes later I have the two names of the men in the pickup and head back to rendezvous with Vinn.

"Did he believe you?" she asks as she grabs the cup of coffee I picked up from some shop with a cutesy name out of my hands before I have a chance to get two steps inside the door.

"I only gave him scraps as far as the fortune-telling ring and left Alvarez out entirely, so he's reserving judgment. As far as the cop, I doubt it. I'm sure he thinks I created the whole story to throw him off our scent and I don't blame him. I'm still not convinced myself. And if Rebecca follows instructions and ignores his calls, he won't be able to verify it with her. He'll still feel obligated to check into it, though, and unless he's secretive about it maybe the heat will force whoever this cop is to lie low for a while."

"We can only hope," she sighs as she makes a face at the cup. Apparently not worth the four dollars and change. "But we've got to assume that Alvarez has some help, not only from this cop but from wherever he got those guys in the pickup. And speaking of, did the names sound familiar?"

"At least one did, I think, but I need to check them out against our notes. I didn't have them with me." I take a few moments to remember where I stashed the notebook as I watch Vinn cross the room and pour her coffee down the sink. I'm just opening it when she returns and settles in beside me. I hand her the crumpled scrap of paper with the names Mendez gave me as a penance for bringing her swill.

"Both of them are here, and to our credit neither one is Josef," she says, sounding relieved. "The first one has an asterisk, so he's probably killed before and was yielding the shotgun. The other one would've been the driver. So that tells us that Alvarez hasn't tapped into some underground network of evil. He's relying on the same Roma men the gypsy women use. That's good to know if true. It limits the number he can call on and we already know who they are."

"And they're not pros," I add. "Still, it wouldn't make sense to underestimate them. Especially if their actions are being directed by Alvarez. So do I tell Mendez what we know?"

Vinn looks thoughtful. "I think not. He may stumble

onto the rest of the men given what you've told him about the setup, but let's not help him get there quicker. If he takes them off the map, Alvarez will have no choice but to find professional help. I'd rather deal with a known quality and I'm confident that these guys aren't up to the same standards. It's the women I'm concerned with."

"Agreed. If looks could kill, or if she had had a letter opener or nail file handy, I think Adria would have inflicted some serious damage on one or both of us. And despite our threats about her daughter, she's still a danger we need to take seriously. Whatever hook we use to reel the entire lot of them together in one place has to include she and Josef."

My comment is met with a frown. "When you say the 'whole lot,' I think you may be overreaching," she tells me. "With the men, yes. Crossing the two from the truck off the list, that leaves four including Josef. Asterisk or not. But if you recall there are over twenty women in this book. It's not like we can arrange a company picnic to gather that many in one place on short notice. We need to narrow the pool."

"I know you're right," I acknowledge, "but it just feels like we're leaving the door open for whoever's left to continue on victimizing vulnerable people."

"That's exactly what we're doing," Vinn admits with a wistful smile. "But it can't be helped. So let's get the worst of them out in the open and maybe with the information we supply Mendez, if we survive, our city's finest can deal with the rest of them. Now assuming that the asterisk works the same for the women as for the men, meaning they'll go to extremes the others won't, let's start with them. How many are there?"

I go slowly through the notebook from the beginning, hearing Vinn count under her breath as I turn the pages. "Six,"

I tell her unnecessarily. "But we also have to include Isadora because of what she did to Chase."

"Agreed. Let's throw two more in at random so that along with the men we get a lucky thirteen."

"One more, you mean. Alvarez will be number thirteen."

"Right." At the mention of his name, Vinn's eyes darken. We've reached the point where the prospect of what we need to do against who we're facing, as well as a clear awareness of our chance of not making it to the other side, becomes something more than a theoretical future event. I watch as her shoulders slump and feel my own emotions nosedive.

Our eyes meet and our thoughts converge. Simultaneously we reach our hands out to each other, rise from the couch, and head to the bedroom. It's been too long, our attention has been diverted to other people, and now's the time for just the two of us. We don't know when or if we'll get this chance again.

"Money," Angela Boswell tells us succinctly through the phone. Our cheap burner phone doesn't have a speaker option, so Vinn and I have it strategically placed between us, balancing on the top of the couch so that we don't need to bend as much to hear. "If you're going to try to lure these women somewhere, that's got to be your bait. Their honor code is complicated and ever-changing and even varies between individuals, so that's not a viable option. I doubt they'd do it as a favor for one of their own, and even though they're mostly related to one another in one way or another it's not like they're one big Hallmark family. If anything, they know one another so well that they don't have an iota of trust to give."

"What sort of payout are we talking about here?" Vinn asks. "And would the promise of riches be enough?"

"That's what you have working for you," Angela

responds. "If you offered them cash up front they'd suspect foul play right off the bat. In fact, it's essential that the two of you stay in the background, so you'll need one of them on your side. Sorry if that's a deal breaker."

"It's not, actually," I interject. "We have some leverage."

"That's good, but any sort of guaranteed payment would still be viewed with suspicion. It's simply not the way their minds work. It's the promise of a big score that'll pique their interest. The bigger the better. Waive a crowd of vulnerable marks in front of them and let their greed take it from there. The kind that are susceptible to the lure of incense and crystal balls and hearing how their deceased husband has something to tell them from beyond the grave. For a price."

"So we'd have to involve innocents in this?" I ask.

"Afraid so, unless you can produce a crowd of confederates with consummate acting skills. Remember, say what you will about the legitimacy of their fortune telling, these women can read people better than anyone and they'll spot a plant. I don't know what your goal is here—although my memory of Malcom's aura gives me an idea—but this will take intricate planning and timing if you're going to catch any of them in a trap. Especially if you want to avoid collateral damage."

"You've certainly given us food for thought, thank you Angela," Vinn pipes in before abruptly hanging up, reflecting the bad mood our brief conversation has put us both in. "Okay, Mal, so now what?"

"Let's talk through the elements of what we need and see if the list inspires one of us to think of a fitting scenario. One, we need to stage an event that will be so enticing to the women on our list that they'll be salivating to attend, which means two, it has to involve the prospect of conning people out of their cash by doing what they do best. Three, we have to make sure that the most they do is take a small amount from their marks with only the promise of more down the line."

"Okay, my turn to play," Vinn edges in, warming to the challenge. "Four, that means we need to look the other way while they fleece members of the public, but limit the amount they take to something that roughly equals the entertainment value of their efforts to ease our own consciences. But that leads to five, this has to be a public event with enough people attending to give them a pool of potential victims."

"Six, and I insist on this," I tell her, "we still need a team in there beyond you and I. And seven, eight, nine, etc., this has to get Alvarez there because our ultimate goal is to take him off the board, which means no cops at least until that gets accomplished and we get out of there. And the only sure way we'll get him there is if he thinks Leo is going to be there, and he won't stay around unless he confirms Leo's there, which means Leo has to be there."

"This is giving me a headache," Vinn moans. "I guess what we're saying is that this needs to be the ultimate, all of our eggs in one basket moment. All in, only one party emerges victorious to fight another day. Him or us."

"When you put it that way..." I don't finish the thought. "And we're going to need Adria's help to put this together and to get the others there. Let's hope she and her daughter didn't have a falling out."

"Now that we know what we want, any ideas as to what form it'll take? Vinn asks.

"Actually, yes," I tell her as a wild idea pops into my head. "And your idea of a family picnic isn't that far off."

TWENTY NINE

"Let me get this straight." Vinn hasn't said a word as I laid out the bare outline of my idea and hasn't betrayed her reaction, so I'm not sure what to expect with her next words. "You want to put together a gypsy fair that's open to the general public, enlist Adria's help to get the Roma women to set up tents on the promise of immunity for her and easy marks for the others, somehow lure Alvarez there, then take him out without anyone noticing?"

When she puts it like that, without the addition of my false optimism, it sounds absurdly impossible. "Yep, that's pretty much it," I respond.

Vinn grins. "I like it. Of course, it means organizing a festival that has to look convincing, which should normally take up to a year, in less than ten days. And the odds of success are low while the risks of something going tragically wrong are high. But lacking a better idea, if we do this right it might be our best chance to kill two birds with one fair. The gypsy women and, most importantly, Alvarez. Let's start with that. The Roma first."

"We'll need to pay another visit to Adria, today if possible, and reinforce our threats to her freedom and to her daughter. Everything depends on her cooperation, so I thought we'd sweeten the pot with a promise that in exchange for her assistance, she'd get immunity from any charges related to the crimes she's committed as a fortune teller."

"You really think that Mendez would go along with letting her slide for her role in multiple cases of grand larceny and murder?"

"Um, no. It'll be a blatant lie," I admit. Vinn actually

looks proud of me, which will need to be a conversation for another time. "She'll buy it because she'll want to believe it's true and because we'll let her know that this is a deal for her alone, and if she doesn't want it we'll go through one of the others. And it will have to depend on her getting all of the women on our list to agree and to have Josef and the men working security so that they're on site as well. Once we've disposed of Alvarez—and Vinn, it has to be us, not the gypsies—the cops can come in and clean up based on a tip as to what these women have done in the past. By that time we'll be gone."

"A tip that's been previously supported by specific proof we've already given to Mendez, I imagine," Vinn says thoughtfully. "Tricky timing, not to mention it requires a face-to-face with our favorite cop, and the first thought on his mind will to be cuff us and bring us in for questioning. Details for later. Now Alvarez."

"Yeah, I don't like this and you won't either, but I don't see any other way. Alvarez has to think that the gypsies, who are scared stiff of him and will do anything he says, have kid-napped Rebecca as a way of getting Leo and ourselves to come out of hiding to rescue her, so that he'll use the opportunity to take care of Leo and, if possible, us."

"Wow," Vinn appears stunned. "Worse than I imagined but I see why your thoughts are going in that direction. To get him there I agree that Leo's presence has to be the bait, although I'm hoping that to reduce the risk of complete disaster we can do so without Leo actually being there. But Rebecca? You know that she'll actually be thrilled to be involved as the purported victim, but she's such a wild card. That and she thinks that she has superhuman powers. So much can go wrong."

"I know. If you can think of any way other than Alvarez seeing an opportunity to get all four of us at once, let me know." I watch Vinn carefully as she takes several moments to think, eventually shaking her head. "We'll have to clear it with her, of course, which won't be a problem, but we'd better have a plan in place to keep her on the periphery."

"I guess we have a little time to brainstorm the details because once we've dealt with Adria and put the wheels in motion, we have an awful lot of planning to do to get this thing together. Share your vision of what you see this fair as. It obviously can't be large in scale but it has to be attractive enough to bring in a decent crowd and not look like a quickly-put-together setup, which of course it will be."

"Ideally I'd like to have it in a park, although that would mean keeping it from the attention of the city because they'd require a permit that we'd never get, at least until we've accomplished what we're setting out to do. After that I don't care. As an alternative, a large parking lot. It has to be in an area that we'll get a lot of locals to drop in, because our time for publicizing it is limited. Tents for the women, a small carnival with games offering cheap prizes and a ride or two for the kids. And food."

"Not too much to ask, there, Mr. Ringmaster," Vinn grins. "And how are we going to pull this off ourselves?"

"We're not. We obviously need help. Anyone we know that seems to have connections to the underground population of the city that knows how to skirt the law and would be looking for an adventure and a quick buck?"

"Right," Vinn acknowledges. "My thought as well. Time is short so we need to split up. I'll go pay a visit to Adria, she's so frightened of me that your presence won't be necessary. You call Chuck."

"That's a tall order," are the first words out of Chuck's mouth after I fill him in. "Not much time to pull a carnival together and to gather a crew to mingle in with the crowd and to act as prey." I feel myself deflate, which he must sense. "But I didn't say it's impossible," he quickly adds. "Believe it or not, the carnival itself is the easy part. I know a guy who makes a comfortable living staging what he calls 'dump and dash' events for churches, charities, and others who want to avoid the cost and oversight of the city inspectors. The rides are assembled overnight in the dark and put on for a single day on a weekend when most of the bureaucrats are off duty, although I think at least one payoff and a fake permit might also be involved. I've never asked. Then it's gone without a trace twelve hours later."

"That would be perfect," I sigh in relief. "What can he get for us?"

"The usual crap. A few of those games like coin toss and popping balloons with darts that no one ever wins. But who needs a giant flammable pink dog anyway? A couple of rides. And a ticket booth or two. Won't exactly be competition for Cedar Point but if what you're looking for is an air of authenticity, it'll be that. And if you let them cheat, which they're going to do with or without your permission, they'll do it for almost nothing."

"What about food?"

"Definitely not the same people unless you want to have paramedics on call. Let me take care of that. Nothing fancy, just dogs and burgers and cardboard pizza and cotton candy.

I'll even throw in a few good sandwiches. All overpriced of course if you want it to look genuine. But I'll provide it in lieu of a fee."

"You're definitely making me feel better," I tell him. "Now, what about a crew, some to act as marks and others just to wander the crowd with their eyes open? Are some of the people we used for the Chinatown tail still available?"

"Some of the regulars, maybe," he says with a little hesitancy. "You have to understand that the pool I draw from is extremely fluid. Many of them live on the fringe, some just travel from town to town, and I'll bet at least a few are currently in jail. Plus last time you just needed some talent skilled at tailing and surveillance. This time around there's personal risk involved and a much less structured idea of what they need to be doing. Narrows the field. It'll help if you can be a little more specific."

"I'll try. We need several to act as naïve victims who allow themselves to be swindled of small amounts at the fair but who hint at having enough wealth to make it look like they can be a pot of gold for the fortune tellers at a future time. Most of the fortune tellers' marks we know about were older. I hesitate to use genuinely older people. I remember at least one of the women from last time who did a remarkable impression of an old, feeble lady. Can we get a couple like that?"

"Not a chance," Chuck replies quickly, surprising me with his vehemence. "Those Roma women make a living sizing people up and there's no one better at penetrating a false front. Even my best would be made in seconds and you'd have those ladies sensing a trap and packing up in no time flat. They have to be genuinely old. Don't worry, I can do that, as well as some younger women and at least one guy who can easily pass off as vulnerable and stupid. What's next?"

"Just as many fairgoers as you can find. On the surface, it sounds easy, but I don't need them just to fill out the crowd. They need to act as spotters, primarily to look for one particular man who's the reason behind this whole charade, but also to watch the carnival workers and the Roma men working security to make sure no innocents get taken too badly. And, I guess, to alert us to anything that just doesn't smell right."

Chuck is silent for so long that I wonder if the call disconnected. "Is there anything you want to tell me about what's going to go down there? If I'm going to put people in danger, they should know about it."

"It's best that no one knows just in case this goes badly. I can tell you that if things blow up, it's most likely my inner circle that won't come out of it. And in that case, your people can just fade away or act as simple fairgoers. I can't guarantee their safety, but if they keep their wits they should be fine. There will be weapons involved for sure, but I suspect that they'll be deadly only if you're up close. No guns."

"All right, done. Counting in my head I can get you at least ten operatives, maybe twelve or fourteen, so I hope it's okay if they visit more than one of the gypsies. If the fates are with us, maybe twice that. Do you need to meet them in advance?"

"Best not to, I think," I reply. "You and I will need to talk again, and you can act as the conduit. For right now, we'll need a location that we can pass on as soon as possible."

"I'll text it to you," he says, "probably within the hour."

Proving that his connections are even better than he hinted, he's true to his word. My phone sounds an incoming text just as Vinn walks in the door.

"Piece of cake," she says before I have time to open my mouth. "Although it did help to promise that she won't be tossed in jail for all that she's done if she helps pull this off. I also told her that she can keep any money she makes off customers at the fair. Sadly, I think the promise of a get out of jail free card and some cash had more to do with her cooperation that my threats about her daughter."

I fill her in on my conversation with Chuck and tell her the location, which turns out to be a large field in Humboldt Park, a spacious city park complete with athletic fields and a lagoon.

"I like his style," Vinn admits. "Right under the city's noses, so audacious that no one would even consider that it's not sanctioned. I'll pass it on to Adria so that she can spread the word. Then I think you know what has to come next."

I do and I'm not looking forward to it. "Yep. We need to have a long talk with Leo and Rebecca. It's high noon and the bullets are ready to start flying. They need to be ready."

THIRTY

It seems like years since I've seen the three-flat I own in the Ukrainian Village neighborhood, and even now Vinn and I are approaching it as if we're ready to infiltrate a well-guarded fortress. We have our Uber drop us off two blocks away and walk in the shadows of dusk as we get near, eventually crouching behind parked cars across the street. Unless Mendez or Alvarez has someone stationed in one of the nearby homes, in which case we're simply screwed, anyone watching the building would have to be in a car. Vinn continues down the block while I circle back to take the other side of the street.

"All clear," she whispers as we meet at my gate. She veers toward the stairs down to Leo's unit while I climb up a flight and do my best at the special knock which Rebecca insisted upon, which is supposed to approximate a song from "Cats." I'm just about to reprise the chorus when the door opens a crack.

"That was pathetic," Rebecca hisses. "Have you no sense of rhythm?"

I bite back every one of the pithy retorts that come to mind in the interest of silence, take her by the arm, and pull her out onto the landing, putting my finger over my mouth to remind her that she's supposed to be in hiding. We quickly descend to Leo's door, which is open a crack. I push it open and step aside to let the diva lead the way.

The apartment is dark save a few candles that are glowing dimly on the kitchen table. It's only when I get close that I can make out the shadows that are Leo and Vinn. I don't even see the glass in front of me until I hear liquid being poured into it. As my eyes adjust, I can't help but notice the large piles of empty bottles scattered around the floor. Leo obviously hasn't been outside for a long time. At least given the number of bottles, I hope it's been a long time.

Always the considerate guest, I take a sip of whatever's been poured and feel a surprising comfort from the sweet burn as it passes down my throat. I glance in Vinn's direction.

"I haven't said a word yet," she tells me, anticipating my question. "Why don't you start?"

Together we bring our two clients up to speed on what we've been doing, answering an occasional question from Rebecca. Leo keeps silent except for an occasional grunt and one belch. We now get to the point of our clandestine rendezvous and start describing the Mystic Fair. Even Leo seems to sit up straighter and opens his eyes past his usual slit.

"This is where it gets tricky," I begin, unsure of exactly what I'm going to say. "Rebecca, we've put you in some dangerous positions before, but nothing close to this. As a kidnap victim, and the bait upon which everything depends, it's likely that Alvarez will want proof that you're there. We assume that he won't venture out to the fair unless Adria can provide it, so hopefully a photo or video clip of your captivity will be sufficient. Once that's provided, any restraints will be released. And one of us will be around to make sure of that."

Rebecca's expression conveys both excitement and doubt, and Vinn also picks up on that. "And if you feel it necessary, you can bring whatever sort of arsenal you prefer." Rebecca looks relieved, even thrilled, but now I have doubts about the wisdom of opening the door to her possibly starting a war or accidentally shooting herself and ruining everything. Vinn looks me directly in the eyes. "It's all or nothing," she says with a shrug.

I turn my attention to Leo. "Leo, I know you, and I know you want to be there when this, whatever this is, goes down. Alvarez will think that you'll ride in to rescue Rebecca and to save us, trying to be the hero, and that's exactly what you think too. I can see it in your eyes. Resist the temptation. Vinn and I discussed it at length, and you need to sit this one out. We've got all the manpower we need to get this done and your presence won't help. It may be a distraction, at least for Vinn and myself."

Leo's eyes flash with anger, just as we knew they would. "We're serious," Vinn adds. "God willing, we'll be at your door Saturday afternoon telling you it's all over. If things don't go so well, then you're free to deal with your brother yourself."

I sense more than see the slightest of nods from Leo, which is the best we're going to get.

"One more thing," I tell both of them. "We hope that the prospect of our being easy pickings at the fair will convince Alvarez that he doesn't need to come after you before then, but he may lose patience. Continue your seclusion and stay vigilant. It's hard, but the end is in sight."

It's only as we exit Leo's apartment that I realize that he didn't say a single word the entire time we were there. Rebecca, on the other hand, has found her voice and won't shut up as we climb back up the stairs.

"...the red one? Or maybe that blue patterned silk number, you know, with the offset sleeves? Do you think they'll put me on the ground, where dry cleaning will be an issue? It's so expensive you know."

Thankfully it's a short trip and soon she's back behind closed doors. I return to Vinn and we cautiously walk several blocks before arranging a ride back to our own hideout, where we have work to do. Time to talk with our man in blue.

"You asked me that last time, Officer Mendez," I chide, "and while I appreciate the invitation, the answer is still no. But I can offer you something that'll help salvage your disappointment in not seeing me and get some nasty people off the streets at the same time. Who knows, you might even get a pat on the rear from your boss."

I didn't wander far from base camp this time, figuring that my phone call to Mendez would be short and calling from an area as dense as Streeterville, he could triangulate my call and still have no idea where I am among the throngs. The idea is to be tantalizing without giving away too much.

"Do you have a pen handy?" I continue, speaking fast. "I'm going to give you an address. When you get there, you'll be given specific instructions and you have to follow them to the letter with no questions asked and no complaints. And it should go without saying that you need to come alone, no reinforcements, no wire. For one thing, we won't be there for anyone to arrest us. Second, you definitely won't want another cop around for personal reasons. You'll understand when you're there. I think deep down you know you can trust us. And it'll be worth your while."

I give him the address and time, ditch the phone, and head back. If we hurry, Vinn and I can split a crabmeat jianbing, a Chinese street food resembling a crepe, near our destination. I may have fibbed when I told Mendez we wouldn't be there. I wouldn't miss this for the world.

We're concealed behind a three-panel jade screen

decorated with botanicals and birds in a small room off the hallway, within listening distance of the entrance to the Three Happiness Massage Spa located on a lonely side street in Chinatown. We're both restless but freeze perfectly still when we hear bells above the main door jingle, announcing the entrance of someone from the outside. Mai Ling, our hostess for the evening who I'd met on a previous sojourn into the area a year before, assured us that no other customers were scheduled this night.

I can't help but smile when I hear Mendez' gruff voice utter an unhappy "What in friggin' hell," presumably in response to Mai's instruction that he follow her to one of the dimly-lit massage rooms, which just so happens to have two hidden visitors behind a jade screen waiting for him. Two sets of footsteps enter the room.

"Undress, please," Mai instructs him pleasantly but firmly. "Lie face down. I will be back shortly."

Mendez begins to object but the door is already closing, leaving him with a choice. Does he walk away and lose an opportunity of unknown value but which may be related to an unsolved murder case or two, or does he swallow his pride and strip. One of us has a hard time repressing a giggle when we hear shoes hit the floor, and it wasn't Vinn.

Per instructions, for no other reason than we thought it would be fun to make Mendez uncomfortable, it's several minutes later that Mai returns. Soft music begins to fill the room, which will help mask the movement that will be taking place shortly. Mendez starts to ask a question but Mai quickly hushes him.

We wait for about ten minutes into the massage before silently emerging. Mendez is still face down, his head nestled into the face cradle of the table, which prevents him from seeing anything but the floor beneath him. He is, in fact, stark naked but for a towel covering his rear. Vinn quietly pumps oil into her hands then deftly exchanges her hands for those of Mai, who grabs Mendez' clothes before exiting the room. Done quickly and professionally, as if they'd practiced all day, he never caught on.

Vinn kneads his back and shoulders for a few minutes before nodding to me to get into position. She leans down to put her mouth inches from Mendez' ear before whispering, "Well hello, Officer, fancy meeting you here" at the same time I snatch the towel. Mendez utters a profanity and reflexively starts to get up before having second thoughts, then quickly lies back down again.

"Good choice," Vinn says soothingly as she continues to massage his back. "Just so you know, your clothes have left the room and are hidden somewhere, so I suggest you relax, enjoy your massage, and listen."

My turn. "Do you remember when we spoke about those fortune tellers and their crimes not long ago?" I begin. Mendez jumps when he hears my voice, but again to my relief doesn't rise from the table. "Vinn and I have filled in the details, with a little help from one of them. They run the whole gamut. Petty theft, larceny, assault, even premediated murder. None of them solved, but we can tell you who did each one and point you in the right direction. It'll still be up to you to gather the evidence, of course, but with our leads and the help of two cooperative witnesses, it should be easy peasy for your fine team of detectives. And we have it all in a folder that's sitting right on top of your pile of clothes, wherever that may be. Well not quite 'all.' We've left off the names and a few other key details that would identify the offenders."

"You see," Vinn picks up the thread as her hands move to Mendez' calves. "We're not quite ready to have you arrest them yet. Soon, though. What do you think, Mal, another week or so? Then you'll get a call, what you in the biz call a 'tip' I believe, from a man or woman who will identify themselves as Mother Nature. You'll want to take that call."

"In fact, you'll want to have a team ready to go," I tell him, "because we're going to do you a big favor and have most of the culprits gathered in one place just waiting for you to arrive and take them in. They won't know it, of course, so be prepared for a little resistance."

I move to the door and open it a crack, Mai's signal to reenter. She expertly places her hands precisely where Vinn's were. Vinn joins me at the door. "That's all we have to say for now," I say. "You still have thirty-five minutes left on your massage, and Mai has been instructed not to bring you your clothes until your time has expired."

"And you do seem tense, Officer," Vinn adds. "You might consider extending the session."

"Do you think he'll stay?" Vinn asks with a chuckle as we leave to head for home.

"Oh yeah. He'll suspect that if he gets off that table we'll have a camera ready or something. By the way, do you still have oil on your hands? My shoulders are a little stiff."

Vinn smacks those shoulders, hard, rubs her hands dry on my shirt, and calls for an Uber.

THIRTY ONE

If I've learned anything over the past nine plus days, it's that time in the short term can drag mercilessly slow, every minute a tortuous lesson in patience, while a deadline that at first seems relatively distant rushes to the present at lightning speed. Vinn and I have spent every waking hour of every day working to get the fair organized, or more accurately overseeing and riding herd on the more experienced and sensible people doing it for us. Had it not been for Chuck's level-headed direction and intervention with his own contacts, and his willingness to tell Vinn and I when to cram it and where, the project never would have had a chance.

As it is, as dawn breaks on Day Zero, we're still not sure what we have. The portion of the park set aside for the fair was roped off with "Under Construction" signs for the past four days and no one from the city has thought to question it. Maybe the bulldozer that was sitting there had something to with that despite the fact that it was, in fact, non-functional and hadn't moved the entire time. When you think about it, though, that's no different from most city projects and might have raised eyebrows if some work had actually commenced. The bulldozer was carted away in the middle of last night when the amusement carnies arrived to set up the rides and games of chance. At midnight, the field was a field. By 5:00 a.m., it was a ghost town of a midway, waiting for the crowds to file in.

If there are crowds to file, that is. Vinn, Chuck, and I spent most of an evening near the beginning debating about how to publicize the fair. Too much and it would get noticed by a dutiful city official who might think to check for permits.

Too little and not enough of the public will show up to satisfy the Roma women and to convince Alvarez that it's a legitimate event and not a trap. In the end we—meaning Vinn and Chuck with me abstaining—voted to wait until four days beforehand to put anything out there in the usual places such as Metromix and social media, but once we started we made it a true blitz. By the time the wheels of government even considered checking us out, it would be too late. Or so the thinking went. We did, however, tease it in local Polish and Ukrainian papers in their own language on the assumption that the authorities have enough trouble reading English, much less a foreign tongue.

Neither Vinn nor I got any sleep last night and the temptation is to go to the site to check for progress, but since the plan calls for us to learn of Rebecca's kidnapping and her presence at the fair only later in the day, it won't do for us to be seen there before the actual time of her snatching just in case there are curious or cautious eyes watching. Chuck promised to call us with updates beginning at 7:00 a.m., and bless his soul my phone rings precisely at that time.

"Good morning," he says, sounding way too awake and cheerful. "As you know the midway was set up overnight. My food people got here about thirty minutes ago and should be starting up the grills, generators, and whatever else within the hour. A couple of the gypsies are already here staking out claims on their preferred spots near the entrance and have begun setting up their tents. Weather looks good. Some joggers and dog walkers seemed curious so hopefully they'll be back."

"How many of your crew did you end up with?" I ask.

"We had twenty-seven at our prep meeting last night,

and a couple more who couldn't make it promised to be here today. Most of them will just be eyes and ears looking for anything unusual and for the appearance of Alvarez. I passed his photo out to everyone but cautioned them not to bring it here today. The last thing we need is for him to see his mugshot sitting on the ground. I have about eight elderly women, all of them sharp as a tack but capable of playing vulnerable, who will make the rounds in the tents, and six younger people to do the same, including two couples. Should keep the Roma busy for at least a couple of hours even if no one from the public were to partake, which is unlikely. People love this kind of thing for some reason. Any idea when whatever's going to happen comes to a head? I can't promise my people will stick around all day."

"If things go according to plan," I begin, ignoring Vinn rolling her eyes at my implication that things ever go according to plan, "between 12:30 and 1:00. So a couple of hours should be enough. I'll let you know when to clear out before the cops arrive. If you don't hear from me by 3:00, or if you hear sirens approaching, pass word to bail."

"Sounds good," Chuck says, not sounding as confident as he did moments ago. "I'll call again about 9:00 and then when it opens at 11:00. Good luck."

Waiting with nothing to do is the hardest part and the next several hours will be agony. Vinn decides to do a weapons check even though we've done it twice in the last ninety minutes. I close my eyes and run through every possible scenario but stop when every one of them ends in disaster in my mind. Like I said, the hardest part.

Chuck's 11:00 call informs us that a small line has formed at the entrance and that several groups are headed that way, which is a good sign. Every one of the Roma women showed up and their colorful tents dot the landscape, while two of the Roma men are working the grounds, allegedly as security but more likely schilling for business on behalf of the women or picking pockets. Adria arranged for Josef and the fourth man to bring Rebecca later.

Time to check in with the kidnap victim.

"I'll be leaving in twenty-five, Malcom, no reason to panic," an excited-sounding Rebecca tells me when I call. "I decided on the blue patterned caftan dress, which should stand out from the dreary fashion the rest of the crowd will bring to the table. Makes me easier to find."

"Rebecca, we shouldn't need to go looking for you," I remind her with an edge in my voice. "Please stay between the curtains in Adria's tent and don't go wandering. Remember, you've been kidnapped and are being held captive. No turkey legs."

"As if," she responds in a huff before hanging up on me. Vinn glances over at me.

"You are pressing a bit," she says. "I know telling you to relax is useless but try not to spread your stress to others. Especially Rebecca. She's high-strung even on a normal day."

I nod in acknowledgment while in my head I begin to calculate the timing. Adria would have already told Alvarez that they took Rebecca in the middle of the night and that they'll be moving her to the fair shortly after it opens, while at the same time notifying Leo that they have Rebecca and plan to wait for Alvarez to show up to dispose of her. Upon hearing that Alvarez will assume, rightly, that Leo would enlist Vinn and I to help save Rebecca. The earliest that we would all get there on our rescue mission would be around

12:30, which means Alvarez would want to be there by 11:45-12:00 in order to scout the location and find the best place to lie in wait. Vinn and I should leave in ten minutes, then, to get nearby so that once Alvarez is spotted, we can make our move.

A lot of moving parts, with any variation in the hypothetical timetable ready to throw off the rest of the schedule. Essentially Vinn and I need to be ready at any time so that once either we see Alvarez from a distance or one of Chuck's spies identifies him, we can close in. Screw ten minutes, we should leave now. I look up from my thoughts to see Vinn standing by the door, tapping her foot. No wonder I love her so.

On a prior visit to the location, we had already identified an elevated wooded area within an easy sprint of the fair and a view of most of it as the best place to wait. We approach it cautiously, though, because Alvarez may have also chosen the same spot from which to scout the premises before approaching. Adria is under strict instructions to keep Alvarez away from Rebecca and her tent until after he takes care of business with Leo and us, but one of Chuck's crew is keeping an eye on it just in case. If Alvarez goes anywhere near her tent, we'll be there moments later.

We nestle in behind adjacent trees. "Adria's tent is the gold and silver one with the striped flag," I remind Vinn as we each pull out our binoculars. She nods in acknowledgement. I silence my phone and check the time. 12:04. As so often in situations where so much is in doubt, I wish we could jump ahead in time by two hours and just view the aftermath of whatever happens.

The grounds are crowded without being overwhelming

and there are short lines outside most of the women's tents, which is exactly what we were hoping for. It takes me about five minutes to find Chuck, who promised to be near the churro stand between 12:00 and 12:15 to make him easier to locate. The green ribbon pinned to his left breast pocket tells me that Rebecca is on site.

Minutes pass as we silently scan the area, then three things happen at once. Vinn utters "Got him," Chuck's ribbon color changes from green to purple, and my phone vibrates. I check my text, which simply says "west side yellow tent."

"He's in fatigue-style pants, a gray shirt, and a green military jacket. His signature Panama hat." Vinn no longer feels the need to whisper. "It's game time, cowboy. Let's go."

We'll lose sight of Alvarez as we make our way to join the crowds, which puts us in a vulnerable position. I'd vetoed the use of earbuds and mics for Chuck's posse to communicate with us as too risky in case Alvarez caught sight of them, a decision I hope I don't regret. Vinn and I choose to stick together, which will give us an advantage when we do meet and prevent Alvarez from picking us off one by one.

As we enter the fairgrounds from between a Roma tent and a balloon-pop game, we take a second to familiarize ourselves with where we are in relation to Adria's tent. First part of the mission is to free the kidnap victim so that we can escort Rebecca off the grounds, eliminating the distraction and worry that Alvarez will ignore Alvia's demand for restraint and go after her first as an initial salvo. We look west and immediately see the flag about fifty yards away. The question now is whether to make our way there among the crowd or from behind the tents.

"Let's stay on the main drag," Vinn suggests. "Harder

to see him, but also more difficult for him to get close to us, which I assume he'll want to do as someone who prefers a knife to do his dirty work. Just keep an eye on our rear and stay off to the side to eliminate one avenue of approach."

We must be a strange sight as we shuffle forward with me walking backward more often than not. Progress is slow and one time Vinn freezes, forcing me to bump into her before she mutters "false alarm" and we continue on. There's a line of about six people outside Adria's tent waiting to go inside. We ignore their shouts of protest as we move past the young couple at the front, push the flaps aside, and enter.

Adria, in full gypsy regalia, is sitting at a table with a pattern of tarot cards neatly arranged between she and a pudgy woman of around fifty with a small pug sitting restlessly in her lap. The scent of incense is heavy and oppressing and the light is dim despite the sunshine outside. Not so dim, though, to cover the flash of anger in her eyes at the interruption.

"Sorry to intrude," I say quickly and with as much an air of authority as I can muster. "Security. We're looking for a lost child, about five, curly blond hair. Have you seen her?"

"No!" Adria responds harshly, at the same time tilting her head to her left, where a barely perceptible double curtain hangs in the shadows. Vinn begins to move quickly in that direction before I grab her upper arm and hold her back. We pause to pull weapons before approaching the hidden chamber with some degree of stealth. Vinn suddenly darts forward and pulls the curtain back in a single motion while I dash past her, pistol at the ready.

"Aarrggh!" I hear, or something to that effect. Rebecca sits on a small canvas stool, her face covered in powdered sugar, a large chunk of fried dough resting on the ground at her feet.

"Now look what you made me do!" she hisses, brushing sugar off of her dress while she mournfully gazes at the ants swarming the remainder of her snack.

"Did you leave the...never mind," I respond in kind. "We need to get you out of here, Grab your purse and let's go."

"No," she says firmly, crossing her arms over her chest. "I'm sticking with the two of you. I'll be a sitting duck by myself wherever you bring me. Besides, you can use the help. I've been useful before, you know."

"Rebecca, if it were Alvarez instead of us a minute ago your ruined pastry would be the least of your problems," Vinn spits angrily. "Now come with us to somewhere safe."

Like a five-year-old child, Rebecca drops heavily back into the chair in a pout, refusing to move. Just as I'm about to add to our argument, a noise from just outside the tent puts Vinn and I on instant alert, scanning the tent for movement that shouldn't be there.

"We don't have time for this," Vinn whispers crossly when no one appears. "Okay fine, but for god's sake at least get off your ass, leave your dessert behind, and grab hold of whatever weapon you brought. And don't even think of wandering off. And if we tell you to do something, you do it. Got it?"

To her credit, Rebecca utters a hasty "Yes, Ma'am" and reaches into her cleavage to pull out a sheath containing a six-inch blade. I grab it from her, use it to cut a long slit in the outside of the tent, then hand it back as we move back outside. Adria can bitch to us from prison.

If Vinn and I looked odd before, the three of us moving into the crowd in a triangular position trumps that by far. At this point, the only strategy is to be alert and to try to stay alive long enough to get the other guy before he gets us. Kill or be killed. Somewhere in this crowd Alvarez is lurking, hoping to see us before we see him. We want to make sure that doesn't happen.

Tense minutes pass as we ignore puzzled glances while moving past the gypsy tents and between food stands, eyes always moving. Twice, once with me and once with Rebecca, we thought we saw Alvarez, but if it was him he was gone in an instant. The feeling of being watched is feeding my paranoia and is terrifying.

We move into the midway, the sounds of barkers mingling with the smell of cotton candy and sweat. A flash of movement from my left catches my eye, then an instant later Vinn shouts "There!" as she points the knife she retrieved from her sleeve over to the booth with the ring toss. I turn just in time to see a green jacket disappear behind the booth. Vinn and I are off and running in an instant, leaving Rebecca to do her best to catch up.

We follow without regard to caution. If one of us goes down, the other can take care of Alvarez. Just as we pass the end of the enclosure into the open space behind the games, I stumble on a tent stake and feel the air move above me. Instinctively I drop to the ground and roll, getting only a glance of Alvarez's back as he disappears to regroup. Vinn knows to give chase without waiting for me, while Rebecca stops to assist me back onto my feet.

"Two inches, Malcom," is all she says as we scramble to catch up. Back in the crowd now, I catch sight of Vinn ten yards to my right, Alvarez twenty more in front of her. He cuts left behind a blue and green gypsy tent. I'm about to shout for her to wait for us when a golf cart towing a wagon full of trash appears out of nowhere immediately in Vinn's path. She slides to a stop, allowing us to reach her before we follow where we saw Alvarez last.

As we again leave the throng and pass the gypsy's tent, Vinn suddenly stops and points in the direction of the back of Adria's tent thirty yards away, where Alvarez and a gypsy woman are in each other's grasp, a deathly struggle. We've barely moved toward them before they fall through the gap in the tent I made only twenty minutes earlier. Eight seconds later we're there, where we find a prone and bloody man on the ground. I look up just in time to see a flash of color enter the woods.

"Go!" Vinn yells and I take off running in pursuit of the mystery woman. Adria? Someone else? As I enter the woods I see her stumbling among the trees, her head scarf catching on a tree branch, and I begin to easily gain ground. I'm only five yards behind when I stop. What am I doing? Why do I want to catch this person? She's done us a huge favor and there's no point in bringing her to justice. Besides, if Vinn and I are on the same page, there won't be evidence of any crime to answer to. I stand and watch as the woman pauses to catch her breath, glancing back to see if I'm following. A small smile of recognition crosses my face. I pluck the scarf off of the branch and stuff it in my pocket as I turn around and head back to the fair.

I emerge from the woods to see a pale and trembling Rebecca standing outside the tent. "Is he alive?" I ask but get no answer other than a hysterical sob. I enter the tent just in time to see Vinn cleaning blood off her knife onto Alvarez's pant leg. "The gypsy put him down but not out," she tells me. I check his pulse before folding the gypsy scarf into a tight section, place it near Alvarez's heart next to a freshly oozing knife wound, then bury the muzzle of my gun deep into the scarf and pull the trigger. We're in this together, Vinn and I. No sense having only one of us carry the burden of what had to be done. We'll never know which actually killed the man, knife or gun, so we can share that guilt together.

Vinn slides over and puts her arm around my shoulder, where we stay without speaking for several moments as we look at the body before us. As if on an unheard signal, we rise and move outside.

"Rebecca, see if you can borrow that garbage cart for a few moments. If there's an issue, ask Chuck to help. Make sure there's a few bags in it."

Five minutes later, Rebecca rounds the corner with the cart. By that time Vinn and I have cut away a large section of canvas and rolled Alvarez inside. We place him in the cart and cover him with the other bags of garbage. Vinn nudges Rebecca to the passenger seat while I climb in back, but not before placing a telephone call and sending an email.

Ten minutes later we're easing Chuck's truck away from the park to the sound of distant sirens closing fast in the direction of the fair.

THIRTY TWO

Once we're a safe distance away, I pull into a gas station with a good-sized minimart. Vinn hops out while I turn to face Rebecca. She's still pale and unusually quiet, breathing fast and irregularly, her heavily mascaraed eyes staring off at some unknown point. I gently take her hand in mine and use my thumb to feel her pulse, which is much too slow. I speak her name but get no response.

The passenger door behind me opens and Vinn scrambles in with an overflowing plastic bag in her hands. She begins to unwrap a chocolate bar and several other varieties of candy, then unscrews the top of a bottle of Coke. She grabs Rebecca's shoulders and firmly turns her so that they're face to face.

"Rebecca, this is Vinn. We're safe now and you need to listen to me. Mal and I need to take a ride so we can't bring you home just yet. It's best you don't know where we're headed, so I'm going to tie this bandana around your eyes. In the meantime, we need you to eat some of this candy and drink this pop. I've been where you are now. It'll help." As she speaks, Vinn places the chocolate into Rebecca's left hand and brings it to her mouth, pushing it against her lips. As if by instinct, Rebecca slowly takes a bite and begins chewing. Vinn stays with her until she finishes the entire bar and part of another and drinks almost the entire Coke before snugly fastening a strip of Adria's tent over her eyes and moving back into the front.

"You too," she tells me as she nestles a large bag of peanut M&Ms in the console between us. "I saved the better stuff for us."

I pull back into traffic and head for the expressway to take us south. Glancing back at the sound of soft snoring, I'm gratified to see Rebecca asleep. Vinn looks as well.

"Her color is better too." She pauses, thoughtful. "We never should have allowed her to stay with us," she says with a disgusted snort. "She's a civilian."

"In our defense," I remind her, "she didn't give us much choice. And she's shown herself to be grittier than you'd think on several occasions. It wasn't that long ago that she was the one driving while you and I were recovering in the back."

"I know, but still," Vinn insists. "It doesn't take much to get pushed over the edge. She's seen dead bodies before, so I'm not sure what triggered her."

"Was he alive when she saw him?" I ask reluctantly.

Vinn nods. "Barely, but still alert. I had Rebecca step outside before..." She leaves the rest of her thought unspoken.

"She probably saw you draw your knife, and she certainly heard my gunshot even though it was muffled. Maybe that crossed a line for her—the idea that the two of us would do that to a defenseless man, no matter how evil he was. Or the fact that it was happening almost at her feet. Anyway, it's done now. She may add an emotional scar to her collection, but she'll recover and the story will grow into something mythical with herself as the heroine over time." I take another glance back. "Do you think she's really asleep or is she listening?"

"Does it matter?" Vinn asks, and she has a point. We continue our drive in silence.

Somewhere in the Google search history of my laptop that I've erased is the phrase "forest preserve dump bodies Cook County," the results of which have led us to a somewhat desolate Whistler Woods Forest Preserve just past the city limits on the southwest side. It seems like its location in the midst of dueling gang territories at one time years ago and its lack of popularity with the general public, combined with densely wooded areas and a river, made it a popular spot for dropping off fresh corpses that wouldn't be found for years, if ever. We're hoping that's still true.

As we pull into the drive of the forest preserve I sigh in relief, as there's little evidence of picnickers even on this sunny weekend day in the summer. Perhaps the gangs are still active enough to scare the public away, but whatever the reason, the lack of activity serves our purpose. We drive slowly deeper into the preserve, angling our way into the more wooded areas beside the river.

"Here," Vinn finally commands. "Pull over."

With no parking lot nearby and no visible trails, it's unlikely that anyone would pick this spot as a starting point for a hike. We leave our doors slightly open so as not to wake Rebecca and pull the tarp out of the back of the truck. It feels heavier than it did forty minutes ago. We mount a small hill, weaving among the trees, then walk until we're about a hundred yards from the road. A large tree that had fallen years ago and was well into a state of decay lay across a slight indentation in the ground. With sighs of relief we place Alvarez on the ground and roll him beneath the tree, still inside the canvas, then cover him with branches and piles of damp leaves. Even standing right next to him, he's invisible.

"Someday someone may find him," I remark to Vinn as we hustle back to the truck. "But even then how will they identify him? Doubtful his dental records are in any system in this country."

We find Rebecca and the truck exactly as we left them,

jump inside, do a quick U-turn, and for the first time in ages, head for home.

Rebecca has recovered enough by the time we park in front of the three-flat to make a few snarky remarks about my driving, but her usual bubbliness is absent. When she stumbles uncertainly exiting the truck, Vinn and I each take an arm around our shoulder and lead her up the stairs to her front door. With more experience than I in locating keys inside a cavernous purse, Vinn takes the lead, gets the door unlocked, and we lower Rebecca onto her couch. I find an old musical on cable, put the remote in her hand, and we stand poised by the door, finally leaving when we see her begin to mouth the words to the chorus of some old love song.

Out on the landing, I look longingly up the stairs at the home I haven't been to in so long, but Vinn grabs my sleeve and starts down. "He'll want to know," is all she says.

Leo's radar is as good as always and his front door opens while we're still at the top of his stairs. By the time we're inside, he's perched on a stool at the kitchen table, an old dusty bottle in the center. Our presence alone appears to preclude having to tell him the results of this afternoon's adventure. He pours healthy doses as we sit, raises his glass, and holds it high until we do the same, then throws it back in a single swallow. Vinn and I know better and take sips. Instead of Leo's usual rotgut, as good as it sometimes is, whatever this liquor is is phenomenal. Our looks of surprise don't go unnoticed by the host.

"Been savin' it," he says before filling his glass and topping off ours. Vinn starts to say something but Leo cuts her off. "No details. Enough that he's gone." Six words is a long speech for him, but it says enough.

I don't know how long we sit and drink, but when the bottle is empty we know it's time to leave Leo to his thoughts and for us to head upstairs to spend a few minutes together in solitude. Chances are it won't be long before Mendez finds his way to my door.

Vinn precedes me outside and I begin to leave, but stop and turn to face the man whose past is no longer a secret or a threat.

"Leo," I say, making sure his eyes are fixed in my direction. "I think you dropped this." I pull my hand out of my pocket and place a colorful gypsy scarf accented with streaks of blood and a bullet hole on a table, then pull the door shut behind me.

THIRTY THREE

Mendez actually waited until Sunday morning to drop by my place. From what I can tell the delay wasn't out of courtesy but because he spent most of Saturday afternoon and evening processing the Roma men and women and trying to unravel the information about the various crimes I had emailed him as a long spreadsheet with exhibits just before Vinn and I pulled out of the park. While our names apparently came up once or twice in interviews with the women, especially with Adria who insisted she had made a deal to avoid prosecution, once we denied that we had been at the Gypsy Fair or knew anything about it he didn't know where to go with the interview. He knew we were behind it and we knew he knew, but since no one reliable could place us there he didn't have any cards to play to encourage us to cooperate. The information we passed on to him was readily available and verifiable online, so Vinn and I simply stuck to the position that we knew no more about the Roma than what we'd pulled off the internet. Mendez left with a warning that he'd be back, but neither of us is worried. There was no mention of the rogue cop.

When Chuck came by to pick up his truck in order to have it washed and detailed, he mentioned that he and his crew also bailed before the cops arrived. I can only imagine the frustration in raiding a fair where no one around can point to anyone in charge. The local news this morning devoted a few paragraphs to the confusion and had a nice photo of a vendor offering an officer in full uniform a candy apple.

Rebecca stopped by shortly after Mendez left but then forgot what she was going to say and left almost immediately, flustered. In other words, she's back to normal. We haven't gone downstairs to check on Leo and probably won't. For the next few days, we need to concentrate on self-care.

Vinn and I are attempting just that as we snuggle close on the couch, television and brand new cell phones silenced, leaving ourselves to each other and our thoughts. I can't remember the last time either of us had a good night's sleep, and that day when I dropped by Vinn's apartment when she was ill hoping to find a crime to solve now seems both distant and naïve. Be careful what you wish for.

Vinn finally breaks our lazy silence with a sigh. "Mal, we can't keep doing this. We both fled from jobs that put our lives in danger in order to find some sort of peace, or at the very least the knowledge that we'd be waking up in the morning. I can't say it hasn't been exciting, and a part of me thrives on the thrills, but I don't want to go on wondering if the next time we stick our necks out it'll be the last."

Vinn has an uncanny skill at expressing what I'm thinking at the very moment a thought enters my mind. Still, I take my time before I respond. "I'm to blame for that, Vinn. You'd found your peace before I arrived."

She twists her head to look directly into my eyes. "In a way, that's true. But if I'm to be honest, I was restless, maybe even bored. And I didn't have anyone that made preserving my life a priority. That's changed." She smiles. "I blame that on you too."

I pull her tighter. "So what do we do the next time trouble comes calling? It seems to have us on speed dial."

"I don't know, Mal. But maybe it's time to think about finding another life, but this time choosing it together. Somewhere where we're not put in a position where we care so damn much."

With that thought we drift again into an easy silence. It seems like I just got to my current situation in Chicago when I stumbled onto things I'd never had before. An engaging and steady job. A home with a bed I'm actually able to sleep in most nights, and not always alone. And people I care about. Could I leave Leo and Rebecca? Chicago? My new life?

It seems like the answer is hovering in the periphery of my conscious thought, but drifts out of reach as I join Vinn in gentle slumber.

ABOUT THE AUTHOR

With age comes wisdom, or so the adage goes, yet despite his advancing years Thomas J. Thorson was fool enough to churn out yet another book in the Malcom Winters series. From a chair by the window of his second-floor apartment in Malcom's Ukrainian Village neighborhood of Chicago, he's but a helpless chronicler of the adventures of the characters he created as they traverse the city leaving havoc in their wake.